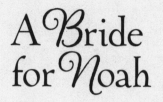

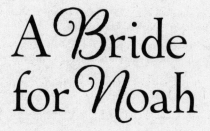

A Bride for Noah

Lori Copeland
Virginia Smith

HARVEST HOUSE PUBLISHERS
EUGENE, OREGON

Scripture taken from:

The King James Version of the Bible

The Holy Bible, New International Version®, NIV®. Copyright © 1973, 1978, 1984, 2011, by Biblica, Inc.™ Used by permission of Zondervan. All rights reserved worldwide. www.zondervan.com

Cover by Garborg Design Works, Savage, Minnesota

Cover photos © Chris Garborg; Bigstock / Andrushko Galyna

Published in association with the Books & Such Literary Agency, 52 Mission Circle, Suite 122, PMB 170, Santa Rosa, CA 95409-5370, www.booksandsuch.biz.

A BRIDE FOR NOAH

Copyright © 2013 by Copeland, Inc. and Virginia Smith
Published by Harvest House Publishers
Eugene, Oregon 97402
www.harvesthousepublishers.com

Library of Congress Cataloging-in-Publication Data
    Copeland, Lori.
    A bride for Noah / Lori Copeland and Virginia Smith.
       pages cm.
    ISBN 978-0-7369-5347-4 (pbk.)
    ISBN 978-0-7369-5348-1 (eBook)
    1. Brides—Fiction. I. Title.
    PS3553.O6336B75 2013
    813'.54—dc23

                          2013010143

Printed in the United States of America

13 14 15 16 17 18 19 20 21 / LB-JH / 10 9 8 7 6 5 4 3 2 1

I lift up my eyes to the mountains—
where does my help come from?
My help comes from the LORD,
the Maker of heaven and earth.

PSALM 121:1-2

Prologue

November, 1851
Elliott Bay, Oregon Territory

That's it! I'd bet my life on it!"

The moment their dugout canoe rounded the Duwamish Head and plunged into the bay, Noah Hughes knew their search had ended. For days their Indian guides had led them on an exploration of the Duwamish River, skirting the vast mudflats of the river delta, but they'd seen no likely place to plant a new city. But here lay a small headland in the center of Elliott Bay's eastern shore. The dense tree line came nearly up to the bank, the vast forest so thick Noah could barely see past the first row of immense cedars. The water of the bay moved swiftly, but even so the surface was smooth enough to be nearly glassy.

"Would you look at that?" David Denny had his eyes fixed on the skyline. Noah had come to respect the young man over the past few months since joining the small group of frontier adventurers who'd recently arrived from Cherry Grove, Illinois.

He followed David's gaze. There, above the top of the trees, stood the tallest mountain he'd ever seen. The solitary Mount Rainier, with its snowcapped jagged peaks, seemed to stand sentry over the primeval forest that covered this lush part of Oregon Territory. Though they'd seen it from their current camp at Alki Point, from this perspective the mountain took on a majesty he had not noticed before.

"Impressive." He scanned the shoreline. Up ahead a flat peninsula of ten acres or so extended into the river, connected to the shore by an isthmus and forming a small tidal lagoon. Just beyond the peninsula a wide tributary emptied into the bay. Though he needed a closer inspection before being certain, it looked deep enough to suit their purposes. "What do you think?"

The shadow of a smile played about David's lips. "It's worth exploring. This bay is isolated from the Puget Sound, so it's probably sheltered from the harsh weather that Arthur is convinced will flatten Alki Point. Let's test the depth." Arthur Denny, David's older brother and the acknowledged leader of the Denny Party in their exploration for a new home, had sent them on this expedition. After several days of fruitless searching, Noah had begun to worry that they would have nothing to report.

He readied the hundred-foot length of rope they'd brought for this purpose, secured a half-dozen horseshoes to the end, and dropped the line overboard. To his surprise, the horseshoes took the line all the way down without touching bottom. Excitement flickered inside as he exchanged a grin with David.

"Let's test over there, closer to the island."

While Noah recoiled their makeshift sounding line, David spoke to their guides from the Duwamish tribe using a few words he had picked up in their language, accompanied by wide gestures and much pointing. When the good-natured natives maneuvered the dugout to the place indicated, Noah repeated the process. The line sank forty feet.

He pointed toward the place where the river emptied into the bay. "I'm guessing the current from the river has dredged a natural channel here. Plenty deep enough for seagoing ships."

They requested that their Indian companions take the dugout ashore, and over the next several hours Noah's certainty that they had, indeed, found the ideal location for their new settlement increased steadily. Timber grew in seemingly unlimited quantities, and yet they discovered several clearings of rich, arable land suitable for farming.

As they entered one such glade, David stopped, a gleam in his eyes as he scanned the landscape. "This is it, Noah. I feel it here." He planted a fist in the center of his chest. "As soon as I'm old enough, I'm going to stake my claim to this spot. I'll build a cabin for Louisa right over there. And then we'll be married."

Noah looked where he pointed. Yes, the landscape was flat here, the foliage sparse. Clearing enough space for a good-sized cabin wouldn't be too difficult. He surveyed the area, surrounded on all sides by cedar and fir trees. Overhead, the sun blazed in a sapphire-blue sky. Birds called to one another from far above, their songs accompanied by the distant sound of water splashing over a rocky bed.

"If I were you," he told David, "I wouldn't wait until I was old enough. I'd go ahead and stake this claim now in someone else's name. Your father's, perhaps, since he isn't interested in living here. I have a feeling this settlement isn't going to stay secret for long."

The younger man's eyes narrowed, and then he nodded. When he looked back at the glade his lips formed a satisfied smile.

Watching him, Noah experienced a pang of…something. Not jealousy, exactly, though any man might envy David for capturing the heart of the beautiful, vivacious Louisa. No, Noah's recent experience with a strong-minded woman was enough to put him off marriage for life. What he envied was the utter happiness he saw in David's face.

Maybe someday the Lord will see fit to send me a bride too.

No. He shook his head to dislodge the unexpected thought. What he longed for after the disaster of the past year was peace and a quiet life. If the Lord really loved him, as his mother used to assure him, He'd grant him a prosperous life free from complications. Let David have the care and responsibility of a wife. Noah would stake his own claim in this fertile land of opportunity, and he would do it alone.

One

December 19, 1851
Elliott Bay, Oregon Territory

*D*ear Uncle Miles,
　　Christmas greetings to you and Aunt Letitia, though no doubt by the time this missive reaches you the season will be long past. I must say, I look forward to bidding the holiday farewell. A fog of gloom has settled over the camp these past weeks, and grows heavier as Christmas day approaches. The men are obsessed with thoughts of past celebrations, and as a result, do not perform their work with the enthusiasm and energy they displayed when we first settled here. At times even the Denny brothers seem to lose their passion for this venture, though only a handful of us are privy to their concerns. Before the men they maintain a confident outlook.

　　Of course, the lack of women in the camp contributes to the sense of gloom. The only women the men have seen since arriving are Mary, Arthur Denny's wife, and her sister Louisa, and they are both spoken for. The men grow heartily sick of one another's company. As for the weather, more than two weeks have elapsed since the sun appeared. The blue skies of autumn are gone, and winter has brought with it an unbroken canopy of gray.

　　And rain. It seems an entire ocean has fallen from the skies in recent days. We pray for snow, because frozen ground would be more conducive to transporting our logs from the forest to the water's edge. Sometimes the *mules are fetlock-deep in mud. Alas, the natives tell us snowfall in these parts is typically light, if it falls at all.*

Regardless, my confidence in this venture continues. If fortunes are to be made in the West, I am convinced they will come from lumber, which we have in abundance. If we can produce a shipment large enough to command the attention of timber buyers in San Francisco, we will move forward with our plans to build a mill and turn this camp into a permanent settlement.

If you feel like visiting this lush land, bring an ax. There is plenty of work for all. Or a wagonload of women, which would do wonders for the men's attitudes! You will be hailed as a hero without splitting a single log. (In my mind's eye I see Aunt Letitia's spine stiffening in outrage. Please assure her that I merely jest!)

> *With sincere regards, your nephew,*
> *Noah*

❧

February 17, 1852
Chattanooga, Tennessee

Mr. Coffinger read the final words of the letter aloud. Though Evie Lawrence did not intend to snoop, there was no help for it. Her employers were settled in their sitting room, and the wide-open archway between the dining and sitting rooms did nothing to prevent her hearing their every word. Taking care to keep her attention fixed on polishing the mahogany buffet until it shone, she hid a smile. The Coffingers' nephew had hit the peg squarely on the head with the prediction of his aunt's response to his jest. The rotund woman's backbone had become as rigid as a fire poker in her seat on the sofa, and her already-thin lips compressed into near invisibility.

"From childhood that boy's sense of humor has been base and uncouth." Her long nose rose into the air to deliver a disapproving sniff. "Were his poor mother still living, I should be forced to inform her of his inappropriate comment. No doubt it would break her heart."

Evie made a final pass with her polishing cloth and then began wiping dust from the crystal and china before returning the items to their positions. Though she kept her back turned away from the sitting room and its occupants, the couple's image was reflected in the glass doors of the hutch.

Mr. Coffinger answered with a guffaw. "My sister would have laughed and then jumped up to assemble a wagonload of women to deliver to Oregon Territory."

After a chilly pause, Mrs. Coffinger spoke in a frigid voice. "Unfortunately you are correct. She may even have *supported* this ridiculous scheme of Noah's from the start. Wisdom and good sense do not run strongly in your family. You are evidence of that, Miles."

Evie held her breath. If her mama had ever insulted her father— God rest his soul—in such a manner, his anger would have flared and, though he had been a patient man, he would have answered with a fiery reply. Nor would Evie have blamed him. But Mama had loved Papa too deeply to ever insult him. Had not her death of a broken heart six months after his passing proven so? Evie closed her eyes against the rush of tears that always threatened when she thought of the loss of her parents. Two years had passed since she'd laid Mama to rest. How long would it be before the memory failed to stir up such a painful response?

Apparently Mr. Coffinger had grown familiar with his wife's barbs. In the months since Evie had been in service here, she'd become accustomed to her mistress taking her vexations out on her longsuffering husband. Instead of becoming angry, he merely folded the letter and slid it inside the breast pocket of his evening jacket. He lifted his glass from the low table between them, leaned back in his upholstered armchair, and sipped the amber contents while watching his wife over the rim.

Mrs. Coffinger seemed not to mind, or notice, his silence. "It begins to sound as though this scheme too will fail. Of course I warned Noah from the start against the foolishness of moving to the wild and unpredictable West. Such a waste of money should not have been permitted." She leaned forward to pick up her teacup from the table. "You should have put a stop to it, Miles. Your responsibility as his uncle and only living relative demanded it."

"The money was his to spend, my dear, left to him by his father," he replied mildly. "He would not have appreciated my interference."

"Interference?" Her teacup clanged down on the saucer with such force Evie thought it might shatter. "*Guidance* is what he needed. And what you failed to provide. Though perhaps Noah was better off without the benefit of your so-called wisdom. Your advice would have done him more harm than good. Since you exercise ignorance more than wisdom in your own affairs, how could you advise others?"

Another haughty sniff, and the sound grated on Evie's nerves like a shovel scraping across a grave. For a moment she considered offering her handkerchief in false concern for her mistress's sniffles, but decided against the sarcastic gesture. She needed this housekeeping job. Besides, after several decades of marriage, Mr. Coffinger could certainly defend himself against his wife's sharp tongue.

His bland response proved her point. "My dear, one would almost think you dissatisfied with our manner of living."

Evie's glance swept the room, taking in the spindly-legged French tables, the elaborately framed artwork on the walls, and the intricate design of the plush rug that warmed the polished wooden floor. She set a freshly dusted crystal decanter in its place on the buffet.

Mrs. Coffinger leaned over her thickset middle to return her teacup and saucer to the table. "It is a miracle that we still have a home after the unwise investments you have made." She shook her head as though chiding a child. "That odious man with the timepieces and that so-called doctor with his ice machine."

"I still say the machine is a sound idea." He drained his glass and rose from the chair to head toward the sideboard. "Imagine being able to produce ice all the year round."

"The man took your money and disappeared to Florida." Double-sniff this time.

Evie balanced the last plate on its display stand and turned from her task to find Mrs. Coffinger's gaze fixed on her. Red spots appeared on the woman's already rouged cheeks. Apparently she had forgotten Evie's presence.

She recovered and straightened on the sofa cushion. "Evangeline, does your young man work for his living?" Her gaze slid across the room to her husband, where he stood near the sideboard sipping from a refilled glass. "Or does he pretend to be an *investor?*" The word slid across her tongue as though it were rancid oil.

Evie glanced at Mr. Coffinger, whose normally placid expression had begun to look strained.

She schooled her voice before answering. "James works at the port, loading cotton and other goods onto the boats."

"A solid job, then." The woman jerked an approving nod. "You can rely on a man who makes his living with his hands." After a pointed glance toward her husband, she rose. "I must check with the cook to make sure dinner will be on time tonight. She has served the meal twenty minutes late twice in the past week, and my consti-tution is greatly affected."

She swept from the room, leaving Evie alone with Mr. Coffin-ger. Gathering her soiled cloths and the jar of furniture polish, Evie avoided the man's gaze. She had never felt sorrier for anyone than she did him for being married to such a sharp-tongued woman. She wouldn't want him to see pity in her eyes.

As she turned to go, she caught sight of his face. He studied the doorway through which his wife had disappeared, his expres-sion thoughtful. He gave no indication he was even aware of Evie's presence. What thoughts circled behind those passive features? The object of his contemplation must certainly be his wife and her sharp words. But Evie saw no sign of anger, or irritation, or even sadness. Only a shade of speculation.

When she headed for the doorway, her rags and polish in hand, he started out of his reverie. The eyes he turned her way focused, and the corners of his lips twitched beneath his mustache.

"Miss Lawrence, please accept my apologies for"—he lifted his glass and gestured toward the doorway—"voicing our private concerns in your presence. Truth is, you're so quiet I'd forgotten you were there. It's no doubt disconcerting to one about to enter the bonds of matrimony to hear an old married couple exchanging tit for tat."

Evie longed to say the conversation had been far too one-sided to be called an exchange, but she bit her tongue. Any answer would only make matters more awkward. Instead she bobbed a curtsy and continued for the doorway.

Mr. Coffinger stopped her. "Your intended. You say he is employed at the docks?"

Though she had no desire to enter into a conversation about James with Mr. Coffinger or anyone else, what could she do but answer her employer politely? "Yes, sir."

"An unstable occupation these days, to be sure, with the railroad gaining strength in Chattanooga. Not tempted by the lure of gold to journey westward, is he?"

More than one of James's friends had packed their belongings and headed west after hearing accounts of gold nuggets as big as a man's fist lying on the ground, ready to be scooped up. Though she and James had differing opinions on many things, concerning the search for gold they were agreed. Only an imbecile would leave behind his family, friends, and livelihood to answer that golden siren call.

She lifted her head and answered Mr. Coffinger squarely. "No, sir, he is not at all tempted by such a fool's errand. James is far more levelheaded than that."

The man's features fell. "Ah, well. I'm sure that's for the best." He waved his tumbler again toward the doorway, this time in dismissal. Then he raised the glass to his lips and drained it.

As Evie stepped toward the doorway to take her leave, he was heading once again toward the sideboard and the crystal decanter.

"Miss Lawrence? One last thing before you go."

She paused in the act of stepping across the threshold and turned to find him watching her. "Yes sir?"

He slipped a hand into his jacket and withdrew the folded letter. A wide grin appeared beneath the bushy mustache as he waved it in the air. "If you ever consider heading west, let me know."

Evie's spine went nearly as stiff as Mrs. Coffinger's had earlier. Why would the man even *consider* that she would travel to the West in his company? And for what? To become a...a *fancy* woman in the wild for that nephew of his? An insult, that's what it was. Her virtue had been called into question, her reputation placed at risk. Why, she should give her notice at this very moment. Throw the polishing rags in the man's face and march out of the house, never to return.

And she would have too, except for the frustrating circumstances in which she currently found herself. Her family home was gone, overtaken by an unsympathetic uncle after her parents' passing. The larder in the small room she rented was nearly empty. Her skirts were mended to the point that she was forced to mend the mends in order to clothe herself decently. If not for this job as Mrs. Coffinger's housemaid, she would be penniless.

Be not rash with thy mouth, and let not thine heart be hasty to utter any thing before God: for God is in heaven, and thou upon earth: therefore let thy words be few.

The verse rose in her mind in time to silence her hasty words. Instead, she lifted her nose in a haughty imitation of the man's wife, gave a dignified nod in farewell, and swept out of the room.

Evie moved through the streets of Chattanooga toward the boardinghouse she called home these days. The draw of Mulberry Avenue was too strong tonight to be withstood. *Railroad Avenue,* she corrected herself. Her childhood had been spent growing up in her grandfather's big house on Mulberry Avenue. Last year, with the completion of the Memphis and Charleston railroad, tracks had been laid down the center of the road and the street's name changed. But in her mind it would always be Mulberry Avenue.

At the corner of Chestnut she hesitated only a moment before turning toward her former home. The name was not the only thing in this area that had changed. As a girl she had played with a pack of children along this avenue, kicking a ball and chasing each other down the center of the street while their high-pitched laughter bounced off the houses. Now the night was filled with different sounds. Though the train track lay empty at the moment, trade establishments that had sprung up at its completion enjoyed a bustling business. Music and light spilled through the doors of several buildings. The pounding of iron on iron came from the new factory where James hoped to find employment soon. Black smoke, a shade darker than the sky, belched from long, narrow chimneys. Evie gathered her bonnet straps securely beneath her chin and hurried past the ugly building, the hem of her dress sweeping across the charred paving stones.

Her step slowed as she approached her childhood home. Though not a grand house like the Coffingers', her grandfather had built a sturdy, comfortable home for him and his wife to raise their two children in. Large columns stood sentry on the porch, and the heavy front door, scratched and scarred from early memory, stood between two wide, shuttered windows. Both Mama and Uncle Jeremy had been born in this house. And Mama had died here. Evie's gaze flew to a dark window on the upper level. Mama's room. After Grandmother's death of consumption, she and her parents had moved in with Grandfather. A kind old man he had been, though never strong of constitution. After Mama's passing, Evie had cared for him until he too claimed his place in the grave a few months ago.

She clutched her handbag and shut her eyes against the faces of her loved ones. So much death.

"Evie! What in tarnation are you doing here?"

The shout from a familiar voice jerked her out of her reverie. She turned to see James, her fiancé, striding down the street, flanked by a pair of young men around his age. His expression spoke of his anger, eyebrows drawn together and hovering just above his narrowed eyes.

"I—I merely…" She wet her lips. James had cautioned her against coming here alone, especially after dark. "I wanted to see the house."

"I've told you and told you, this street is not safe." He grabbed her upper arm in a grip that, had she not been wearing a thick woolen coat, would no doubt have left a bruise. "There are men along this way who would do you harm."

In one part of her mind she acknowledged the truth of his warning. Her gaze flickered behind him, past his two friends, to take in the activity on the street. Two men had spilled out of one of the ale houses and were rolling on the dusty ground, fists flying, while a handful of watchers cheered them on.

Anger erupted in the other part of her mind, fed by the iron grip James had on her arm. He had no right to treat her so. They were not married, not yet.

"But this is *my* house." She stabbed a finger across the tracks. "My family home. If I want to walk past it…"

He gave her arm a shake that rattled her entire body and stirred her anger to greater heights. "Not two nights ago a woman was found not far from here, beaten and bloodied. Are you so ignorant to think you will escape the same fate?"

Had she seen an ounce of real concern in his face she might have softened. And had he not chosen that moment to glance over his shoulder at his two friends, who watched the exchange with matching smirks, she might have attributed his brusque manner to worry on her behalf. But one of the men crossed his arms and ducked his head toward James as though to encourage him, and James straightened to a domineering height over her diminutive figure. He even swaggered, so much as he could standing still.

Why, he is not concerned for me. He is merely putting on a show for his workmates. Showing them how he handles an errant woman.

She wrenched her arm free of his grip. "Are you saying you think me ignorant?" It was one of the insults Mrs. Coffinger had flung at her husband during their most unpleasant disagreement not an hour past.

James returned his attention to her. "Foolish is as foolish does. Besides, you know it is not your house any longer."

She jerked as though slapped. That his words were true made no difference. Her gaze flickered sideways to the family home she loved. The one her uncle had taken from her. Her shoulders drooped.

He took her arm again, though not so roughly this time. "Come on. I'll see you safely home." To his chums he said, "Sorry, boys. You go along without me. I'll join you for that drink after I run this little errand. Duty before pleasure, you know."

Duty? The word was a cold slap in the face. Was that what she represented to James? A duty? As the men waved a cheery farewell and headed toward the closest ale house, she walked stiffly beside her fiancé, her thoughts churning.

"I am not a child." She cast him a sideways glance. "I resent being treated like one."

"I'll treat you the way you deserve." Now that he was no longer posturing for his chums, he spoke in a softer tone. "It is my responsibility to protect you from the consequences of your own foolish actions. Acting in ignorance could get you seriously hurt, or even killed."

That word again. "There were people all up and down the street. It's not as though I wandered down a dark alley alone." Evie's gait became more of a march as she placed each step with more force than strictly required. "And is that all I am to you, a responsibility?" She glared sideways. "A duty?"

His eyes rolled upward. "Lately it seems you are determined to be a headache as well."

Her spine stiff as a railroad tie, she planted her feet on the paving stones, forcing him to halt as well. "A headache?"

His jaws bulged as he ground his teeth and he gave an irritated sniff. "When you act unreasonably, as you are now, yes."

The sound of that sniff shot through her ears to her irritated nerves like a savage's arrow. At that moment a trio of men pushed between them, their steps unsteady. Evie took the opportunity to draw in a few deep breaths. That's why Mrs. Coffinger's arrogant sniffles had grated upon her so. She'd not been aware of it before now, but James had the same annoying habit.

I am not angry with James. The Coffingers' argument has upset me is all.

And yet…was there a basis for her irritation? Of late she had felt James's treatment of her was less caring than earlier in their relationship. He was short with her more often than not, and avoided answering her questions concerning the date of their upcoming marriage.

She tilted her head and looked him in the eye. "Tell me, James, why you asked for my hand in marriage."

The abrupt change of subject seemed to startle him. His eyebrows arched. "What do you mean?"

"I mean," she said slowly, "what reason do you have for wanting me to be your wife? I have nothing besides the hope chest my mother put together for me. No fortune." She swung a hand back toward her grandfather's house. "No property. So why do you want to marry me?"

"Well…" His gaze searched the darkened sky. "I've no fortune

myself, you know. Not yet, though I hope one day to be a man of"—
his gaze slid behind her head, toward the house that was no longer
hers—"of property. We will have to work for it now, is all."

Suspicion niggled its way into Evie's thoughts. James had been
quite upset when her uncle came unexpectedly from Boston to
claim the family home after Mama's death. Evie herself had been
sunk in a fog of grief and shock, especially when her uncle insisted
that she find other living arrangements. James had been outraged,
she assumed because of his concern for her. Perhaps another reason
lay beneath his disappointment.

*Did he want to marry me under the expectation that I would inherit
Grandfather's house?*

"And besides." James reached toward her, his hand sliding down
her arm to take her hand. "I'm quite fond of you, you know."

Not exactly a profession of undying love from the lips of her
intended.

"Fond of me," she repeated dully.

"Of course. You're attractive enough, and you're a fair hand at
cooking when you put your mind to it." He tucked her hand in the
crook of his arm and resumed their walk. "Besides, your job as a
housemaid brings a decent wage. I've intended to talk to you about
an idea I have. Word is in a few years the railroad is going to build a
new station over on Chestnut Street. Property there goes for a song."
He gave a low whistle. "So I thought if we wait a while before the
wedding and put our money together, we can buy a place over there."

Her mind went numb. "Wait to be married? But why?"

"Think about it, Evie. Your room at the boardinghouse doesn't
cost much and neither does mine. When we're married we'll have to
get a place for the two of us to live together, and we'll pay a lot more.
Instead, we could spend our money buying property on Chestnut.
When the railroad announces their plans for the station, prices will
turn. We'll make a bundle. Then we can get married." He patted
her hand. "Shouldn't be more than a year or two. Three at the most."

Her feet continued to move, though she was unaware of her surroundings. Three more years at the boardinghouse. Three more years of housework for Mrs. Coffinger, of listening to the woman berate her husband for his "ignorance." And afterward countless years of being called a fool herself, of James "taking care" of her because of the depth of his "fondness."

They arrived at the boardinghouse and James pulled her to a stop.

"There. Safely home. You go on inside and think about what I said. I'll come calling on Wednesday, like always."

He bent to place a chaste kiss on her cheek and then turned without waiting for a response. The sound of his whistle followed after him as, hands in pockets, he sauntered back in the direction they'd come to join his friends at the ale house.

Think about what I said.

Evie watched his retreat until he rounded the corner. Oh, she'd think about what he said, all right. She'd think long and hard.

About that, and a few other things as well.

Two

Elliott Bay, Oregon Territory

Hughes! Got a minute?"

At Arthur's call, Noah glanced up from trimming branches from a felled tree in preparation to bucking it. The air rang with the chopping of blades and the deep voices of the men calling instructions to each other. At the edge of the clearing, Arthur raised an arm and gestured for him to come. Noah set his ax down on the log and hopped across it. Beside Arthur stood the unmistakable figure of the chief of the Duwamish along with a handful of his tribal clansmen, all of them watching the work of the lumberjacks with the keen interest they displayed in everything the white settlers did. Their village was located several miles from this new settlement, close enough that from some places on the land to which Noah had laid claim he could hear the distant beat of their drums.

Noah nodded a greeting to Chief Seattle as he approached. The man commanded respect, though there was nothing physically impressive about him. He stood at average height, several inches shorter than Noah, and his build leaned toward slender. Even so, he held himself with an ease born of confidence in his position as the chief of nearly four thousand men, women, and children. He watched Noah's approach through intense black eyes set in a broad face.

Arthur welcomed Noah with obvious relief. "Could you talk to Chief Seattle for me? David's working over at the skids so he's not available."

David had made a concerted effort to learn the language of the Duwamish. Though nowhere near as proficient as David, Noah had picked up a few words from the almost constant Indian visitors to their camp.

"I'll try," he told Arthur. "What do you want to say?"

"It's Mary and Louisa. They're all worked up because a pair of braves have been hanging around the cabin, staring at them and the children."

Noah wrinkled his brow. "Just staring? They haven't tried to hurt them?"

"No," Arthur was quick to say. "No, they just watch, like they do here. But yesterday the women left the cabin door open to get some fresh air, and these two wandered inside. Apparently they walked around the cabin, touching the beds and the stove, inspecting the cookware, and they even rubbed little Margaret's curls."

A smile threatened Noah's lips, but he worked hard to control it. Arthur and Mary's second daughter had a head full of wild red curls, no doubt fascinating for the Duwamish. He schooled concern into his expression. "I can see how that would be unsettling for them."

"So if you can make the chief here understand they shouldn't do those things, perhaps he might speak with his people."

Chief Seattle watched their exchange with his usual impassive expression. Noah wasn't sure how much English he understood, since the man refused to speak anything but his native tongue. David insisted the man possessed a keen intellect, so he probably understood the gist of Arthur's request already. At least, Noah hoped so. He knew enough Duwamish to barter salmon or hire a guide, but beyond that his vocabulary was limited.

He faced the chief. "Chief *Si'ahl*." He awarded the man the respect of using the tribal pronunciation of his name and ducked his head, though taking care not to lower his eyes.

Without a noticeable change in his expression, Seattle fixed polite attention on Noah.

What's the word for woman? Noah cast about in his mind. "Ah, the *klootchman* in the cabin that way." He pointed eastward in the location of the Denny cabin.

Seattle's eyes followed his hand, and then he indicated he understood with a nod. Not surprising, since there were the only two white *klootchman* within a hundred-mile radius. No doubt everyone knew their location.

By using gestures and a few words he had picked up, he managed to communicate Arthur's request. At least, he hoped the message came through accurately. The chief turned his head and spoke to his tribesmen in a commanding voice. Then he turned to Arthur and regally lowered his head as if to indicate that the request had been granted.

Relief flooded Arthur's features, and he extended a hand toward Seattle. "Thank you. You don't know how I appreciate that."

The chief hesitated only a moment before shaking the offered hand. Behind him, the braves chuckled and mumbled to one another in low voices. The Duwamish did not shake hands with one another but their leader's willingness to learn the white man's customs, if not his language, spoke of his respect and hopes for a peaceful future relationship.

Noah bid the visitors farewell and returned to his work. As he picked up the ax, he shook his head. Women. Nothing against Mary and Louisa, who were both upstanding and hardworking, but life was much easier without the burden of protecting and caring for a woman, especially in the rugged environment of this part of Oregon Territory. The crew obviously did not agree, and continued to complain bitterly about the lack of female presence in the new settlement.

To Noah, though, that was one of the appeals of the place. Hard work during the day and solitude at night. That was the life for him.

If only he'd figured that out before he'd squandered his inheritance on that deceitful woman back in San Francisco.

☞

Chattanooga, Tennessee

The morning was well underway when Mr. Coffinger finally put in an appearance downstairs. As was her custom, Mrs. Coffinger would linger in her upstairs sitting room until after lunch, when Evie could clear the lunch tray and begin her afternoon duties cleaning the bedrooms.

Mr. Coffinger hummed a monotone tune as he descended the stairway. He nodded absently toward Evie, who was sweeping the hallway carpet runner, and continued past her to the library. A moment later the heavy oak door closed behind him with a soft click.

Particles of dust rose in puffs from the carpet as Evie changed the direction of her efforts and swept toward the closed door. Sleep had eluded her last night, so tumultuous were her thoughts. In the past five days she had become more certain that James's true intention in marrying her had been to gain control of Grandfather's house. One moment she'd berated herself for her uncharitable attitude toward him, but the next she remembered the neighbors selling their properties one by one to business owners as the railroad track down Mulberry Avenue had neared completion. She remembered the men who knocked on Grandfather's door with their offers, which he had sternly refused to entertain. And James's words from that night had echoed in her mind. *You're attractive enough. I'm fond of you.* And, of course, the ones that rankled. *Are you so ignorant? Foolish is as foolish does.*

James was a fine man, not afraid to work. He had goals, and ambition enough to attain them. She also had to admit that he was something of an opportunist, no doubt a necessary quality for a man with lofty aspirations. He would make a fine husband for someone.

But not for her.

The realization brought with it a curious sense of relief. The fact that she was not devastated at the idea of ending her relationship with James proved that what she had assumed to be love had been something else entirely. Fear, perhaps, of being alone in the world after Grandfather's death. Anxiety at the approach of her twenty-third birthday, an age at which most young women were safely wed and raising a family. Marriage had seemed a logical step to relieve her of the looming fear of a lonely spinster's life. But not marriage to a man she did not love and who described his affections for her as mere fondness.

With the coming of dawn this morning, clarity had arrived. Why must she rely on anyone else to make her future? Many women made their own way in the world without the benefit of a husband. Look at Mrs. Browning, the widow who ran the boardinghouse where she lived. Evie was certainly as capable of earning her way.

Leaning her broom handle against the wall, she paused for a moment in front of Mr. Coffinger's library to gather her thoughts. Swallowing past a lump of nerves, she lifted her hand and rapped quietly on the door.

"Yes?" came the muffled reply from inside.

She cleared her throat and cracked open the door enough to stick her head through. "Might I have a word with you, sir?"

He was seated behind the big wooden desk, his head bent over a paper. Dark pouches dragged at the skin beneath red-rimmed eyes. He must have had as restless a night as she.

She looked around the room, curious. Her housecleaning duties excluded this room, which was Mr. Coffinger's domain. Book-shelves lined the walls, though most were only half-filled with bound volumes. Stacks of papers occupied much of the writing table and many of the shelves as well. Though sunlight filtered through the tall windows behind the desk, the odor of lamp oil clung to the air.

He raised his head to look her full in the face and leaned back in the tall leather chair. The mustache twitched, indicative of a hidden smile.

"Of course, Miss Lawrence. Come in and be seated." He gestured toward a wooden chair resting against one wall.

Evie lowered herself into the chair, nerves doing battle in her stomach. In the predawn light, her resolve had been firm. Now she wasn't so sure. Perhaps she really was the fool James claimed her to be.

"If you've come to ask for an increase in your wages, let me save us some time and tell you I am not in a position..."

"No," she hurried to say. "That's not it at all. I'd like to continue our conversation from a few nights past."

Mr. Coffinger rested his elbows on the arms of his chair and entwined his fingers across his middle. "I must confess to some surprise. When we spoke I had the impression I'd offended you."

No use denying the truth. "I was...taken aback by your parting comment. But I've since considered your words and have some questions."

A gleam of interest appeared in his red-rimmed eyes. "Questions concerning my nephew's letter?"

She nodded. "That and your offer."

His eyebrows rose. "I wasn't aware I had made an offer."

She realized she had twisted the fabric of her skirt into a knot, and smoothed it out. "You said I should speak with you if I decided to go west. I am considering such a move."

Surprise colored his features. "Don't tell me you've been bitten by the gold lust."

"No, but it has occurred to me that there are many opportunities in the West besides the quest for gold. Your nephew's venture, for instance."

He leaned back, eyes narrowed. "Has your fiancé a mind to try his hand at logging?"

Heat rose in her cheeks, and she lowered her gaze to a point on the desktop in front of him. "We have…ended our agreement. *If* I decide to pursue a future in the West"—she met his eyes directly as she placed an emphasis on the word—"I will be alone."

A long silence followed, during which Evie forced herself not to shift in her seat. She had not actually told James of her decision yet. Nor had she informed him of her determination to end their engagement.

Mr. Coffinger said, "I see. And tell me, exactly what do you intend to do when you get there?"

That very question had occupied her thoughts throughout much of the early morning hours. Her initial assumption upon hearing Noah Hughes's jesting request for "a wagonload of women" was that it had been a thinly veiled invitation for women of low reputation, which of course was out of the question for a Christian lady such as herself. But he wrote with such conviction of the bright future of the settlement he and the others were striving to establish. If so, there would be opportunities for upstanding women, especially if they were not afraid to work.

She cleared her throat. "Every successful town needs commerce to thrive. Dry good stores, and clothiers, and blacksmiths…the list goes on."

Mr. Coffinger's expression became thoughtful, and he nodded slowly.

Evie took his silence for encouragement and straightened in the chair. "I've considered many opportunities—perhaps a restaurant?"

Clearly, that had not been the answer he expected. His brow furrowed. "A restaurant?"

Ignoring his lack of enthusiasm, she continued. "Just one possibility. The opportunity for business in a new settlement is practically unlimited, and I must consider my talents. I am a fair hand with meat and bread—and a needle, so a trade as a seamstress is a possibility. Surely men who work out of doors have mending needs and since there are very few women in the settlement, the demand for a full-time seamstress is undoubtedly limited."

He steepled his fingers in front of his mustache and dipped his head. "Go on."

Folding her hands in her lap to keep them still, she continued. "I've a good mind for finance, which would help in any number of ventures. Running a mercantile for instance."

"Certainly a necessity to a fledgling town," he commented.

Encouraged, she nodded. "There is a good deal of work involved in opening such a business. Suppliers must be secured, inventory purchased, trade routes established." She spread her hands. "I have no contacts in the area, so forming these relationships would take time, and a great deal of money."

"Opening a restaurant would also require suppliers and the purchase of inventory."

"Yes, but the initial expenses would not be as high. We would not need to purchase inventory to stock shelves, merely cooking equipment and a good supply of basic ingredients." She reached into her apron pocket and drew out the list she'd made. "Tables and benches, but surely in an area rich with timber those would not be difficult to find." She glanced down. "Oh, and table linens of course. We want to provide a homey atmosphere so the men will feel welcome and relaxed. Our restaurant would be a hospitable place, a respite from the demands of their labor."

As she spoke, Mr. Coffinger's eyebrows edged upward toward his hairline. "*Our* restaurant?"

Evie busied herself in folding her list. "That is the matter I hoped to discuss with you. Though I am able to run such a business competently, and am confident enough in my cooking ability to have no fear about my ability to attract a satisfactory clientele, there is an obstacle." She slid the paper back into her apron and settled her hands once again in her lap. "I have no money to finance such a venture."

"None?"

Her thoughts turned to the small sum secured in her hope chest at the boardinghouse, squirreled away from her meager wage as Mrs. Coffinger's housemaid in anticipation of setting up a home as James's wife. "Very little." She cleared her throat. "I am aware that in the past you have occasionally invested in causes you deem worthwhile." With that thought she fell silent, the unspoken question deafening in the silence that fell between them.

His mustache twitched from side to side, and she fancied she could almost hear the faint tapping of his steepled fingers against one another. Then she realized the noise was the sound of her own pulse.

Finally, he spoke. "I see merit in the venture." Her chest inflated with a hopeful breath as he continued. "There is only one problem."

"And that is?"

"In an unsettled territory the amount of money to finance a fledgling business is significant." He splayed his hands. "In all conscience I cannot entrust such a large investment to someone I hardly know. Especially a woman."

Was he saying she was untrustworthy? Evie stiffened her spine but remained silent when he raised his finger.

"The journey to Oregon Territory is arduous, and doubly so to a woman traveling alone. You must first arrive in California and book passage from there. If you travel overland, you risk starvation, thirst, and attack by savages. The journey by sea is hardly better, with the threat of cholera, malaria, and pirates in the waters to the south."

The breath deflated from her lungs through a suddenly constricted throat. It appeared that Mr. Coffinger had spent at least some time investigating the possible routes. How would she, who had never ventured beyond the borders of the Chattanooga valley, hope to undertake such a journey? She swallowed. "I assume there are wagon trains that one may join?"

"A young woman alone, carrying a large enough sum of money to start a business?" A scowl scrunched his features. "In the past I've been known to hand over money for likely ventures only to have it disappear with the borrower. It is a foolish man indeed who repeats his past mistakes."

And a foolish woman who would ask him to.

Her shoulders slumped. The idea had held such promise in the dark of night, without the light of logic to point out the shadows of uncertainty. But he was right. This was a fool's errand. She rose to leave, an apology for wasting his time on her lips.

"Wait."

She stopped in the act of standing.

"On the other hand, I do not intend to repeat the same mistake." The ends of his mustache rose with a smile. "This time I shall keep watch over my investment and oversee the spending personally."

For a moment his words made no sense. Then their meaning became clear. Hope flickered to life again. "Do you mean to accompany me?"

His smile widened. "Of late I've had a desire—a deep longing to see the land my nephew describes in his letters. What better opportunity?"

The memory of his wife's disdain for Noah Hughes's undertaking in Oregon Territory returned. Evie had a hard time imagining her standing idly by while her husband sank money in the venture. "Will Mrs. Coffinger agree?"

"Leave Mrs. Coffinger in my hands." He rose and crossed the room to open the library door, a clear gesture of dismissal. "But perhaps it would be best if you did not mention our plans until after I speak with my wife."

Releasing an audible sigh, Evie nodded. With Mrs. Coffinger's disdainful sniffle and arrogant countenance in mind, that was a request she had no trouble granting.

Three

Chattanooga, Tennessee

Evie folded the final skirt and laid it in the steamer trunk atop the rest of her belongings. It had hurt to sell the beautiful wooden chest that had once been her hope chest and replace it with this ugly trunk, but that had been the only logical step to take. The chest's polished wood would no doubt have been scarred and scratched during the journey across the country and the sea voyage upon which she was about to embark. Besides, the chest had brought a higher price than she expected, and this trunk cost far less than she had planned for. She had been delighted to add the balance to her restaurant fund.

She ran a hand across the fabric. The past two weeks had held far less pleasant tasks than selling her hope chest. Informing James of her decision to end their relationship was much harder than she expected. She closed her eyes against the image of his stunned expression.

"But…but what of our plans?" he had stammered, looking as though he'd suffered a physical blow.

"Your plans," she'd corrected. "I had no say in them."

"We can discuss them. I am open to considering your opinions, Evie."

It was only in retrospect that she realized he had not offered to change his course of action, only consider her opinion. And that he had not once during the difficult conversation professed his love, or acted in the least hurt. Merely surprised, and perhaps even a bit angry at the disruption in his plans. At the time she'd steeled herself against an unexpected wave of guilt and repeated as gently as she could that she had changed her mind and would not marry him.

She did not tell him of *her* plans, and had battled more guilt in the ensuing two weeks. In the back of her mind she'd feared James would decide to join her in her restaurant venture, something she most definitely did not want. Better to let him learn of her departure after she was gone.

She closed the trunk lid, clicked the clasp into place, and then turned to survey the room that had been her home since she'd lost Grandfather's house. The narrow bed looked stark without linens, the small night table bare after having been stripped of its adornments. Her dressing table and chest of drawers crowded this tiny space more than she'd realized. Those too had been sold, leaving the room empty and looking a bit forlorn.

A rap at the door interrupted her thoughts.

"The carriage has arrived." Mrs. Browning's whisper was barely audible from the hallway, in deference to the sleeping guests who did not wish to rise before the sun.

Evie opened the door and watched as a burly man hefted her trunk onto his broad heavyset shoulders. She picked up her travel bag and followed him through the house and out into the predawn mist. While he secured the trunk on the back, Mr. Coffinger exited the enclosed carriage.

"Good morning, my dear." His voice boomed through air heavy with moisture.

"Good morning, Mr. Coffinger."

"Since we are to be business partners, I think we can dispense with the formalities. You may call me Miles. And may I call you Evangeline?"

His request pleased Evie. She had intended to have a discussion with him to clarify that their arrangement was to be a true partnership and she no longer wished to be thought of as his employee. It appeared there was no need. She inclined her head in agreement.

"Have you had word from Mrs. Coffinger?" The one detail that left her feeling uneasy was her departure from Mrs. Coffinger's service. Miles had insisted that she not discuss their venture with his wife, and in fact not mention a word of her impending departure. Instead, he preferred to handle what was sure to be a volatile discussion himself. Last week Mrs. Coffinger had gone to Knoxville to visit her sister, presumably due to her extreme irritation with her husband's decision to invest in Evie's business venture. Evie would have preferred the opportunity to discuss her plans, or at least to say a proper goodbye.

Miles grimaced, and then quickly replaced the expression with a smile. "Only the letter telling me she arrived safely and would return in two weeks' time, after we are well on our way." He patted her coat sleeve. "Not to worry. She will get over her prickliness. She always does."

He offered his arm, and Evie turned to wave goodbye to Mrs. Browning before allowing him to help her climb into the carriage.

When she entered, she was surprised to see there were already three occupants inside. She slid into an empty place on the rear-facing bench beside two of them, and nodded a greeting as Miles entered and took the seat across from her. Apparently they were to share the carriage for at least part of the trip.

Miles settled himself and then cast a smile around the inside of the carriage. "Allow me to conduct the introductions. Miss Evangeline Lawrence, may I present Miss Lucy Burrows, her sister, Miss Sarah Burrows, and Miss Ethel Strapp."

The sisters, who occupied the bench with Evie, shared several family traits including exceedingly high foreheads, equine-like noses, and hair the color of wet straw. They were very close in age, which Evie guessed to be around eighteen or nineteen. The third lady appeared to be several years older and far more sturdily built. Her strong features bordered on masculine, and though it was hard to see much beneath her travel cloak, her figure left a great deal to be desired.

"Pleased, I'm sure." Evie nodded a greeting to each lady. "How pleasant to have company on the first part of our journey. Will you travel with us all the way to Charleston?"

The women turned startled expressions on Miles, whose hearty laugh filled the carriage. "Most assuredly," he replied. "They will accompany us all the way to Oregon Territory."

"Oh?" Evie frowned. Was Miles doing as his nephew asked and delivering a wagonload of women? A warm flush crept from her collarbone toward her cheeks as she glanced again at her traveling companions. They didn't *look* like fancy women of loose morals.

"They are to be your employees, my dear."

Evie's glance returned sharply to Miles. "My employees?"

"We will need staff to help us," he explained. "There will be a lot of work to get things going in our restaurant, and we cannot count on help from anyone else. The men have work to do in cutting down trees and splitting logs, or"—he waved a hand vaguely in the air—"whatever lumberjacks do."

A wave of irritation washed over her. The story was a thinly veiled excuse to answer his nephew's jesting request to bring women to the isolated lumber camp. Perhaps these three were not fancy women—she didn't think so—but they were women. What had Noah Hughes's letter said? If Miles brought women, he would have the admiration of the camp. Evie's teeth clamped firmly together.

If she were to have employees, she preferred to select them herself. Beyond that, she could not afford the expense. She clutched the handle of her travel bag, which contained her carefully detailed lists. Tasks to be accomplished, supplies to be purchased, projected initial costs and ongoing operating expenses. There was no room on her lists or in her budget for employees.

She cleared her throat. "The cost of wages—"

Another wave of Miles's hand cut her off. "We will go over that. After all, we have a long journey ahead of us. Plenty of time to discuss the details."

Evie bit back a heated reply. He was, after all, responsible for the major part of funding this venture. If he thought they needed employees, then he would simply have to pay for them. But at the first opportunity she intended to inform him that running the restaurant, including directing the work of any employees, would be her domain. On that she would insist.

With an effort, she relaxed her grip on the bag. When they stopped for the night, she would update her lists.

❧

May 12, 1852
Elliott Bay, Oregon Territory

Noah was running a tally when Arthur approached from the direction of camp.

"How does it look?" Arthur dipped his head toward the ledger in Noah's hands.

Noah finished his second count of the felled and cleared trees along the shoreline and recorded the results before answering. "It will be close. We have one week before this shipment is due to leave, so there's still time. We'd better pray the weather cooperates, though."

Both men's glances traveled upward to the cloud-filled sky. They were high clouds, thank the Lord, and white enough not to be a threat. At least not today.

Behind them, the *rip, rip, rip* of a saw played a rhythmic background to the chopping sound of multiple axes chewing into wood. The break in the rain had improved morale somewhat, and the men were finally working with something that approached their former enthusiasm. Or it could be the approaching deadline that boosted their flagging efforts. Once the timber was delivered to San Francisco and the initial payment had been made, they would all receive their promised pay. Though what they intended to do with it, Noah couldn't imagine. There was nothing to spend it on out here, and the second installment of lumber was due to ship a mere six weeks later. That left no time for traveling to any of the nearby cities to release pent-up energy. At least, Noah hoped no one intended to leave. If they lost even two men now, meeting their next deadline would become impossible.

"David and I have been talking about the delivery." Arthur lifted one booted foot and planted it on the nearest log. "We'd like you to handle things down in San Francisco."

"Me?" Noah frowned. "Don't you think you should be the one to deliver the first shipment? After all, you worked out the contract."

Arthur's face contorted, his lips cocked sideways and his eyebrows drawing together to form a single ridge. Finally he gave a sheepish grin. "Mary prefers that I stay here."

A laugh stirred in Noah's belly, but he deemed it wise to stifle it. Arthur was a strong, proud man, and admitting that he would bow to his wife's wishes must have galled him. "David volunteered to go," Arthur continued, "but I think it best he stay here. The men look up to him."

Noah saw the wisdom in that. Arthur was a natural leader, but David worked side by side with the men. He was a part of them in a way Arthur was not. If anyone could convince them to continue working after the first shipment was on its way, it was David. The Denny brothers were beginning to make a name for themselves in these parts.

"Well, of course I'll go. Glad to do it."

Arthur clapped him on the back. "Good man. I know I can count on you to handle things. Probably better than I would myself."

As Arthur left, Noah stood straighter, his spirits high. It felt good to have earned the trust of a man like Arthur Denny.

A moment later, another thought occurred to him. If Arthur was an acknowledged leader and David accepted by the men as a fellow worker, Noah knew himself to be somewhere in between. He had felled his share of trees at the outset of this venture, and he fancied he had gained the respect of the hardworking men in camp. But Arthur had quickly recognized that his strengths lay in his mind more than his back and reassigned Noah to the role of ink slinger, in charge of the business end of things.

In other words, his role was important, but when it came to the actual work, he was probably the most expendable man in the camp.

A fact Noah intended to change.

Four

June 3, 1852
San Francisco, California

Evie hurried out of the hotel onto the busy street. She was late for her meeting with the greengrocer, and her insides were a jangle of nerves. Tardiness was a sign of unprofessionalism, something she abhorred. Since their arrival in San Francisco, Miles had made a habit of sauntering into appointments fifteen or twenty minutes after the scheduled time, and she felt the indifference reflected badly on her. They were, after all, partners.

If I am late, it might teach him a lesson. Let him sit alone in the back office with Mr. Langley popping in every few minutes to see if I have arrived yet.

The problem was that neither Miles nor Mr. Langley would wait before conducting their business. They would proceed with the meeting whether she was there or not, and that rankled. Though Miles constantly proclaimed that they were equal partners in this venture, every supplier with whom they met spoke almost exclusively to him. They clearly preferred to deal with a man, and the knowledge chafed. Several times she'd been forced to insert herself into the negotiations in order to stop Miles from making poorly thought-out decisions.

She increased her pace. A busy crew unloaded cargo from a newly arrived schooner, stacking a pile of crates along the wooden pier. When she passed, one of the sailors paused in his efforts to whistle. His mates responded with laughs and a few calls in her direction. Though she had grown accustomed to the inappropriate behavior of the men who worked the pier, a blush still warmed her cheeks. Did James behave thusly when a woman passed by back in Chattanooga? She highly doubted it. Men in the East seemed to have more manners than those she had encountered in California. She kept her face pointed straight ahead and marched past without the slightest acknowledgment.

To her right lay the town, a collection of closely built wooden buildings that housed a variety of businesses, most of which she had visited since their arrival two weeks before. Every café and diner in San Francisco had been inspected, even if she'd been able to afford nothing more than a cup of coffee and a roll. She paid attention to everything—the table settings, the service, the variety of offerings on the menus. A mental image of her restaurant took shape and solidified daily.

As often as not, Sarah and Lucy accompanied her. During the two-month sea voyage and arduous trek across Panama she'd grown fond of the Burrows sisters, and increasingly irritated with Miles for his dealings with them. Though pleased to discover that they were not girls of loose morals, she worried that their expectations would not be met. Miles had promised they would find husbands in Oregon Territory, and that was the only reason they had agreed to come. Ethel too, though she had suffered with such a terrible case of seasickness that Evie didn't have as much opportunity to talk with her as with Sarah and Lucy.

Of course there was nothing to prevent them from finding husbands among the lumberjacks in Oregon Territory. In a place where men outnumbered women in huge amounts, surely even homely Ethel—

Cheeks warming, this time with guilt, Evie stopped from completing the thought. No doubt Ethel possessed many fine qualities that a man would find desirable in a wife. For instance, in the past two weeks as she regained the strength lost during the miserable sea voyage, she'd shown signs of a wicked sense of humor.

Distracted by trying to assemble a mental list of Ethel's finer qualities, Evie entered Mr. Langley's establishment. A bell jangled above the door, drawing the attention of the clerk, a young man bent over a crate of tomatoes. He rose and cast an inquiring glance her way, wiping his hands on a stained white apron.

"I'm here to see Mr. Langley. I believe he is expecting me." She glanced around the small shop, but saw no sign of the proprietor.

The boy jerked his head toward a door on the rear wall. "He's in the office wi' a gen'lman."

It seemed Miles had been on time for once. "Thank you."

The clerk looked like he might stop her as she made her way toward the office, but then shrugged and returned to his tomatoes. Evie gave a quick rap on the door with gloved knuckles and entered without waiting for an invitation.

"Gentlemen, please forgive—"

She fell silent when she caught sight of the man seated in the small room with Mr. Langley. It was not Miles. A much younger man rose from the spindly chair and fixed his gaze on her. Chagrin settled over her. She had interrupted a meeting with someone else.

Flustered, she took a backward step. "Pardon my intrusion. I thought you were my…"

The words died on her lips, snatched by a sudden confusion. Did she know this man? He had a familiar look about him. High cheekbones, a finely shaped nose, and a thatch of dark hair. Perhaps she had seen him in a café, or on the street?

Thick eyebrows rose. "Your what?"

"My…" Her tongue was possessed by an unaccountable awkwardness. She cleared her throat. "My business partner."

Mr. Langley had also risen. "He has not yet arrived."

"I'm sorry to have interrupted." Evie turned to exit. "I will wait outside."

The young man stopped her with a raised hand. "Please don't go. We were merely passing the time. Our business is concluded." He looked at Mr. Langley and nodded. "I'll expect the shipment to be delivered to the pier by nightfall in two days' time. We sail at sunrise the next morning."

She settled into the chair he had vacated. The man's ship sailed at the same time as the *Commodore,* the one she and Miles had hired to take them and their supplies to Elliott Bay. On the other hand, San Francisco was a busy port town. No doubt many ships arrived and left at the same time.

"Agreed." Mr. Langley nodded, and his gaze slid to Evie. "I'm afraid this means I will not be able to supply the full shipment we discussed, my dear."

Evie stiffened. "I beg your pardon?"

"Due to weather, some of my larger deliveries have been delayed." The man spread his hands. "I only have so much produce on hand, and I've just sold half of it."

She looked at him in dismay. "But we had an agreement."

A smile spread across the man's lips as he patted a canvas bag resting on the corner of his desk. The clink of coins was clearly audible. "But he had the funds."

"What do you mean? My partner has paid you."

Mr. Langley laughed coldly. "I've had nothing but talk from that one as yet."

She reeled back in the chair. Miles had not paid the man? He had assured her he'd settled the financial arrangements with all the suppliers with whom they'd met in the past two weeks. Would this happen again? Would the dry goods she needed be sold out from under her too?

Indignation stole over her. She rose and stood squarely in front of Mr. Langley on her side of the desk. "This is outrageous."

He waved off her protest. "I'll still be able to cover half of your order. Potatoes, onions, and lettuce are all good. It's the oranges, peaches, and tomatoes that'll be short."

No fruit meant no pies, no marmalade. And no tomatoes? How could she run a restaurant without tomatoes? It would be a disaster.

The younger man cleared his throat. "I'll be going now."

"No, wait!" Evie whirled and covered the space between them in two swift steps. Perhaps if she explained her situation. She took a deep breath to calm herself. "I need that produce for my business. Without it I will be understocked for the first few months of operation, which are critical to my success."

Sympathy flashed across his features. Her hopes rose, only to deflate again when he spoke.

"I'm sorry, ma'am." He ducked his head in farewell and made as if to leave again.

Panic clenched her stomach. This was Miles's fault. Why hadn't he followed through with his responsibilities? But regardless of blunder, the success of her restaurant was about to walk out the door. She couldn't let that happen. She whirled to confront the man about to depart. "I'll buy them from you. Name your price." It would serve Miles right if he had to pay twice what the produce was worth.

The man shook his head. "I need those supplies too. I've got a crew of hungry men to feed."

Frustration erupted as she sensed her plans crumbling. She stomped a foot on the wooden floor, her hands clenching into fists. "But you don't understand. You'll be the ruin of me before I even begin."

The full, dark eyebrows rose again, and disapproval shone in his blue eyes. "Madam, there is nothing to understand. This is a business arrangement, not a personal vendetta. I suggest you speak with your partner. Perhaps he can explain the error to you."

Heat kindled in her chest and erupted into her face. From his condescending tone, the implication was clear. She, a mere woman, couldn't understand the intricacies of business without a man to explain it in language simple enough for her to grasp. Well, Miles did have some explaining to do, but it wasn't about the nature of business arrangements. And this arrogant young man could use a lesson in the abilities of an independent woman like herself.

She drew herself up to her full height, trying to ignore the fact that even so the top of her head came only to his nose. "I assure you, sir, that I am capable of comprehending an agreement between two *professional* people of business." She cast a disdainful look toward Mr. Langley. "I am proposing such an arrangement. You have the supplies I require. I will purchase them from you at your price."

A brittle smile twisted the trim lips. "And I am afraid I must decline your proposition. Good day, madam."

With that, he left the office. Evie stood staring after him, her breath coming hard in her chest. Mr. Langley's soft chuckle so infuriated her that she dared not look his way lest she say something that would endanger the transaction for the rest of her supplies.

The bells on the outer shop door jingled. Should she go after him and try once again to persuade him to sell her the fruit she needed? Then she heard a familiar voice.

"Noah!" exclaimed Miles. "Good to see you, my boy! What are you doing here? I thought you were tucked away in the wilds of Oregon Territory."

Whatever answer the man spoke was lost to Evie, whose thoughts clamored in her mind. The arrogant man who had stolen half her supplies was Noah Hughes, Miles's nephew. No wonder his looks were familiar. Now she recognized the family resemblance to his uncle. That meant the ship that sailed in three days' time, the one he would sail on, was the same one that would take them to Elliott Bay and the settlement where she would open her restaurant.

The men Noah needed to feed were the same men she hoped would frequent her restaurant.

Leaving Mr. Langley behind, she stepped out into the shop to find Miles and his nephew shaking hands vigorously. Miles caught sight of her and his face brightened even further.

"There you are, Evangeline. You'll never guess who I've just run into. This is Noah, my nephew, the very one we are joining. Noah, let me introduce Evangeline Lawrence, my partner in a venture I think you'll find quite interesting."

Noah turned and his earlier smile faded.

At least she had the satisfaction of seeing that he was as stunned as she.

~

"No, I do not understand. You told me you would handle the finances, and I expected you to uphold your end of the bargain."

Noah kept his eyes fixed on the mug resting in front of him, though he was keenly aware that across the table creases had formed in Evangeline Lawrence's high forehead.

"And I shall, my dear. Don't worry." Uncle Miles reached out and gave her hand a paternalistic pat, a gesture Noah would not have dared. Judging from the fire blazing in the young woman's eyes, he risked pulling back a bloody stump.

"Do not patronize me, Miles."

No, this woman would not tolerate being patronized. Everything in her bearing said so, from the rigid set of her spine to the way she thrust her delicate jaw forward. Her shapely lips formed a hard line.

"Perhaps he means…" Noah fell silent when she turned those blistering eyes on him. He picked up his mug and took a long pull at his cider. Let Uncle Miles explain himself.

Beside him, his uncle's expression became solemn. "All right. I won't patronize you." His low, careful tone commanded the attention of both Noah and Evangeline. "The truth is I was unable to put my hands on all the money we needed before we left Chattanooga."

Evangeline's jaw went slack. "But I thought you said you could provide the funding for my restaurant."

Noah glanced up. "What restaurant?"

They both ignored him.

"I did, and I have. Just this morning I concluded my business with the bank and have secured the funds we need. I had hoped to have the arrangement in place before now, but an investment of this sort requires multiple levels of approval."

Evangeline leaned across her teacup to hold his eyes. "Do you mean you *borrowed* the money? I thought you were the only investor, that the money was yours. You told me you were coming with me to ensure that the expenditure of *your investment* was handled correctly."

Uncle Miles shifted in his seat, his hand on the glass in front of him. "Yes, well, that didn't work out as I had hoped. Some of my previous investments haven't produced the anticipated income, and I found myself running short."

Now it was Noah's turn to stare at his uncle. "You've run short of money?" Though Noah didn't know details of his mother's family fortune, he remembered from childhood visits the opulence of Uncle Miles and Aunt Letitia's lifestyle. Miles's inheritance from his father had been significant, and Mother had told him that Letitia's dowry was considerable.

"Of money to *invest*," Uncle Miles corrected. "I could not, in all conscience, put at risk the amount it will take to establish a successful business in the wilderness from my personal funds."

Hot, angry blotches covered the creamy skin of Evangeline's neck and face. "I thought you believed in this venture."

"Oh, I do," Uncle Miles rushed to say. "And so does the bank manager, which is why he agreed to loan us the funds we need."

"Us?" Her voice, shrill with alarm, drew the attention of those at nearby tables.

He frowned. "It's your business too, my dear."

With an obvious effort she lowered her voice, though she could not look at him as she spoke. "Are you saying you borrowed money on my behalf, in my name?"

"Of course. After all, we are partners in this venture, as you keep reminding me."

The flush on her face deepened to an alarming shade of purple, and her hand trembled. "Your role in our partnership was to provide the funding." Her voice shook, and she clamped her teeth together for a moment before continuing. "If you have failed in that, then our partnership is no longer valid."

"Oh, my dear, of course it is. I have secured the necessary finances, just as I promised."

"Using my name," she ground out.

"Using *our* names." He leaned back in his chair. "That was why the approval process took so long. The bank managers are not accustomed to loaning money to women." His shoulders lifted in an apologetic shrug. "Without my assurances that I would personally oversee the venture and do all in my power to ensure its success, their answer would have been no."

The color in her cheeks faded, and her mouth opened and closed several times as she tried, and failed, to speak.

Noah had listened silently long enough. He'd followed their conversation enough to draw a few conclusions, and he didn't like what he heard.

"Am I to understand that the two of you intend to open a restaurant at our settlement?"

Evangeline tore her glare from Uncle Miles and turned it on him. "That is correct. At least, that was the plan before you stole half of the produce we need."

Noah ignored the accusation. Clearly she was upset and lashing out wherever she could find an easy target.

"I think the idea has merit." Uncle Miles's finger traced the thick rim of his glass. "A new town needs trade to thrive."

"What town?" Noah shook his head. "You don't understand. The settlement isn't even a proper lumber camp. There are no buildings, no blacksmith, no general store. There is no place to put a restaurant."

Doubt darkened the round eyes across from him, but Uncle Miles dismissed him with a wave. "Not yet, but there will be. In your letter you spoke of your dreams to turn that camp into a proper settlement." He slapped Noah on the shoulder with a large hand. "We believe in your dream, boy, and we're prepared to invest in it."

Noah shook his head. "But a restaurant? The men eat for free. We provide their meals at the camp."

Now Evangeline's jaw softened enough to speak. "And what does your cook make, Mr. Hughes? Beans and salt pork?" Her tone dripped scorn.

"Actually, we have a pretty good cook at the camp." He went easy on the praise because of late the men had grumbled about the number of meals consisting of beans and boiled venison.

"I am better than *pretty good*." She spoke with confidence.

"And not only that," put in Uncle Miles. "She's a woman. And there are more coming with us."

Noah turned toward his uncle. "You brought women with you?"

"Only three. Four, counting Evangeline. But that's four more than you've got now. And all of them are unmarried."

She cast one more glare toward Uncle Miles and then turned a sweet smile on Noah. "Don't you think the men would prefer a delicious home-cooked meal served by a woman to beans and salt pork around the campfire?"

"We have a cook shack."

She sniffed. "Our restaurant will be more than a 'shack' and will allow the men a choice. I gather there aren't a lot of choices in this camp?"

Noah was forced to concede that she had a point. The men would probably flock to the establishment, and if the other women were as pretty as Evangeline they'd stampede to get there. Still, he had a bad feeling about this idea. What would Arthur say?

He shook his head. "I still don't think you understand. There is no town."

"You let us worry about that." Uncle Miles picked up his glass and drained it. "We've clearly thought this through and arranged for everything."

"Everything except tomatoes, oranges, and peaches." Evangeline aimed a scowl his way.

Noah bit back a sigh. She may be an attractive woman, but he had a hunch she was going to continue her harangue about fruit all the way to Elliott Bay. The voyage was sure to be one big headache on a ship the size of the *Commodore*, where there would be no place to escape her. And *three* others like her?

He'd rue the day he'd sent Miles and Leticia that Christmas card. He shook his head. Restaurant. At the logging site.

Five

*E*vie held on to the rail, her gaze fixed on the land as the ship skimmed the shoreline. Never had she seen anything so beautiful as this part of the Oregon Territory. The dense forest grew almost up to the riverbank, trees taller than any building and as big around as a dozen of the largest oaks back home. When they'd left the southern part of Elliott Bay and entered the Duwamish River, she had been unable to tear her eyes from the mountain peaks towering above the tree line in the distance. In Tennessee the mountains rolled with the landscape, their peaks smooth and tree-covered. These were steep, sharp, and majestic, their snow-capped peaks thrusting boldly toward heaven. She drew a deep breath into her lungs and tasted the difference in the air. Here it was cleaner, and so fresh with the scent of cedar that it was almost sweet on her tongue.

"Look!" Beside her, Sarah pointed to a place on the shore far ahead of them. "Is that a pier?"

Evie squinted through the misty drizzle that had begun an hour past. That brighter spot might be a clearing in the tree line, and the dark structure in the river could be a pier.

"I wouldn't call it anything so grand as a pier." Noah's voice behind her made her start. She hadn't realized he had joined them. Throughout the last leg of this journey he seemed to go out of his way to avoid her, and that was just fine. "A small dock is more like it. Just big enough to moor the ship and unload her cargo."

Ethel, who had dragged herself from her bunk to join them on deck, turned her head to answer. "I don't care if it's nothing more than a gangplank, so long as it gets me off this boat and onto dry land."

Evie awarded her a sympathetic smile. Though the journey had been smoother in the days since they left the open ocean, Ethel still suffered terribly from seasickness. Even now, when the ship's deck was nearly as steady as a wagon on an even road and the river almost flat, her skin held a slightly green tint and her red-rimmed eyes were dull and watery. Not blessed with beauty to begin with, she looked truly dreadful. No doubt it would be several days before she recovered.

A shout from the shore drew their attention.

"Oh, look." Lucy gestured toward a figure standing just outside the tree line, one arm waving above his head. "It's a man!"

She and her sister exchanged an excited glance, which made Evie smile. The man on the shore apparently caught sight of the passengers lining the ship's deck. His hand rose to shield his eyes, and then he thrust both arms in the air to wave with more energy. Giggling, Sarah and Lucy waved back. The man turned and shouted something into the forest and then took off running upriver toward the clearing.

"Ladies, I believe you've been spotted." Noah's dry tone drew Evie's attention. She turned her head in time to see his lips twist into a wry grin. "No doubt they're flipping coins to see who gets to escort you off the ship."

"Good." Miles joined them from below deck. "They can help unload the cargo."

Evie turned her back on him. He had tried to charm her ever since they left San Francisco, but she had not yet forgiven him for misleading her about the finances or for signing her name on the bank loan. His promise to the bank manager that he would personally oversee the restaurant chafed. If he intended to meddle in the day-to-day operation of her business, he had another think coming. No doubt they were going to butt heads in the coming months.

The drizzle thickened and became a cold rain as they neared their destination. Evie pulled her cloak close against the chill and considered going below in search of shelter, and thereby avoid Miles's company. No, she was already so wet it would make no difference. Thank goodness the brim of her bonnet was wide enough to shield her face, though the water dripping off the back had long since saturated her hair.

The ship's captain began shouting orders to his crew and sailors ran to the ropes. On shore, a small crowd of men had gathered to watch their approach.

"Would you look at the size of that one," murmured Ethel.

There could be no mistaking the one Ethel meant. He stood a full head above the others, his blond hair slicked tight to his head by the rain. Evie tore her gaze away from him and realized all of the men on shore were big, with hulking shoulders and muscles she could see even under their flannel shirts. Most wore beards, and to a man their hair was long and unkempt. Any one of them would make James look like an altar boy, and her former fiancé was a strong man. Sarah and Lucy were almost bouncing with enthusiasm.

Plagued by a sudden fit of nerves, she turned to Noah. "I see no ladies. Did you not say there were women and children?"

"A few. Their cabin is a bit of a hike from here." He waved toward the group on shore. "These, m'lady, are your future customers. Not a pretty bunch, are they?"

"They are…" She cast about for a word. "Big." *And dirty.* But she kept that observation to herself.

"Most of them are massive," he agreed. "They have to be strong. Jacking is hard work."

She cast a questioning glance his way. "Jacking?"

"Lumberjacking. You saw the size of those trees. Takes a lot of muscle to fell and ross a tree like that."

For the first time, Evie's confidence wavered. She had no idea what it meant to *ross* a tree. These people had a language all their own. They obviously didn't bathe regularly. She and the other ladies would be true foreigners in a land where the rules were different from those at home.

"I've been wondering something." Noah met her stricken gaze. "Exactly how did your partnership with my uncle come about?"

She made a show of studying the shoreline, thereby avoiding his gaze. Under no circumstances would she tell him she had been his aunt's housemaid. If he thought her nothing more than a servant, he would never take her seriously as a businesswoman. "We met through a mutual friend," she answered vaguely. "When he received your last letter, we began discussing the opportunities a new settlement in the western frontier presented." A movement on the shore, off to one side, drew her attention. Thank goodness. An excuse to turn this uncomfortable conversation away from her. Straightening, she pointed. "Who's that?"

A trio stepped out of the forest, though they held themselves apart. They were not as tall as most of the lumberjacks, and were dressed differently. Two wore loose shirts of an indistinct color made from a fabric that seemed to repel the rain. With a start, Evie saw that the third man was nearly naked. He wore nothing but a long fringed skirt hanging low on his hips. They all had dark skin and straight black hair nearly as long as hers.

"Why, those are Red Indians!"

Noah followed her gaze and nodded. "They're Duwamish. Their village lies in that direction, but there are usually a few tribal members hanging around. They like to keep an eye on the camp."

She turned her shoulders away from Sarah and the others and lowered her voice for Noah's ears alone. "Are they safe?"

His lips twisted sideways into a crooked grin. "You're not losing your nerve, are you?"

"Of course not," she rushed to reply. "It's only that I feel responsible for the others."

A shrug. "They're safe enough. Their chief has taken a liking to us." His glance swept the group of lumberjacks, and his grin faded. "I'm more concerned about the crew than the natives."

Startled, Evie looked once again at the men who would, hopefully, be her customers. As she watched, two more hurried into the clearing to join the crowd. Their stares were fixed on her and the other ladies, and as the boat drew alongside the wooden platform that served as a dock, she couldn't help but notice their hungry expressions. A shiver crept down her spine. It was not food they craved.

She started to say something to Noah, but he had caught sight of someone.

"There's Arthur." Relief saturated his voice. He spoke without taking his eyes from the shore. "You ladies stay onboard while I talk to him."

Evie was only too happy to comply.

A couple of lumberjacks hopped onto the dock and caught ropes thrown to them by the sailors onboard. Noah didn't wait for the lines to be secured, but climbed up on the railing and leaped onto the platform before the boat had completely stopped its forward movement. Wiping a splattering of rain from her eyes, Evie couldn't help but admire the effortless way he landed and strode forward without even a pause. He wasn't as tall or as broad-chested as some of the men on the land, but he moved with an athletic grace that a heavier man could not have managed.

Lucy turned away from the railing and fixed eyes clouded with doubt on her. "Where are the houses?"

She almost asked *what houses,* but swallowed the words. Surely when the women who lived here heard of their arrival, they would open their homes until suitable housing could be arranged. "Noah said they are a little distance away."

Ethel's thick eyebrows drew together. "Not too far, I hope. There's no sign of a carriage, and I don't fancy trudging through this rain."

Sarah swept a hand across the sodden shoulder of her coat and water splashed onto the ship's deck. "What I want are some dry clothes, a warm fire, and a hot cup of tea."

"As do I." Evie forced a confident smile onto her face. She had to do something to brighten their scowls. "Look at the bright side. No matter how far the house is, we've arrived safely and the ghastly journey is over. And we won't have to carry our own bags. I think we'll have plenty of volunteers for that."

The women focused on Noah, who had pulled a tall, dark-haired man aside to converse with him away from the crowd. A hand gestured in their direction. The conversation continued for some minutes, during which the lumberjacks' eager gazes grew weighty enough that even Ethel began to shuffle on her feet uncomfortably.

Miles sidled up to them, and Evie drew close enough to his side that the sleeves of their coats touched. She might still be irritated with him, but at least he was familiar, and no threat.

"Do you know that man Mr. Hughes is talking to?" asked Lucy.

Miles squinted in Noah's direction for a second and then shook his head. "If I were to hazard a guess, I would say that is one of the Denny brothers."

Ah. The bosses of this lumber venture. Evie turned to study him as he gave a nod and broke away from Noah. The man strode to the platform of the dock with a confident step and planted his boots in the center. When he raised his hands, every man present gave him his attention. Yes, definitely a leader, someone they respected.

"Men, I have an announcement." His voice, a deep baritone, rang out in the clearing. "As you may have noticed, our ink slinger has brought some visitors with him."

A loud cheer broke out, and Evie's cheeks grew warm at the wide smiles suddenly fixed on her and her companions.

"Visitors?" she mumbled quietly to Miles. "Did Noah not tell him of our intentions?"

"All in good time, my dear," came the whispered reply. "Have patience."

The man on the dock continued. "Before we welcome them ashore, I would like to point out that these are ladies."

A voice called out from the crowd. "We already figured that out ourselves, Arthur!"

Rough laughter answered him from all quarters.

"Arthur Denny." Miles gave a satisfied nod. "The leader of the Denny Party. I'm glad we shall meet him first off."

Arthur raised his hands again and the men fell silent. "You may have noticed that they are female, but I'm telling you they are *ladies*. I expect each and every one of you to treat them as such." His voice lowered and took on a menacing tone. "The man who doesn't will answer to me. Do I make myself clear?"

Evie let out a breath when the men all murmured agreement. She glanced at Noah, and found him looking at her. He touched a couple of fingers to his forehead in a silent salute and then returned his attention to Arthur.

"All right then. Let's welcome our guests."

The sailors, who had been waiting until he finished, opened a gate in the ship's railing and lowered a gangway. Miles offered his arm and when Evie took it, escorted her to the ramp. At the top, he halted and stepped aside.

"Ladies first." He swept a hand toward the ramp in a magnanimous gesture.

Stomach fluttering, Evie glanced at the others and then stepped onto the ramp. At that moment the heavens opened and the steady rain became a downpour. An omen, perhaps? She thrust the thought aside and lifted her soaked skirts to step forward. Small strips of wood had been nailed in place to supply footing. A good thing, since the leather soles of her shoes were not intended to traverse surfaces such as this.

The bottom of the ramp ended in a step of eight inches in depth. She hesitated, and then stepped forward. When her foot touched the dock, her sole skidded across the sodden surface. She tried to regain her balance, but the toe of her other shoe caught on the edge of the gangway and she pitched forward…

…into the strong arms of a fast-moving lumberjack.

A voice boomed in her ear as she was lifted off the ground. "I gotcha, little lady. Uh, I mean, ma'am." He flashed a triumphant grin.

Hovering mere inches from her nose was the face of the giant man they had seen from the ship. The thick blond beard covering his face parted to reveal a set of yellow teeth between smiling pink lips. Though thankful that he had saved her an inglorious fall in front of the entire camp, a blast of malodorous breath brought the sting of tears to her eyes.

"Thank you," she managed, trying hard not to wince at the tightness of the huge hands around her waist.

In the next instant, she was surrounded by a wall of flannel and flesh as the men surged forward, presumably to help the others from the ship. She was carried through the crowd, her shoes hovering at least a foot above the ground. The combined odor of unwashed bodies and dirty wet hair assaulted her nostrils while rain poured down on her from above. The first rule she would make for her restaurant would be a requirement of baths before dining.

Finally clear of the crowd, she was set down. Her feet sank ankle-deep in mud at the exact moment the brim of her hat succumbed to the relentless assault of rainwater and collapsed into her face. She lifted it away from her eyes with a hand that trembled, whether from chill or nerves she didn't know. At the moment she was consumed with both.

Soon Lucy and Sarah were deposited beside her, followed shortly by Ethel. They huddled close to her sides, the object of intense stares from the men who formed a circle around them.

She cleared her throat and raised her voice to be heard above the pounding rain. "Is there someplace dry we can wait while our things are unloaded?"

"Uh, we-ell." A dark-haired man cocked his head sideways and scratched his beard with a finger. "Thar's the tents back at camp."

"Tents?" Despair stretched out Lucy's word into something that resembled a wail.

Evie placed an arm around the girl's shoulders and squeezed. "How far is your camp?"

A young man who looked to be around fifteen pointed in the opposite direction from the river. "About half a mile up that-a-way."

Someone else shoved an elbow into his stomach. "We can't haul them up to camp. There ain't no empty tents, and you heard what Arthur said. These are ladies."

The youth glared at him. "I didn't mean they'd share with us. We'll have to double up for a while is all."

Evie spoke before a fight could erupt. "Perhaps there's somewhere we could sit until we figure out where we'll be staying."

"There's a log over here." The giant who had carried her shoved a couple of men sideways. "Get out of the way and let the ladies go sit down."

An opening appeared as men scrambled to move. Someone offered a soaked flannel-covered arm to Evie. When she took it, a dozen more arms were offered to the other girls to help them to their seat. With an effort she pulled her foot out of the mud. Her shoes were unrecognizable. There was a sucking noise beside her and Ethel gave a cry. She stood with one stockinged foot hovering in midair.

"Here, ma'am. I'll get ye." A lumberjack swept Ethel off her feet while another pried her shoe out of the mud.

In the next moment, Evie found herself also being scooped up in strong arms and carried across the clearing to be deposited on a dead tree at the edge of the forest. The others were soon seated beside her, Ethel with her muddy shoe in her lap.

"There's naught but a tent to sleep in." Her tone held the stress they all felt. "No fireplace."

Lucy shook her head. "No warm bed."

"Or hot tea either, I wager." Sarah's shoulders slumped.

"There's coffee," said one of the men. "Cookee's always got some going. By this time of day it's thick as axel grease, but at least it's hot."

"No tea?" Ethel sniffled as rain ran in rivers off of her bonnet. "Coffee does merciless things to my digestion."

Evie patted her leg. "I'm sure the captain will let us have some tea from the ship's stores. We can heat water over the cook's fire."

"Yes," agreed Lucy glumly. "But the captain's setting sail tomorrow."

Ethel sniffed again. "And we'll be left here."

She dropped her face into her hands and began to weep. In a moment Lucy followed suit, and the misery plain on Sarah's face said she may soon join them. Evie put one arm around Ethel and the other around Lucy and pulled them close, with Sarah huddled on her sister's other side. The men standing around them watched, their faces a series of helpless masks. Though she tried to think of an encouraging word, Evie came up blank. If there was a bright spot in this moment, it was too buried in gloom and rain for her to see.

Someone ran up from outside the group to stand behind their log, and in a moment rain stopped pelting against her head. She turned to find Noah holding a dirty yellow Macintosh like a canopy above her.

"Here, some of you men, take these and give the ladies some shelter."

He tossed more coats into eager hands, and before long the ladies sat beneath a canopy of rubber and thick wool. Then Noah rounded the log.

"Here, what's this?" He crouched down in front of Ethel and gently pulled her hands from her face. "Are those tears? I can't tell for all the rain."

The poor woman's puffy eyes were as red as her nose, but her shoulders heaved in a half-hearted attempt at laughter. "Truthfully, I can't either."

He turned a grin toward Lucy. "I'd give you my handkerchief, but it's as wet as my shirt."

That brought a trembling smile to the girl's lips. Some of the pressure in Evie's stomach lessened at the sight of it.

"There. That's better. Now, as soon as this rain lets up, we'll get you to camp."

A dangerous prickle started behind Evie's eyes. Had he spoken harshly she could have steeled herself, but a show of kindness was enough to bring her to tears.

"Is there room for us?" The note of despair that crept into Evie's question made her cringe.

"Sure there is. Arthur and I have it all settled. You'll stay in the command tent tonight, and then tomorrow we'll figure out a more permanent arrangement."

His confidence gave her a flicker of hope. "Command tent?"

"Sort of like a field office. We'll move everything out of your way and scrounge up some cots." Even his grimace held a hint of kindness that set loose a warm spark deep in her shivering body. "Not ideal, but they're more comfortable than the bunks on the ship."

The ship. She looked toward the dock, but the rain obscured everything in the distance behind a dismal gray curtain. "I am sure the captain would let us remain in our bunks for one more night."

"No." Ethel's reply was instant and insistent. "I shall not spend another night in that miserable, heaving cabin. Even if it means sleeping in a wide open field, I am staying on dry land." She extended a hand into the downpour. "So to speak."

It was clear there would be no persuading her to return to the ship, not that Evie could blame the woman after the terrible sickness that had plagued her all the way from Charleston.

Evie turned a smile toward Noah that she hoped was not as brittle as it felt. "Thank you." She meant the words to hold gratitude for more than arranging their beds for the night. He might be irritating most of the time, but at least he could be gracious when it counted.

And so could she.

❦

Dark had fallen by the time the ship's cargo was unloaded and the ladies settled for the night. Noah had fended off so many questions from men eager to know how he came to find four women willing to come to the lumber camp that he couldn't bring himself to go to the cook shack to eat. Instead he grabbed a plate of venison stew and headed for the tent he would share with the Denny brothers and Uncle Miles for the night. He hadn't been there long enough to eat a bite before the flap opened and Arthur entered, his brother David on his heels.

"What were you thinking to bring them here?" Arthur covered the distance between them in two long strides to stand squarely in front of Noah, fists planted on his hips. "A lumber camp is no place for women."

Noah almost took a backward step at the force in his voice and blazing eyes. Though he was in complete agreement with his boss, he held his ground.

"It wasn't my idea. It's that woman, Evangeline. She's got a mind to open a business here."

"A business?" Arthur's brows knit. "What kind of business?"

"A restaurant."

The anticipated explosion followed, and it took all of Noah's strength not to wince at the creative curses that filled his ears. He waited until the flood slowed before trying to insert a comment.

"I told her it was a harebrained idea. Neither she nor my uncle would listen to reason."

Arthur's eyes narrowed. "What exactly does your uncle have to do with this scheme?"

Noah detailed what he knew of Uncle Miles's and Evangeline's partnership, though he left out his own unwitting role in the scheme. If Arthur discovered that it had been an off-hand jest in Noah's letter that had given Uncle Miles the idea of bringing women to the camp, he might find himself sleeping with the mules tonight.

David had remained silent thus far, but when Noah finished speaking he ventured a comment. "They're right about one thing. We've said all along we want to plant a city here. Every city I've ever been in has places to eat."

Arthur swung around to face him. "First, before anything else? We haven't named our town yet."

Noah admired the way David, who was at least ten years his brother's junior, held his expression impassive in the face of his brother's sarcastic bite. "I've been telling you we need to come up with a name. As for the business trade, if this timber venture works out, there'll be other investors to come soon enough." He switched his calm gaze to Noah. "How did things go at Malcher's Mill?"

Relieved to have something besides Evangeline and Uncle Miles to talk about, Noah leaped at the change of subject. "Fine. Great. Malcher was impressed with the quality of the logs and satisfied with the quantity of the first shipment. Paid the full thousand dollars and seemed glad to give it over."

Grim satisfaction settled on Arthur's face. "He still wants the second shipment in a month?"

Noah nodded. "He told me to relay the message that if the second shipment is as satisfactory as the first, he'll be amenable to a long-term contract. He says since San Francisco keeps burning down he's got plenty of customers for milled lumber, and he'll take as much cedar as we can produce."

Grinning, David gave his brother a hearty slap on the shoulder. "That's exactly what we wanted."

"Yes, it is." Triumph shone in Arthur's eyes as he rubbed his hands together. "At least until we build a mill of our own. Then we'll be the ones selling the lumber."

"Plus shipping lumber will be easier than logs." Noah shook his head. "There were a few times on the way down I was sure we were going to lose the whole cargo."

"Well, you didn't." Arthur awarded him an approving nod. "You did just fine, Noah."

Noah basked in his taciturn boss's rarely given praise. In the next second, Arthur's stern expression returned and the breath stuck fast in his lungs.

"Nothing can interfere with meeting our quota for that next shipment. I want that clearly understood. Those women are not to distract the crew from their work."

Judging by the way the men had flocked around the ladies down by the river, his concern was valid. His mouth dry, Noah nodded his agreement. How was he going to keep a horde of female-starved lumberjacks from becoming distracted with four single ladies right beneath their noses?

David must have shared the same thought. "It might be best if they stayed at the cabin with Mary and Louisa and the children. At least for a month or so, until the next shipment is on its way."

Arthur looked at him for a long moment and then nodded. "They'll be out of sight there. I'll speak with Mary about it. But tonight you'd better stand guard outside their tent," he said to Noah. "I don't want any of the men getting ideas about those four alone only a few yards away."

"Me?" Noah stiffened, but his protest died on his lips when Arthur continued.

"You're the one who brought them here. They're your responsibility."

He was trying to think of an appropriate argument when the tent flap opened and Uncle Miles entered.

His uncle's face brightened when he caught sight of Arthur. "Ah, Mr. Denny. Just the person I hoped to find. Might we have a word? There are several matters I'd like to discuss with you."

Arthur answered graciously. "Of course, Mr....Coffinger, was it? I've just been talking with your nephew about your plans for our fledgling city. My brother and I are eager to discuss our vision for this part of the Oregon Territory."

While Arthur conducted the introduction between Uncle Miles and David, Noah picked up his bedroll and his untouched supper plate. Arthur's final words to him had killed his appetite as surely as if they had been delivered by means of an arrow to the stomach. Evangeline and the other ladies were *his* responsibility? He'd been afraid something like this would happen, even back at their first meeting in the greengrocer's store. Evangeline Lawrence, with her grand ideas and headstrong determination, did not strike him as the kind of person who meekly submitted to anyone's authority.

Especially not his.

❦

Seated on the edge of her cot, Evie sopped the last bite of stew from her tin plate with a corner of crusty bread. She had to admit that the food was tastier than she'd imagined. And it wasn't beans, either. The man who brought it to their tent had identified himself as Cookee, apparently the one responsible for feeding the crew of lumberjacks. Short and slim, almost scrawny, he stood only an inch or so taller than Evie and was the only man so far who had seemed entirely unimpressed by the arrival of four women in camp. Except for Noah, and he didn't count.

"The pusher said for me to bring this here meal to ye," he had told them as he placed a small pot of stew, a loaf of bread, and a pie on

Evie's trunk in lieu of a table. His scowl clearly announced his disgust at having to make a personal delivery.

"The pusher?" Ethel had asked.

"The boss of the camp. Arthur Denny."

Lucy almost gushed. "How nice of him to think of our comfort that way. The boss, you say?"

Cookee's scowl deepened. "Ain't nice at all. He's jest trying to keep you away from the jacks on account of he's afraid ye'll cause a riot or something. And he's hitched, lady."

The news sobered them all. Evie let him leave without asking any of the dozens of questions she'd noted on her list for the camp cook.

"I'll say one thing for that little fellow." Ethel held up a heaping spoonful of raisin pie. "He's a lot better cook than that hash slinger on the ship."

"How would you know?" Sarah held a piece of bread in front of her mouth and spoke in a teasing voice. "You never ate anything but bread and broth the whole way here."

Evie gave the woman a kind smile. "You're probably starving for a decent meal. Hardtack and water would taste good to you. Still, I have to say, this stew is better than I expected."

She couldn't help but feel disappointed. That she could produce food this good she did not doubt, but better enough that the men would pay extra to eat it? Perhaps a better strategy would be to offer a diversity of dishes. And, of course, the satisfaction of being served by a woman. She glanced around the room at Ethel finishing her pie, Lucy daintily picking a piece of venison out of her stew, and Sarah lying back on her cot with drowsy eyes. Perhaps in including them Miles had stumbled upon the answer after all.

A scratching sound outside the tent interrupted her thoughts, followed by the loud clearing of a throat.

"Are you ladies decent?"

At the sound of Noah's voice her stomach gave a leap. The

reaction irritated her, and she answered in a sharper tone than she intended. "Who wants to know?"

Ethel raised her eyebrows in Evie's direction. Noah paused and then responded in a subdued tone. "I am alone. May I come in?"

Three pairs of eyes turned toward her, and with an abrupt sigh, Evie shrugged and then busied herself stacking the dirty dishes. Lucy opened the tent flap and let Noah inside.

When he entered, the confines of the tent shrank. Four trunks and cots occupied most of the floor space, leaving only a small space which his manly form dominated. His boots pounded with a hollow sound against the plank floor.

"Ah, you've had supper, I see."

Though she made a point of keeping her back turned, Evie sensed that his comment was directed at her.

Lucy answered in her stead. "We have. Served in person by someone who identified himself as Cookee."

"Ah, so you've met him. Good."

A sudden suspicion overtook her, and Evie rounded on him. "Why?"

She could see she had startled him with her sharp tone. His eyes widened. "No reason. Only that you are both cooks. I thought since you hope to serve meals to the crew, you might enjoy meeting someone who has done so for the few months since this venture began."

Evie forced herself to put on a calm demeanor. The man meant no harm. In fact, he seemed intent on providing them with a hospitable welcome to this wretchedly primitive place. She pasted on a smile, though it faded almost as soon as it fell into place. "We appreciate your thoughtfulness."

She would have felt better about the conversation if he had managed to hold her eyes, but after a brief meeting of gazes, he turned his head to look around the tent.

"Though far more primitive than you're accustomed to, I hope you'll be comfortable here tonight. Arthur has arranged more suitable accommodations on the morrow."

"Oh?" Sarah stood from her bunk, her expression hopeful. "Has a proper building been found for us?"

He returned her gaze with a cautious one. "Not exclusively for you. Arthur's wife, Mrs. Mary Denny, lives with her sister and children not far from here. He is certain she will welcome you into her home until appropriate arrangements can be made."

Something about his words disturbed Evie. She sidestepped between the cots to stand before him so he would be forced to look her in the eye. "What arrangements?"

His mouth opened and then closed again. Finally he managed an answer. "Whatever arrangements are determined to be appropriate."

A rod of steel slid into her spine. "And who will decide what is *appropriate*?" If discussions were to take place concerning the future of her and the ladies for whom she had become responsible, she intended to make her voice heard.

A flash of alarm crossed Noah's features at the ferocity of her tone, but he exerted a visible effort to relax his stiff shoulders. "I don't know. Everyone in camp is committed to meeting our next delivery deadline in four weeks, so no one has much time to spare."

Evie narrowed her eyes. In other words, no one wanted to be bothered with them. They intended to tuck them away in Mrs. Denny's cabin and think about them at a more convenient time. Well, she would not submit to being tossed aside as though she were nothing more than a bothersome dog who had stumbled upon their camp.

"Mr. Hughes." She straightened her posture and held her chin high. "Please inform Mr. Denny that we are grateful for the offer of shelter in his family's home. However, at his earliest convenience, I request a meeting to discuss the possible sites for my restaurant and for hiring the labor to construct a suitable building."

Surprise crossed his features, and then quickly settled into a polite smile so brittle it might shatter with a word. "I'm afraid

Arthur's time to discuss frivolities is limited. If you require something, let me know."

"You?" She frowned. She was to be shuffled off to an underling?

"As for hiring labor..." Noah shook his head in what he probably intended to be a regretful gesture, but to Evie's eyes held the touch of a smirk. "Every man in this camp is hard at work meeting our next shipment. No one can be spared."

She became aware of their audience. The three ladies had observed the conversation in silence, their eyes traveling back and forth between the two of them. Lucy and Sarah wore wide-eyed expressions of astonishment while worried furrows carved deeply into Ethel's forehead.

Drawing herself up to her full height, she spoke in a polite tone. "Mr. Hughes, may I speak with you in private?"

A muscle twitched in his cheek. "Certainly, Miss Lawrence."

Ignoring her sodden bonnet, she picked up her cloak from the pile of wet clothing in the corner. Noah held open the tent flap and, with a gentlemanly gesture, indicated that she precede him outside. Head high, she passed out of the tent.

The rain had finally stopped, thank the Lord. Relieved, she hung her dripping cloak over a nearby low-slung branch. Though the moon was hidden behind a firm wall of clouds, her vision was no longer obscured by a dense curtain of rain. She found herself in a wide clearing, surrounded on all sides by the giant trees she had seen from the ship. A long row of tents had been erected at the far end of this clearing, and from inside she heard the sound of men's voices. Beyond them lay a long building made of uneven, rough-cut logs. So they did have buildings in this camp. Or at least one.

She turned to place the solid trunk at her back and faced Noah. No need to draw this conversation out with polite banter. "Are you determined to thwart my efforts?"

His eyebrows arched high, apparently surprised at her directness. Then he shook his head. "No, of course not."

"They why can you not spare a few men to build my restaurant?"

He scrubbed at his chin in a gesture of frustration. "You seem to think I have a personal vendetta against your venture. That isn't true. We have a quota of lumber to fill and not a lot of time to do it. After that shipment is gone, I'm sure you'll have more volunteers than you have tasks to give them."

"And how long will that be?"

"The shipment is scheduled for delivery by the middle of July."

Evie drew in a sharp breath. A full month before she could start generating income to repay the bank loan? Unacceptable. "I can wait a week, perhaps, but no longer."

He snorted a laugh. "I'm sorry. A month's the best I can do."

She detected not even a hint of sorrow in his demeanor. Folding her arms across her chest, she clutched her forearms in tight fists. "From the moment we met you've been determined to ruin my plans."

The set of his jaw became stubborn. "From the moment we met you've tried to blame me for every obstacle you encountered."

"You stole my shipment," she snapped.

"I conducted a business deal," he returned in a tone every bit as unbending as hers.

She searched for a sharp reply, but the steel in his gray eyes lashed at her so sharply that she could not manage a rational response.

Finally, he broke the uncomfortable stare by raking his fingers through his hair. "Look, I've made no secret that I think your idea of a restaurant in what is, at this point, nothing but a lumber camp is a foolish one."

She drew a sharp breath. How dare he call her foolish?

Oblivious to her reaction, he indicated the camp. "We don't even have a name for this settlement yet. In fact, there won't be a settlement unless we can prove this place can support a town or city. Once we've established a viable lumber trade there will be plenty of opportunity for other businesses. First and foremost, this endeavor will be built on lumber, not on home-cooked suppers."

Her fingernails dug through the sleeves of her dress, but she managed not to shout. "Was it not Napoleon Bonaparte who said an army marches on its stomach? Somehow I doubt a lumber camp is much different."

A grim determination stretched his lips into a hard line, and he leaned closer. His eyes held hers in an unbreakable grip. "Evangeline, listen closely. I cannot allow you to disrupt this camp. You will keep your women out of sight and let the men get their work done."

Fury shot down her spine. How dare he bark orders at her as though she were one of his lumberjacks! "And I cannot allow you to disrupt my plans. I *will* build my restaurant, even if I have to do it myself."

A genuine laugh rose from his throat into the night. "I'd like to see that."

"See it you shall," she snapped. "That is, if you can come down out of the trees long enough to watch."

With a flounce of her skirts she marched away, her nose high in the cool night air. Her stomach churned, whether with anger at his infuriating manner or at the monumental task she had just boasted she could accomplish, she wasn't entirely sure.

Of one thing she was certain. She had no idea how to split a log for firewood, much less build a restaurant.

❧

Noah unrolled his bedroll directly in front of the women's tent entrance. From inside he could hear the ladies' voices as they discussed the events of the day, though his own thoughts almost drowned them out. If Evangeline spoke he would blatantly eavesdrop, because he needed every advantage over that stubborn woman he could get. But she remained silent.

He crawled beneath his blanket, thankful that he'd had the foresight to grab a rubber sheet as protection against the soggy ground.

Though cold mud conformed to the shape of his back, at least he would sleep dry.

What was wrong with that woman? Did she really expect the entire camp to stop work in order to help get her settled? No, apparently anything that interfered with her plans was *his* fault. She seemed determined to blame him for everything that went wrong.

He pillowed the back of his head in his hands and stared upward. The tops of the trees that surrounded the camp were barely visible as dark shapes against a black sky. Inside the tent, the ladies fell silent while in the distance the loud rumble of a snore came from the direction of the jacks' tents. Must be Big Dog Carter. Noah pictured the camp giant as he'd been this evening, leaping onto the dock to catch Evangeline before she fell and then carrying her in bear-sized hands as if she were a child. He'd been taken with her. And no wonder. She was a mighty attractive woman, even with her dark hair hanging in wet strings down her back and her hat collapsed around her head.

Noah rolled onto his side and pounded a lump in the mud until it lay flat beneath his bedroll. Looks counted for nothing. He'd learned that lesson months ago, when Sallie disappeared with his money and left his prospects for a decent future in shreds.

Pretty women meant trouble, that's what he'd learned. It was not a lesson he intended to forget.

Six

*E*vie awoke before dawn to the sound of men's voices. Sleep still dragged at her eyelids and fogged her brain. Beside her Lucy breathed the slow, regular breath of one who is deeply asleep. Ethel's rumbling snore from the far side of the tent indicated that she too slept.

And no wonder. When Evie pried her eyes open, the blackness in the tent was as complete as it had been when they fell into an exhausted sleep the night before. Her body told her dawn was still several hours away, and yet she knew she would not drift off again. Too many thoughts crowded her mind, driving sleep away.

She became aware of sounds outside. Men's voices. Morning might be hours away but the camp was stirring. Or perhaps morning had already arrived. For all she knew the sun never shone in this wretched place. Regardless, she could not lie there a moment longer.

The dry skirt and waist shirt lay across her trunk where she had put them in readiness for the morning. Moving as quietly as she could, she crawled to the end of her cot and donned her clothing. Sarah stirred when she opened her trunk to retrieve her brush, but then fell back into a deep sleep. The other two slept on.

Evie unfastened the flap and slipped out. She half expected to have to step over Noah, but she found the space in front of the tent empty, his bedding rolled into a neat bundle and set off to one side. With a touch of chagrin she realized he had risen before her, though why that thought should leave her feeling unsettled she didn't know. Who cared when that man slept and when he rose? Certainly not she.

A slight breeze stirred the branches of the trees far above her. The air held very little chill from yesterday's rain and was tinted with a wild, fresh sweetness that shot energy through her tired limbs. She inhaled deeply and realized that other aromas also rode on the wind. The tangy bite of salt pork frying and the delicious smell of baking bread. Her stomach rumbled to life as though she had not eaten a full meal only a few hours before.

A glance around the clearing revealed a glimmer of lamplight seeping through cracks in the long structure she had noticed last night. The voices came from that direction as well, and with her eyes adjusted to her dim surroundings she could see the shadow of smoke trailing into the sky. That building must be the cookhouse. Good. She wanted to get a good look at it.

Stepping with caution across the muddy clearing, she made her way to the structure, following the sound of male voices. When she drew near she spied a door standing open at the far end. She paused a moment to smooth her skirts and settle a sudden case of nerves. Then, with her head held high, she marched inside.

It took a moment for her eyes to make sense of the jumble of activity. Lamps created glowing circles of light throughout the room. Long tables stretched the length of the building. A closer inspection revealed that they were nothing more than wide logs that had been split down the center to form a roughly level surface. On top was piled the biggest feast Evie had ever seen. Stacks of flapjacks, platters piled high with meat, tubs of butter, and huge bowls of delicious-smelling fried apples. The benches pulled up to each one followed the same design as the tables, though obviously on shorter legs, and filled with men.

A dark-haired lumberjack on the far end of the room caught

sight of her. He jumped to his feet and pointed. "There's one of them now."

At his shout all talk in the room ceased. Every head turned her way, and Evie found herself the center of attention. Her breath became a frozen lump in her lungs. Perhaps Noah had been serious in his cautions about her safety in a camp full of men. In the next moment benches tumbled backward as the men leaped up. Knit hats were snatched off heads and those seated nearest the door rushed forward. A dozen deep voices wished her good morning, and she found both of her hands tucked in muscular arms as she was pulled forward. A bench was hastily righted and she was invited to sit.

"I'll bring you a plate, Miss," a brawny blond offered eagerly.

"I'll git your coffee." The man next to him edged him away by planting his hands on the table and leaning toward her. "We got honey for sweetin'."

Though moments before her stomach had complained of emptiness, Evie suddenly found the idea of eating in this crowd intimidating. The men formed a seemingly endless circle around her, their eyes roaming over her like so many starving dogs hovering outside a butcher shop. No doubt her every bite would be watched.

She declined a plate of food with a polite shake of her head. "Though I would appreciate coffee with a touch of honey." Coffee was not something she normally cared for, but she remembered their chagrin yesterday at Ethel's request for tea.

Three men whirled and banged into each other in their haste to meet her request. The rest quickly closed the circle. The odor of unwashed bodies threatened to overpower that of the bacon, and she masked an unpleasant flutter in her stomach with a quick smile. She was answered by a dozen or so wide grins.

Someone pushed between two beefy lumberjacks and stepped into the circle. With a jolt, Evie looked up into Noah's unsmiling face.

"Miss Lawrence." His voice held a chilly courtesy. "I didn't expect you to be up at this hour."

"You'll find that I am an early riser, Mr. Hughes." She poured extra sweetness into the smile she awarded him. "Especially when there is so much work to do."

His jaw tightened, and he looked as if he would have answered except that her coffee arrived at that moment. A man inserted himself into the circle and carefully set a steaming tin mug in front of her.

"There you go, miss. A dollop of honey." He did not move, but hovered with an anxious expression.

Evie picked up the mug and took an experimental sip. Scalding hot and bitter, she had to school her expression to hold back a grimace. "Delicious," she lied. "Thank you, Mr.…."

The man straightened to attention. "Smithers, ma'am. George Smithers."

"George?" A guffaw came from somewhere behind him. "Don't go trying to put on airs, Pig Face."

He glared at the chuckles of his crew mates. "George is my given name."

Unfortunately, his nickname was well earned. The tip of his nose pointed toward the sky, granting Evie an unobstructed view of two round nostrils that did hold a more than passing resemblance to a pig's.

"Thank you, Mr. Smithers." She set the mug down on the table and let her smile travel around the circle of faces. "I am Evangeline Lawrence, recently arrived from Chattanooga, Tennessee."

Her audience began calling out names so quickly she could do no more than give a brief nod of acknowledgment to each man.

"Lester Palmer."

"Randall Miller, ma'am."

"Red Anderson." That one, at least, she would have no trouble remembering, thanks to a thick thatch of orangey-red hair that topped a face round as a melon.

Her gaze was drawn to the giant from the dock, which towered a full head above the others. "And your name, sir?"

"Jacob Carter, ma'am." His hands twisted a knitted hat into a ball. "But everybody calls me Big Dog."

She nodded, and then spoke to the lot of them at once. "I am pleased to make your acquaintance, gentlemen. I hope we will become friends in the days ahead."

"Miss Lawrence, may I have a word with you outside?" The disapproving scowl on Noah's face left no room for refusal.

Rather than cause a scene, Evie opted for a show of manners. "Of course, Mr. Hughes." Taking her mug in one hand, she slipped off of the bench. The men moved out of her way, disappointment clear on their faces, and allowed her to head for the door.

A flash of color caught her eye. Toward the center of the table stood a bowl of oranges. Her oranges, of course, all the way from Mr. Langley's greengrocer in San Francisco.

She exclaimed with delight. "Oh, look at that lovely fruit." Rounding her eyes, she turned an innocent look on Big Dog. "Do you think I might have one?"

Men fell over themselves rushing toward the table. A moment later she found the entire bowl thrust into her hands.

"The other ladies might like them too," Big Dog said.

"Oh, I'm sure they will, Mr. Carter. Thank you for being so thoughtful." She gave him her widest smile before following Noah out of the building.

She found him standing off to one side, scowling, with his arms folded across his chest. "I will not stand by and watch you toy with those men for your own amusement."

Outrage warred with the tiniest stab of guilt in her. She *had* been putting her best foot forward, fully aware that the men would be charmed with a feminine presence. Yet how dare he accuse her of toying with them? "I am not toying with anyone." Her whisper rasped in her throat.

"Of course you are." Assuming a simpering smile, he batted his eyelashes and he clasped his hands together beneath his chin. "*Oh, look at those lovely oranges!*"

His high falsetto rubbed on her nerves like gravel. Under no circumstances would she ever simper like that.

"My oranges!"

"They were on my table."

She felt like she could spit. "You are the most annoying man I have ever met."

"And you…" A struggle twisted his features, and then he snapped his mouth shut. When he spoke, it was in a controlled tone. "I must request once again that you and the other ladies make an effort not to distract the men from their work."

"May I remind you that I too have work to do? Can we not do both at the same time?" The rim of the bowl pressed into her stomach, but she managed to keep her voice low. "It is not my intention to distract anyone from anything, and the other women have done nothing but comply with your directions." As far as she knew they were still sound asleep in the tent.

He shook his head. "Oh, you're a distraction all right."

Torn between determination to make him see her point and pleasure at the compliment, she said nothing. A moment later she was saved from replying when Arthur Denny strode into the clearing. Catching sight of them, he covered the distance and fixed her with a wide smile.

"Miss Lawrence, I have good news. My wife and sister-in-law are delighted to have you and the other ladies stay with them. They both say they've missed the opportunity to talk with women, and they look forward to having you for as long as is needed." He rubbed his hands together, obviously well pleased with the arrangement. "Noah will escort you to the cabin this morning."

Evie hesitated, unsure how to proceed. Making demands to Noah was one thing, but Arthur's stern countenance did not invite discussion.

"But my things, my supplies—"

He dismissed her concern with a shake of his head. "Your personal belongings can go with you, of course. As for the rest, Noah will make sure they are stored and secured to your satisfaction."

The issue thus resolved he started to turn away.

Evie stepped hastily in front of him. "Mr. Denny, I would like to talk with you about my restaurant."

"I've spoken at length with Mr. Coffinger, who is, I believe, your partner?"

She nodded, though reluctantly.

"He knows my thoughts on the matter. Now, if you'll excuse me, I need to give the men their orders for the day." He stepped around her and disappeared before she had a chance to stop him again.

Evie turned to find Noah scowling after him. Apparently he wasn't any happier about being her escort than she was to have him. *If they think I will meekly be scuttled out of sight like a bothersome child, they are in for a surprise*, she thought to herself.

First, though, she needed to know what Miles discussed with Arthur. Then she could make plans from there.

"Where is your uncle?"

Noah shrugged. "Still asleep, would be my guess."

"When he wakes, would you tell him I'd like to speak with him?"

At his nod, Evie gathered her skirts in one hand and, carrying her bowl of oranges, marched across the muddy clearing to wake the others. They had a busy day ahead of them.

❧

Evie, Sarah, Lucy, and Ethel perched on one of the rickety benches in the otherwise empty cookhouse in front of plates of flapjacks and fried apples. Gone were the astounding quantities of food she had seen piled on the tables an hour past, devoured by men whose appetites surpassed anything she had imagined. When asked, Cookee haughtily informed her that men needed real food, and lots of it, if they were to have energy to do the hard work of a lumber-jack. Her lists concerning quantities and serving sizes would need to be revised before she opened the doors of her business. The white linens carefully pressed and stored were definitely out, as were the lovely glass vases intended for a single flower.

Though Miles had no plans to pick up an ax, he sat on the other side of the table with a plate as full as that of any of the lumberjacks she'd seen earlier.

Evie eyed the huge bite of molasses-soaked flapjack that he was preparing to place in his mouth. "If you continue to eat this way, you'll end up paying me to let out the seams of your trousers."

The fork paused in front of his mouth. "You would charge your partner? My dear, how mercenary of you." The food disappeared behind smiling lips.

"Business is business, and money is money. As you know, I have a loan to repay."

Still, she couldn't stop an answering smile. Though Miles had misled her and misused her name without her knowledge, it was impossible to stay angry with someone whose enthusiasm shone in his countenance. He had entered the cookhouse this morning hum-ming, his spirits contagiously high.

"I understand you've spoken with Mr. Denny concerning the restaurant." She took a cautious sip from the tin mug. The coffee's bitterness was beginning to grow on her, especially when, halfway through the first cup, her mind fairly buzzed with an energy she'd never experienced from tea. "Did you discuss a likely location?"

"We didn't get so far as that, though he did outline his plans for the new town. If this next lumber sale goes through, they hope to attract investors for building a mill. Of course that will be located near the river's head—perhaps a more ideal place for our restaurant?"

She conjured an image of the bay, though the rain had been fall-ing so hard and her nerves had been so jangled, she hadn't gotten a clear look at anything. "Near where the *Commodore* is docked now?"

Nodding, he washed down a mouthful of bacon with coffee. "Precisely. Naturally the town will spread outward from the mill."

Ethel pushed her empty plate away. "So that mud hole we had to tromp through will become the town center?" A scowl curled her nose. "I don't think much of that plan."

Actually, Evie agreed with her. The ideal location would be near enough to the bay to take advantage of the view, but far enough inland to provide protection from the elements during storms and heavy rains, such as yesterday's. There must be a suitable location nearby.

"Did you express to Mr. Denny the urgency of our situation?" She set her coffee down and planted her forearms on the splintery surface. "He seemed eager to avoid the subject when I saw him this morning."

"The topic did arise." He speared an apple with his fork. "You see, everything rests on the Dennys' ability to meet this next shipment of logs. Until that happens, the future of this settlement is uncertain."

Evie's lips pressed together. The same tale Noah was so fond of repeating. "I cannot understand why these men will not see reason. I've no doubt lumber will be an important part of the town's future, but lumber alone will not do it. The sooner a variety of commerce is established, the stronger the settlement's chances of survival." She leaned forward and caught him with a direct stare. "You must make them see the logic in that, Miles."

"Not to worry, my dear. The time will not be wasted." Renewed enthusiasm shone in his eyes. "This territory is brimming with opportunities. Why, do you know what Captain Johnson is doing today? He is buying salmon from the Indians."

He flashed a wide grin on all the ladies, obviously pleased with his revelation, though Evie couldn't imagine what a ship's captain trading with natives had to do with her restaurant. Was he saying she should purchase salmon from the Indians and cook it for her customers?

Before she could reply, Lucy voiced a question. "Is that allowed?"

"Of course. The local natives are quite willing to barter. Salmon is highly prized in California, and available in abundance here. They say the fish practically leap out of the stream and into the nets. The problem, of course, is transporting it quickly enough that it doesn't spoil."

Ethel shook her head slowly. "I don't see what this has to do with us."

"Why, my dear, if the salmon are so easy to catch, why can we not do it ourselves?"

While he beamed at a bemused Lucy and Sarah, Evie exchanged an uneasy look with Ethel. He wanted them to stand in an icy stream and catch leaping fish?

"Don't you see?" He gripped the edge of the table. "We can preserve the salmon in a brine solution and pack it in barrels. If we spend the next month working industriously, we can have several hundred barrels ready for the *Commodore's* return." Folding his arms across his chest, he settled back on the bench. "We will make a fortune."

"Look here." Sarah's features formed a scowl. "None of this is getting us what we signed up for. Miss Evangeline says this boss wants to tuck us out of sight in a cabin some ways from here. If we do that, how are we ever going to snag a husband?"

With a frown fixed on Miles, her sister nodded agreement.

Miles reached across the table and covered Sarah's hand. "Have no fear on that account. We mustn't appear uncooperative, after all. But did you see the enthusiasm with which the men welcomed you yesterday? Why, by the end of the summer you'll have your pick of husbands." With a paternalistic pat on her hand, he straightened. "And then Miss Evangeline and I will have to find more ladies to help in our restaurant while you're off raising babies to fill your new homes."

The glowing expectation seemed to appease them, at least for the moment. Lucy picked up an orange and began peeling it, a dreamy smile on her lips.

Uncooperative? Evie tapped the dirt floor with an impatient foot. Arthur Denny and Noah were the uncooperative ones. It appeared they'd lured Miles into their way of thinking as well. Apparently they were so set on their own goals that they failed to see reason, even when it was laid out plainly before them. Well, so be it. Let them follow their own plan. She intended to do the same, with or without their help.

Evie maintained a stubborn silence during the fifteen-minute walk to the Denny cabin. Noah took the lead, trading isolated words with one of the Indian braves who seemed to accompany them wherever they went. He held the mule's lead rope loosely in his hand. She felt sorry for the poor creature, laden as he was with four trunks and as many bundles as they could attach to his back. Riding high atop the rest was a crate of chickens who, judging by their protests at the jostling pace, wouldn't lay for weeks to come. The mule didn't seem overly burdened and plodded obediently behind Noah like a trained puppy.

The path, if it could be called that, wound through the dense forest in such a jagged line that she nearly lost her sense of direction. Though she took care to search for landmarks, there were few to be noted in the never-ending stretch of immense trees. At least the sun did shine overhead, though so many branches lay between the sky and the ground that the shade was at times nearly as dark as twilight.

Though she had no desire to speak with Noah, she and the others took care to stay close to him. The tail of their party consisted of two more natives, both of whom eyed the ladies with undisguised interest as they trailed behind, making no more noise than a bird in flight. Their disturbing lack of proper clothing kept Evie's cheeks burning, and the smell of the oil with which they covered their bodies provided a constant reminder of their presence.

"It's quite a long way, isn't it?" Lucy caught her eye over the mule's neck. "How long do you suppose we've been walking?"

Before Evie could answer, Ethel ventured a breathless guess. "An hour at least."

The poor woman looked as though she might collapse from exhaustion. Red splotches rode high on her cheeks and her ample bosom heaved with the effort to breathe. Strands of mouse-colored hair had rebelled against the binding at the back of her neck and waved freely above her head.

"I hope it's not much farther." Sarah's tone contained the hint of a whine. "These shoes weren't meant for tromping over miles and miles of wilderness."

At the lead, Noah turned his head to speak in their direction. "We haven't gone a mile yet." The amusement that lightened his words served to further irritate Evie. "But don't worry. It's not much farther."

She held her tongue, in part because she was feeling rather winded herself. Back in Chattanooga she had walked much farther than this to and from her rented room at Mrs. Browning's boardinghouse, but that had been on paved, even streets. Trudging over grass and winding around trees over land that dipped and rose in no apparent pattern was an entirely different kind of travel. Besides, the delightfully fresh air here seemed not to satisfy her lungs as well as the heavier air she'd grown up breathing.

When they reached the end of their journey, Noah brought the mule to a halt. Evie stepped out of the trees into a clearing and stopped, awed by the sight that met her eyes.

The sun, unimpeded by the dense forest, sparkled in a dazzling blue sky, casting its warm light downward like liquid crystal and turning the grass from ordinary green to a shimmering emerald. Clusters of ferns decorated the lush ground, their giant feathery leaves swaying in a gentle breeze. Along one side of the glade a shallow stream splashed over a rocky bed, the water so blue it might have been a ribbon of sky. Fir trees of all hues and sizes formed a protective circle around the glade, their bushy branches joining together to create a green rainbow wall. And towering above all, the ever-present cedars stretched toward the deep blue heavens, their moss-covered trunks straight and mighty.

"What a beautiful place." Evie's voice, breathless with wonder, broke the silence that had descended on the party.

Eyes round, Sarah agreed in an awed whisper. "I've never seen anyplace so lovely."

A cabin lay on the other side of the clearing, a rectangle made of rough log walls and a steeply pitched roof covered in wood shakes. An odd-looking half door punctuated this side, the top part pushed open. Did they close the bottom to keep forest animals from wandering in? Evie spared a sideways glance at Ethel, who had made no secret of her fear of wild animals.

Noah cupped his hands around his mouth. "Ho, the cabin!" His shout echoed in the clearing.

A woman appeared at the cabin door and inspected them with a sharp glance. Her head turned, as though speaking to someone inside, and then the bottom half opened. Two little girls tumbled out.

"Uncle Noah! Uncle Noah!" The high-pitched voice of the youngest rang with delight as she ran toward them on chubby legs. The child's head was covered with a mass of red curls which shone in the sunlight.

Her dark-haired sister, whose legs were longer, reached them first and skidded to a stop in front of Noah. "Papa said you would come today and bring our visitors." She turned a shy but curious glance on Evie, and dimples appeared in her round cheeks. "You're pretty."

Smiling, Evie bent down to put her face on level with the girl's. "So are you. What's your name?"

"Louisa Catherine. And this is Margaret." Her eyes widened when she caught sight of the mule's burden. "You have chickens!"

Laughing, Evie straightened. "Yes, I do."

Margaret arrived, puffing with the effort of catching up with her sister, and threw herself at Noah, who swept her up in his arms. "Good morning, sweets. Did you save me a bite of your biscuit from breakfast?"

The child became serious. "No, Uncle Noah. I ate it all." She brightened. "But Aunt Louisa made extra 'cause she knew you were coming."

Aunt Louisa? Evie's ears perked to attention. And the children called him Uncle Noah? While on the *Commodore* he had told them all he was not married, but was he, perhaps, spoken for? She tried to ignore the tickle of disappointment at the thought. What did she care if he had an arrangement with a woman? Not a thing.

Two women exited the cabin and waded through the thick grass toward them. The older held a baby propped on one hip, and though she had a kind smile, when she neared Evie saw signs of fatigue in the creases that circled her eyes. Arthur Denny's wife?

Her companion lengthened her stride and came toward Noah with her hands extended, delight apparent on her face. And a lovely face it was, with smooth cheeks that curved around high cheekbones and eyes that danced with welcome.

"Noah, how lovely to see you. You've been too often absent lately." The last was spoken in a teasing reproach that was belied by the deep curve of her pink lips.

When Noah set the little girl down and took the extended hands, Evie experienced a stab of jealousy. He had never smiled at her that way. The most he'd ever given her was a scowl and a lecture. Not that she gave two figs about Noah Hughes's smiles, but he could have at least afforded her the respect he showed this lady. Surely she deserved that.

"Arthur keeps me too busy for visits." He grinned into the

woman's face. "Perhaps he is doing it on purpose, to keep me away from here."

She threw her head back, and laughter lilted toward the heavens. "That would be a completely un-Arthur-like thing to do. He is far too focused on real work to try to come up with worthless distractions." Leaning close, she said in a mock-whisper, "Now, David might attempt such a scheme."

While Noah chuckled, she finally released his hands. The older woman spoke up as she did so. "I am Mary Denny. My husband told me of your arrival and your need for suitable accommodations. Our home is not large, but we will gladly make room. You're welcome here for as long as you care to stay."

"Thank you. I am Evangeline Lawrence, and these are my... friends." *Employees* sounded almost haughty, and besides, the four of them had become friends in the months since leaving Chattanooga.

Ethel stepped forward, her eyes fastened on the child in Mary's arms. "Thank you for taking us in." She bent forward and smiled into the little face. "What a lovely little lad. May I hold him?"

"This is Rolland," said Mary as she handed the little boy over, and Sarah and Lucy immediately crowded around, cooing and chucking his chin.

"They've made a friend in Mary, that's for sure." The voice beside her lilted with laughter, and the young woman turned toward Evie. "I'm Louisa, Mary's sister. Arthur told us of your soggy arrival last night, and of the crew's response to you. He said they fell all over themselves trying to help you ashore." A mischievous spark twinkled in her eyes. "That had to be entertaining."

Grandfather used to say he could form an impression of a man within ten seconds of meeting him. At that moment, Evie believed him. In spite of herself, she was drawn to Louisa's wit and ready grin.

She couldn't stop a chuckle. "It was rather comical, though I wouldn't admit that to Ethel. She was quite upset by the whole thing."

With a laugh, Louisa tucked her arm inside Evie's and pulled her close. "You and I are going to be friends, Evangeline. I can see that already." She spoke over her shoulder as she guided Evie toward the cabin. "Noah, bring the ladies' things inside, will you?"

A backward glance showed her that Noah stood staring after them with heavy creases on his brow. For some reason, his bemused expression stirred up a giggle that she had to swallow to keep in check.

She fell into an easy step with her new friend. "You can call me Evie."

Seven

His Indian companions helped Noah unload the mule, though he noticed they were careful to leave the ladies' belongings piled neatly outside the cabin door. Apparently Chief Seattle had followed through on his promise to prohibit his tribesmen from entering the white women's home. After thanking them in their language, Noah opened the half door and entered.

While he and the others worked the women had talked nonstop, their female chatter drifting outside. Unaccountably, the sound had lifted Noah's spirits. It had been several days since he'd heard Evie's voice in anything but a sharp tone.

Correction. Evangeline. I haven't been granted permission to become that familiar.

The thought frustrated him, but as he entered her delighted laughter filled the cabin, and the sound settled lightly in his ears. Not once during the journey on the *Commodore* had he heard that happy tone from her.

"What's so funny?" he asked.

She turned with a start and the laughter evaporated, her lips tightening into the arrangement he had come to recognize as her annoyance with him.

Louisa's answer floated on a giggle. "Evie was telling us about the first time she heard of Elliott Bay and the Oregon Territory, when you wrote to your uncle asking him to bring a wagonload of women here."

Mary gave him a playful scowl. "Did you really say that, you naughty man?"

Noah dug a toe in the hard-packed dirt floor. "It was only a joke."

Evangeline's dry voice came from the corner where she had retreated. "Not a very funny one, to my way of thinking."

He met her gaze warily. "I never thought he would take me seriously. I was trying to needle Aunt Letitia."

The corner of her lips twitched. "Did it ever. You should have seen her expression." They exchanged a grin, the tension sinking away with a chuckle.

Sarah, Lucy, and Ethel had each claimed a stool and a child, and were happily engaged in playing with the family's youngest members near the fireplace.

"Noah, come sit next to me." Mary vacated a chair at the table and scurried across the confined space to the iron stove in the corner. "Louisa made an extra big batch of biscuits this morning and we opened one of the last jars of strawberry jam we brought from Illinois." She bestowed a twinkling smile in his direction. "I know how you love my jam."

"Only save some for David." Louisa adopted a mock-stern expression. "I'll not have you shorting my beloved to feed your own greed."

Evangeline started to full attention. "Your beloved?"

"Yes." Louisa paused in the act of wrapping biscuits in a linen napkin, a dreamy mist settling over her features. "David Denny, the most handsome man in the world." She drew and expelled a deep breath. "Have you met him?"

"No, not yet." She glanced at Noah.

"Oh, just wait." Louisa's enthusiasm practically bubbled. "He is wonderful, and intelligent, and works harder than any three others. He is clearing a plot on his land to build our cabin, and then we'll be married." A happy sigh escaped as she smeared jam on a fist-sized biscuit and set it in front of Noah. Then she turned back to Evangeline with a teasing grin. "Only I'm a bit apprehensive to introduce him to someone as pretty as you. I wouldn't want him getting any ideas."

Everyone in camp knew that David Denny's affection for Louisa Boren was true and unbendable. Noah started to voice his opinion when his gaze fell on Evangeline and he saw her as David would, with fresh eyes. She was quite beautiful today. A becoming rose-colored blush rode high on smooth, round cheeks the color of rich cream. She'd fixed a ribbon in her hair at the back of her head to pull her tresses out of her eyes but left dark waves cascading down her back, their ends dangling at a waist so tiny he could easily encompass it with his hands.

With a start, he realized he was staring, and that Louisa was watching him with a secretive curve to her lips.

Mary, perched on a stool near the fireplace, shook her head. "David is smitten with you, Louisa. You know that."

Dimples creased the girl's cheeks as she handed another biscuit to Evangeline. "I know. And I him."

Evangeline took the plate to Ethel, who appeared to be enraptured with little Rolland. When she turned, she caught sight of something at the door and gave a tiny scream.

The three Indian braves who had accompanied them from camp stood there, crowded together to stare inside the cabin.

"Oh, them." Louisa patted Evangeline's arm. "Don't worry. You'll get used to them. They show up from time to time to watch us."

Evangeline raised a hand to her throat. "Watch?"

"They seem fascinated with everything about us," said Mary. "That's why we keep the bottom half of the door closed. When it's open they wander right in for a closer look."

Amused, Noah watched her rise from her stool, cross to the stove, and take three biscuits. These she distributed to the Indians with a smile.

"Here you go," she said, handing them out. "We're going to close the door now. No offense intended. Goodbye."

Though they obviously didn't understand a word, the men took the offerings, bobbing their heads in unison as she closed the top half of the door. Darkness settled over the cabin, with the only light coming from a small glassless window in the back wall.

"They'll come around the back," said Mary as she lit a lamp and set it on the table in front of Noah. "It's a nuisance on a sunny day like today, but they don't mean any harm. At least these don't."

Evangeline turned a wide-eyed look her way. "What do you mean?"

Noah broke off a piece of biscuit. "They're from the Duwamish tribe. Their chief is a peace-loving man who is committed to maintaining good relations with the white settlers. Some of the tribes to the north, though, are not of the same mind. It's a good idea to stay clear of them." He raised his eyebrows in Evangeline's direction to ensure that she understood the gravity of his caution.

She sank into the empty chair across the table from him, lost in thought. She was a gutsy woman. "There are some things about the Oregon Territory that we must get used to."

He nodded and put the biscuit in his mouth. As long as she understood, perhaps she would act wisely, even if he wasn't nearby to make sure she did.

❦

Evie stood in the beautiful little clearing for several long minutes after Noah left, staring at the place where he and the mule had disappeared into the trees. Their Indian companions had left with him, and the cabin felt strangely bereft with only the women and children there. Though he'd been nothing but a trial since she laid eyes on him in San Francisco, she'd grown accustomed to his presence.

Louisa came up beside her. "Noah is very handsome, don't you think?"

"He's comely enough, I suppose." She avoided Louisa's gaze. "Though he's prickly as a cactus most of the time."

"Oh? I haven't noticed that. He's always struck me as polite and courteous, though guarded. I suppose the hurts of his past have affected him."

Evie gave her a sharp look. "Hurts of his past?"

She nodded. "We've gotten to know him a little since he joined our party in Portland last November, but he has never spoken in more than generalities. I gather he was in love with a lady he met in California, and the relationship ended badly."

Suffering from a broken heart? That was a new aspect of Noah that Evie had not considered. Yes, he was polite enough, but he seemed to use courtesy as a shield behind which he allowed no one. Courtesy for others, anyway, and a wall of cold stone for her.

"Ethel and the girls would agree that he is handsome as well as mannerly." She grimaced sideways at her new friend. "Apparently it's only me who brings out the beast within the man."

Louisa stared at her a moment. Then she bent down and plucked a wildflower from the grass at their feet, twirling it absently as she talked. "When I was a little girl in Cherry Grove, there was a neighbor boy who took great pleasure in teasing me. He pushed me down in the dirt and pulled my hair in church. Every time I saw him I ended up running home in tears. For a full summer he was one of the terrors of my childhood." She wore a dreamy, far-away look as she ran a finger softly over the flower's delicate petals.

"What happened?" Evie asked, interested in spite of the fact that she knew a lesson would be forthcoming.

Louisa emerged from her reverie with a start. "My papa spoke with his papa, who made him apologize and promise to treat me nicely from then on." She leaned forward and tucked the flower behind Evie's ear, her grin broad. "A promise he has kept to this day, and vows he will for the rest of our lives."

Realization dawned. "The boy was David Denny."

She nodded, and then looked at the barely discernible path by which Noah had left. "Perhaps..." She shook her head, and spoke brightly to Evie. "Come and help us figure out where we shall all sleep. We'll be cozy for sure."

Evie lingered for another moment, thinking about what she had learned. Someone had broken Noah's heart. That did partially explain the guarded manner he assumed whenever they spoke. Perhaps she reminded him in some way of the lady, the same color hair or other feature that pained him to see. The thought left her a little sad.

"Coming, Evie?" Louisa asked from the doorway of the cabin.

Plucking the flower from her hair, she turned toward the house. There was plenty to do without worrying about Noah's broken heart. She had a restaurant to build.

And finally she had an inkling of how to go about it. Surely six capable and determined women working together could accomplish anything they set out to do.

All she had to do was to convince them to help.

⁊

Noah transferred the mule to Cookee, who would use it to deliver lunch to the cutting site. In the command tent he found that the crate containing his ledgers and papers had been moved back inside, along with the flattened log they used as a desk. He ran a hand over the rough-cut surface. Finally, things could get back to normal. The journey had taken valuable time from his schedule, and he felt a pressing urgency to reconnect with work. The success of this lumber venture meant more to him than any man present, with the exception of the Denny brothers. If they succeeded, he would settle here with prospects for a good future as full as anything he'd left back in Tennessee.

If they failed he'd be left with nothing, destitute. Again.

He took a moment to read through the ledger, noting David's hurried scrawl beside his neatly formed script. In his absence, Squinty had been sick with ague for three days and Red Anderson had missed one day with a shoulder injury. He underscored the notations so he wouldn't miss them when it came time to calculating their pay and then put the ledger back in the crate. Time enough later to compute the men's wages, a task that could be performed by lamplight. While the sun still shone he needed to get down to the skidway and talk to a man about his time. Snatching up the cheat stick he used to measure the logs, he strode out of the tent.

The sound of men's labor echoed through the forest long before he reached the cutting site. Deep voices called to one another over the background of saws and axes, sounds that had become as natural in this area as that of water rushing through the streams or wind rustling in the branches. He stepped out of the trees into a swatch of cleared downward-sloping muddy ground. With a smile of satisfaction he noted the skids. There had to be close to thirty logs piled high on platforms built for that purpose. The men had not wasted any time in his absence.

A mule came into view, led by Palmer and pulling a log by skidding tongues along the moist ground toward the skidway. When Palmer caught sight of Noah, his expression turned eager and he urged the beast to a faster pace.

"Did you get the ladies settled?" he asked when he drew close enough for speech.

Noah held back a groan. Apparently every conversation would now revolve around the women. "Yes, they're well settled." He gathered his brow and turned a stern look on the man. "And they are not to be bothered."

The man's shoulders sagged. "We wouldn't bother 'em none. Nothing wrong with talking to a purty woman, is there?"

"Nothing at all," agreed Noah. "As long as the work gets done. Work first, at least for the next month."

"Yeah, yeah, the boss already told us that." A scowl scrunched his face. "But it sure would be nice if they was a bit closer, to my way of thinking."

"That's exactly why they're where they are."

"How's a man supposed to find a wife around these parts?"

Noah had plenty of answers to that, but kept them to himself. Instead he helped Palmer guide the mule and position the log before unfastening the skidding tongs. When the man had disappeared up the trail, he set about his task of calculating the board feet of lumber in each of the felled logs. He kept careful records, and as he measured each log he marked it with the stamp hammer that identified it as belonging to the Arthur Denny camp. As he worked, muscles in the back of his neck that had been tight for two weeks relaxed. This was what he needed—to immerse himself in man's work and forget for a while the complications that came with females. Especially one diminutive female with wavy hair and a stubborn set to her shapely chin.

So engrossed was he in his work that he didn't hear the approach of someone from the direction of the camp.

"There you are, Noah. I've finally found you."

He turned to find Uncle Miles striding toward him, his face blazing with exertion and his normally neat hair plastered to his damp forehead.

"I've looked behind every tree in this forest and got myself turned around more than once." He stepped into the soft, moist soil of the skidway and then lifted a foot and inspected it with distaste. He gave a vigorous shake to dislodge the mud that clung to his boot and stepped more gingerly across the trail. "I need you to speak to the Indians for me."

Noah closed his eyes and sent a silent request for patience toward heaven. Uncle Miles might prove to be as much a distraction as Evangeline. "I'm busy at the moment."

"Oh?" He looked at the ledger in Noah's hand as though he'd just noticed it. "Well, I'm sure whatever you're doing can wait."

Noah cocked his head. "What business do you have with the Duwamish?"

Uncle Miles straightened. "I intend to pickle their salmon."

Noah stared at him blankly. "What?"

"Or rather, I'm going to purchase salmon from them as well as what I catch on my own, and preserve it. Then I'll sell it in California." He rubbed his hands together, a wide grin on his face. "According to Captain Johnson, I am practically guaranteed to triple my investment in a single shipment."

Pickle their salmon. Noah stopped himself just before his eyes rolled upward. He was well aware of Uncle Miles's propensity to investing in schemes of all kinds. He couldn't recall one that had worked yet. His partnership with Evangeline and his very presence here in Oregon Territory was proof of that, and now he wanted to pickle salmon. Did Evangeline know that his investments had never shown a profit? If not, he certainly would not be the one to tell her so.

On further consideration, the salmon idea held promise. It was true that every time Captain Johnson visited this distant place on Elliott Bay he set aside time to sail along the shoreline, stopping at all of the native villages in the area in order to buy as much salmon as they would sell him. Afterward, he made haste to return to California before the fish spoiled.

Even so, Noah couldn't allow himself to be distracted from his work.

"I'm sorry, but I don't have time to take you to the Duwamish village right now." He held up the ledger. "Next month, when we've settled this contract, I'll gladly help any way I can."

Uncle Miles's lips drew together into a tight bow. "I begin to see why Evangeline has become so ill-tempered at hearing that answer." He paused a moment, during which time Noah bit his tongue against a heated reply, and then his face cleared. "Ah, well. No harm done. I shall visit the chief myself. I understand he's a man of intelligence and honor."

The idea of Uncle Miles trying to make himself understood when faced with Chief Seattle's perpetually impassive expression almost made Noah smile. But he had no time for amusement, not with forty more logs to scale.

Uncle Miles turned to go, and then stopped. "One more thing. Where can a man go to have a drink in these parts? My brandy supply will run low before long."

One other aspect of Uncle Miles of which Noah was well aware was the older man's taste for brandy. He sighed. "I've wondered when the subject would come up." He softened his voice to deliver what he knew would be a harsh blow. "Arthur Denney doesn't hold with strong drink, and doesn't allow any in the camp."

Shock overtook Uncle Miles's features. He slapped his chest with a hand and staggered backward. "Do you mean the man's a teetotaler?"

A smile struggled to break free on Noah's face, but he wrestled it into submission. "I'm afraid so. All of the Dennys are."

"But...but..." The hand left his chest to wave in the general direction of the camp. "All those men, those lumberjacks. They accept this restriction?"

"They do if they want to work here."

Uncle Miles considered the information, and then delight broke out on his face. "I've just had a marvelous idea. What this new town needs is an ale house. Why, the man who opens that establishment will be rich in a matter of weeks!" Noah didn't have to answer, merely pasted on a heavy scowl, at which his uncle's face fell. "I suppose not. It wouldn't do to fly in the face of the town's founder at the outset. Perhaps later. In the meantime, I'll focus on my salmon until we can get the restaurant business settled." He squared his shoulders once more. "I'm off to visit the Indians, my boy."

Shaking his head, Noah watched him saunter back into the woods. Someday one of Uncle Miles's schemes would pay off. Who knew, maybe it would be pickled salmon. Or Evangeline's restaurant.

The thought of her brought her image clearly into focus. Her expression when he left the Denny cabin hovered in his mind. She seemed almost sad, her eyes dark with emotions that went unvoiced. He'd halfway expected her to ask to return to camp with him. Or maybe urge him to stay there with her. The thought wasn't all that unpleasant…

He snapped the ledger shut and picked up the stamp hammer. A ridiculous notion. She'd made it clear from the beginning that the only thing she wanted from him was his assistance in accomplishing her business goals. Denied that, she would rather avoid his presence.

With a mighty stroke, he swung the hammer at the flat end of the nearest log. The iron dug into the wood with satisfying force. Sometimes numbers weren't enough to clear the mind of unsettling thoughts.

Sometimes a man had to exert his muscle.

Eight

$\mathcal{E}$vie slept dry and cozy in Mary Denny's cabin, though there wasn't much room to move around after they'd set up four cots. Louisa and the two little girls climbed a ladder to a small loft, leaving the bed to Mary and Rolland. Apparently Arthur would sleep at the camp while Evie and the ladies remained guests at his home. She was determined that she would displace him for as short a time as possible.

On her second morning in Oregon Territory, Evie awoke far more refreshed than the first. She opened her eyes to find Margaret standing over her cot, watching her with intense concentration.

The child's face lit, and she announced, "She's awake!"

Evie sat up and rubbed sleep from her eyes, her thoughts taking a moment to come into focus. When she looked around, she was embarrassed to discover that she was the last to rise. Ethel, Lucy, and Sarah had already tucked their cots and blankets out of the way, and were clustered around the table at the other end of the cabin. Mary, still dressed in a modest white flannel nightgown, stood over the stove.

Evie sat up and threw her feet over the side of the cot. "My goodness! Why didn't someone wake me?"

Louisa's face appeared over the edge of the loft. "You were sleeping so deeply we figured you needed the rest."

Little Margaret fixed a solemn gaze on her. "We had to be quiet until you woke up." She lifted her face toward the loft and shouted. "But she's awake now, Louisa Catherine!"

Mary turned from the stove with a stern frown for her youngest daughter. "That is quite enough. Ladies do not shout inside the house, Margaret."

The child ducked her head submissively, but Evie had to hide a grin when she spied a rebellious twinkle in her eyes.

"Would you care for tea, Evie?" Mary asked. "Or, as the jacks say, 'swamp water'?"

Tea! Oh, what a blessing. Ethel and the others at the table cradled earthenware mugs in their hands. "That would be wonderful."

She watched as Mary poured steaming liquid into a mug and accepted it with a thankful smile. "We brought tea with us from California. When I can get to the rest of my belongings, I'll be happy to replenish your supply."

"No hurry. We've plenty to last a while."

Margaret took up a stance in front of her, hands clasped behind her back. Her hair had been brushed, and she wore a fresh frock this morning. "May I feed your chickens?"

The chickens. She'd forgotten about them. "Yes, certainly you may help me. Have you chickens of your own?"

Red curls waved as she shook her head. "The coyotes ate ours."

"Coyotes?" Ethel half-stood, alarm ringing in her voice.

Louisa, dressed in a pretty skirt and waist shirt, descended the ladder. "That was shortly after we arrived. Now the coyotes don't come near the cabin so much."

"Or the cougars either," said Margaret.

Evie caught Ethel's eye and attempted a confident smile. The poor woman looked like she might jump out of her skin. "I'm sure it's quite safe for people."

"Usually." Mary spoke without turning from the stove. "Only we're careful not to let the children wander outside without one of us nearby."

Blood drained from Ethel's face as she sank back into her chair, leaving her skin a pasty color. "Lord, help us!" She snatched up her mug and took a deep draught.

Evie's confidence sagged. Of course she'd known wild animals were a given in an unsettled territory like this one. But coyotes and cougars? If they would attack a child, wouldn't they also attack a lone woman?

Louisa's laugh rang in the cabin. "It's not as bad as that. They mostly leave us alone. The trick is to make a lot of noise."

Sarah turned in her seat. "Why?"

Louisa shrugged. "It scares them off, I suppose. David says we are not their natural prey, and our presence here confuses them. So most of the time they prefer to stay away from us, unless they sense that we're weak and smaller than they."

"Where can I find a pair of stilts?" asked Ethel in a weak voice.

That brought a chuckle from the others that lightened the tension in the cabin.

Margaret remained quiet for a moment, and then said in a guileless manner, "I'll bet those poor chickens are hungry."

Evie laughed and ruffled the child's curls. "You're right. Let me get dressed and then we'll feed them together."

Lucy and Sarah rolled up her bed linens and tucked her cot out of the way while she dressed and tamed her hair into a semblance of order. From one of her bundles she extracted a sack of grain. Taking Margaret by the hand she headed outside, leaving the top half of the door open.

Another sunny day awaited them. The morning air held a crisp, honeyed scent that sent her spirits soaring. At the far end of the grassy area surrounding the cabin a pair of black and white magpies splashed in the shallows of the gurgling stream.

Margaret dropped her hand and covered the few yards to the chickens' crate with her curls bouncing. She bent to peer inside the wooden slats and turned with a smile. "They're still here."

"What a relief."

Chuckling, Evie started after the child. Something caught her eye, and she stopped. Leaning against the side of the cabin were three long poles. Designs had been painted on them in brilliant reds, yellows, blues, and greens.

"Why, I don't remember these from yesterday." She stepped closer, bending to examine the intricate pattern painted on the one nearest. It was quite lovely, and the paint so vivid. She reached out a hand to touch one.

"Stop!"

At the urgency in Louisa's shout she jerked her hand away. Turning, she found her friend standing in the doorway, watching her with an odd expression.

"What are they?" she asked.

"I'm not sure what they're called, but they were made by Duwamish braves and left here during the night." Rather than alarm, Louisa's mouth quirked with amusement. "David told me about them. Apparently you've gained some admirers in your short time here. They're an invitation of sorts."

"An invitation?" Evie turned to inspect them once again. The markings on each pole were unique, though all as colorful and intricate as the first. "To what?"

"To marriage."

Her jaw dangling, Evie stared at her friend.

"It's a custom of the Duwamish tribe," she explained, her tone dancing with mirth. "When more than one man is interested in a woman, they each make one of these poles and lean it against her tent at night. In the morning, she chooses her husband by picking up one of them."

Evie stepped back, her hands clasped behind her back. "Do you mean if I had grabbed that pole...?"

Louisa nodded. "You would have selected your husband."

The earth wavered around her. "But…" She swallowed hard, staring at the poles as if they were serpents. "But what do we do with them?"

The humor faded from Louisa's face. She raised her head and scanned the surrounding woods. A shiver crept down Evie's spine. Were there three braves waiting in the forest, watching to see which pole she chose?

"Leave them," Louisa advised. "There's probably nothing to worry about, but we'll need to send word to Arthur and let him know."

Probably nothing to worry about. Hair rose along Evie's arms, and she folded them across her middle. Coyotes, cougars, and now amorous Indian braves. The Oregon Territory was turning out to hold dangers she had not anticipated.

Probably, if she were smart, she should leave now.

⤜

Evie made the announcement after breakfast.

"I'm going to the camp and ask Mr. Denny about those poles. I want to get a look at the settlement site anyway, and check on my supplies." She looked across the table at Louisa. "But I need someone to show me the way."

Margaret leaped up from her stool beneath the window, where Louisa Catherine had been showing her how to make her letters. "May I go with Evie?"

Gathering up the plates, Mary shook her head. "I'll not have you tromping through the woods. Your father would be furious."

"Oh, Mama." The child sank back onto her stool, her lower lip protruding.

Louisa took the stack of plates from her sister. "I'd be glad of the chance to visit the camp. It has been several days since I've seen David, and I miss him."

Sarah exchanged a grin with her sister. "We'll go. I wouldn't mind getting a closer look at that camp myself."

"I've never seen lumberjacks at work." Lucy's eyes sparkled with excitement. "Besides, we might get a better look at those men."

Ethel, who had once again taken the baby on her lap and was letting him chew on her knuckle, gave an expansive shudder. "I'll stay here, thank you. I saw enough." She glanced at Mary. "That is, if it's all the same with you."

"I'm glad for the company." A frown gathered on her forehead, and she faced Evie. "But I don't think you should disturb the men at their work. Arthur wouldn't like it."

Disturbing the men's work wasn't her goal. She did want to let Arthur know about the Indian poles, but other than that she hoped to avoid spending any more time in the men's company than necessary. For what she intended to do, she preferred not to have Noah hovering over her, scowling disapproval.

❦

"Noah, did you see this?" Arthur approached, waving a piece of paper above his head.

The cutting site was alive with activity today. The men's spirits seemed as high as the sky, and the air was filled with snatches of songs and good-natured jibes. More than once already the deep shout of "Timber!" had echoed in the forest, and now Noah was applying his ax to the limbs of a felled cedar tree.

He set down his tool to give Arthur his attention. The *Commodore* had delivered a sack of mail, which Noah had sorted last night and distributed this morning. "Looks like a letter."

Arthur shoved it under his nose. "Yes, but look at the address."

The flourishing script read, *Arthur Denny, Duwamps, Oregon.*

"Duwamps." A grimace creased the man's face. "Who dreamed that up, I'd like to know?"

"Someone at the Territorial Legislature office?" Noah guessed.

Arthur scowled. "A terrible name. Hideous. We've got to come up with something better."

"The Duwamish people call this place *Skwudux*."

"That's even worse." He slapped the letter against his thigh. "Think on it, will you?" He caught sight of something behind Noah and strode off, shouting, "You there! Anderson! Watch where you sink that wedge."

Shaking his head with a smile, Noah picked up his ax. That man had a million things going on in his mind at the same time. How he managed to keep them all straight was a mystery, but he never let a thing drop. Next week he'd probably come to Noah expecting a list of name suggestions for the settlement.

Another shout, this one from high up, rang through the clearing. "It's the women!"

Noah jerked upright to scan the area. Sure enough, four ladies sauntered down the trail from the direction of camp, their skirts swishing around their ankles. Following closely behind was Uncle Miles. Noah slapped a hand to his forehead when he recognized Evangeline and Louisa in the lead.

A silent pause seemed to grip the forest, and then the jacks erupted into a flurry of activity. Tools were dropped as men hurried toward the ladies. Men descended trees like a herd of squirrels, chunks of wood flying from the spikes on their boots as they maneuvered their safety straps with blazing speed.

Arthur turned, his expression going stern when he caught sight of their visitors. His gaze sought Noah's, dark with disapproval.

Biting back a groan, Noah dropped his ax and hopped over the felled tree, intent on confronting that frustrating woman. He had no doubt that Evangeline was responsible for this impromptu visit. She *knew* his wishes on this, and Arthur's too. Why was she determined to cause trouble for him?

By the time he arrived, a cluster of lumberjacks surrounded

the ladies. Making liberal use of his elbows, Noah pushed his way through until he stood inside the circle. Sarah and Lucy were all smiles and fluttering eyelashes as they answered the men's questions concerning their comfort at the Denny cabin. Louisa extended her neck to its fullest, trying to see over the heads of the tall men surrounding them.

But it was Evangeline who drew his attention. She stood silently, a half-smile on her face and her eyes dancing with mischief. When she caught sight of him, her jaw thrust ever so slightly forward.

"There you are, David." Delight lightened Louisa's voice as she stepped forward to embrace her beau.

Wearing a slightly stunned expression, David returned her hug and then held her at arm's length to search her face. "What are you doing here? Is everything all right with Mary and the children?"

"Yes, of course. They're fine."

Noah stared at Evangeline, who refused to meet his eye. Instead, she watched Louisa and David with what might be described as a longing expression. The sight of it made Noah's fists clench at his sides.

"Something's come up that we thought you should be aware of." Louisa's eyes grew round. "Evie has attracted some admirers."

"What?" The word came from Noah before he could stop it.

Arthur's deep voice took command of the situation. "All right, men, you've spoken to the ladies. Back to work."

A disappointed grunt answered him, and with sorrowful expressions the circle slowly started to break apart.

Before he left, Pig Face stepped up to Lucy and asked hopefully, "Will you be staying for lunch, then?"

"No." Noah barked the answer, his glance daring Evangeline to contradict him. "They'll be on their way in a few minutes."

He was the recipient of reproachful stares as the men slowly returned to work. David lingered, Louisa's arm firmly entwined with his.

Arthur waited until they were all out of earshot before asking in a low and surprisingly patient voice. "Now, suppose you tell me why you're here."

Uncle Miles, who had remained quiet until now, stepped forward. "It seems some of our Indian friends have taken a shine to the ladies and have taken steps to proclaim their feelings."

Louisa turned to David. "Do you remember telling me about the poles? There were three leaning against the cabin this morning."

"Poles?" asked Arthur.

While David explained, Noah studied Evangeline. It was not like her to remain silent so long.

"What makes you think they were intended for you?" he asked.

Her eyebrows arched. "I don't presume to know who they were intended for. They may have been meant for Lucy or Sarah or Ethel." She looked at Louisa. "Or even you, Louisa."

Louisa shook her head. "No, the natives are used to me. It must be one of the new arrivals, or maybe more than one of you. Perhaps they were waiting to see which of you choose a pole."

Both Sarah and Lucy appeared alarmed at the suggestion. Clearly they had not considered that one of them might be the object of the braves' amorous attention.

"We left them where they were," Louisa continued, looking at David. "But we felt you should know."

"I'm certain this can be cleared up." Uncle Miles spoke in a knowing tone. "I'll just have a word with Chief Seattle. I spoke with him yesterday and though language is a bit of a barrier, I found him to be a most amiable man."

Arthur jerked his forehead toward Noah. "You go with him, so there's no misunderstanding."

Uncle Miles slapped his hands together. "Excellent. We'll go first thing in the morning, after I've had a chance to pull some things together. And while we're there you can help me settle a few of the finer points of our bargain that I was unable to explain."

Noah closed his eyes and focused on taking deep, even breaths. How had he been pulled into his uncle's latest scheme? It was Evangeline's fault. He opened his eyes to find her watching him with wide-eyed innocence.

Arthur started to turn away, and then stopped to fix Noah with a look full of meaning. "Would you please make sure the ladies get back home safely?"

The only answer Noah could manage was a nod. Arthur stomped off, his boots abusing the soft soil.

Noah glanced at Evangeline. "May I speak with you privately, please?"

Without waiting for an answer, he hooked a hand under her arm and pulled her off to one side. When they were out of earshot, he rounded on her.

"What are you *doing* here?" His voice hissed with a ferocious whisper. "I thought I'd made myself clear that you were to stay at the cabin."

Her expression cold, she stared pointedly at his fingers around her arm. He realized his grip was firmer than he intended. Chagrined, he released her and tucked his hand behind his back.

"I was not aware that your *orders*"—she drew out the word—"applied when we were in danger from the natives."

"You're in no danger." He straightened and crossed his arms. "If anyone is in danger, it's the tribesman who thinks he wants you for his squaw."

She drew herself up, outrage plain in the stiffening of her spine. Before she could deliver what was sure to be a blistering reply, Noah raised a hand. "I'm sorry. That was impolite." A dull ache began in his head, and he pressed his forefingers and thumbs against his eyes. "I only wish I could make you understand the pressure we're under."

"And I am under none?" The words fired at him like gunshots, but then she drew in a breath and continued in a softer tone. "I don't wish to make trouble for you, truly I don't. The fact is we are both under a great burden."

His shoulders relaxed a fraction. "Thank you for recognizing that."

Her expression had lost some of its sharpness, which gave Noah a flicker of hope. Perhaps today she would listen to reason.

"You see what happens when the men see you and the others."

He waved a hand in the direction of the lumberjacks. Work had resumed, but with nowhere near the previous enthusiasm. The men's gazes were fixed on the ladies. A few made halfhearted attempts with ax or saw, but their attention was obviously elsewhere. Lucy and Sarah were enjoying the attention, tossing their hair and waving with waggling fingers. Several of the men returned the gesture, either unaware or uncaring that they looked like besotted idiots.

"Somebody's going to get hurt. A lumber camp is no place for women."

"Hmmm." Observing the men, Evangeline's expression became thoughtful. "I see what you mean. We should leave immediately."

Noah straightened, pleased that she was finally open to hearing reason. In the next instant suspicion set in. What was going on in that lovely head of hers?

"Yes, I think that would be best. Let me get my tools and I'll escort you home."

"Oh, no need for that." She spoke quickly, her face a mask of concern. Laying a hand on his arm, she said, "I hate to take you from your work. We can certainly find our way back."

He cocked his head, studying her. He'd never known her to be so considerate of him. She returned his stare without blinking, her smooth forehead clear of guile.

"Perhaps Uncle Miles won't mind going along, just to be safe."

She opened her mouth as if to argue, then appeared to change her mind. "If he doesn't mind," she said in an agreeable tone, and patted his arm before removing her hand. "Don't worry about a thing."

Without waiting for an answer, she whirled with a swish of skirts and rejoined the other ladies. She gestured toward the watching men and toward him, and Uncle Miles nodded and headed down the trail toward camp. David placed a kiss upon Louisa's cheek and then returned to his work while she and Evangeline fell in behind Uncle Miles. With obvious reluctance and an occasional backward glance, Lucy and Sarah followed.

Noah stared at the trailhead long after they had disappeared. That woman had taken pleasure in irking him since the moment he laid eyes on her. He'd come to expect it. A cooperative Evangeline left him mildly alarmed.

❦

On the way back to the logging camp, Evie kept glancing over her shoulder. Would Noah follow to make sure they returned to the cabin? He would certainly interfere with her exploration plans if he knew she had no intention of going back home immediately.

The only sign of life at the camp was a steady stream of smoke rising from the chimney of the cookhouse. The aroma of bacon lingered in the air, along with the savory scent of roasting meat.

She lengthened her stride and caught up with Miles. "Before we head back to the cabin, I'd like to take a look around."

"Oh?" His brow creased. "Why?"

"We were hurried off so quickly yesterday I haven't had an opportunity to see anything. I want to see the area where we will build our restaurant. And I want to get a few things from our supplies for Mary."

Louisa glanced back down the trail. "I'm not sure Arthur would approve."

He certainly would not. Arthur and Noah both cared only that

Evie remained neatly tucked out of sight. And if that's what they wanted, then so be it. She didn't intend to hover about beneath their noses begging for help anymore. Upsetting *Mr.* Hughes.

"Why would he mind? We won't be distracting anyone from their work except Miles, and he doesn't matter."

Miles drew himself up. "Here now. I wish you wouldn't put it like that."

"You know what I mean." She smiled an apology to take the sting out of her words. "This is your venture too, you know. Aren't you at all interested in exploring the place where our fortunes will be made?"

He cocked his head. "When you put it like that, yes."

Louisa took a long moment to consider, and then shrugged. "You're right. Besides, Arthur doesn't need to know that we didn't go straight home."

Sarah and Lucy were agreeable. The five of them took off down the trail toward the dock where they had landed two days before. The *Commodore* had left early this morning, according to Miles, and Evie regretted that she hadn't an opportunity to bid farewell to the crew and Captain Johnson.

They hiked for some ways over a trail that sloped gently downward. The night before last the ground had consisted of muddy sludge. The center of the path was still soggy, even after a day and a half without rain. They kept to the sides, where the soil was moist but easy to traverse. This trail was more defined than the one between the Denny cabin and the logging camp, and the forest slightly less dense. Obviously this area got more use. She spied signs indicating the men had done some clearing to widen what had probably been a natural path leading away from the bay. Had Noah helped select the site for their logging camp, or had that decision been left up to the Denny brothers?

Shortly before they reached the beach, she began to get glimpses of the bay. Snatches of blue shimmered between the endless stretch of trees, and the gentle sound of water lapping against an unseen shore provided a peaceful background to the noise of their feet crashing through pine needles and fallen leaves. Miles had taken the lead, but now Evie lengthened her stride, straining to see ahead.

They came out of the woods suddenly. She stepped from shadow to sunshine, her eyes dazzled by a view so beautiful it snatched the breath from her lungs. The bay stretched out before her, sunshine sparkling on the rippled blue-green surface. The last time she saw this bay it was through a gray curtain of rain, but today the air was sharp and clear, and she could easily see the distant shoreline covered with the same dense forest. Above the treetops rose the magnificent mountains she had noticed from the deck of the *Commodore*, but today their snow-capped peaks stood out starkly, appearing to carve a jagged line in the sky. The glassy surface of the bay reflected a clear image, so that whether she looked up or down she saw their majestic form.

Beside her, Lucy gave a gasp. "I've never seen anything so pretty in all my born days."

"It is lovely, isn't it?" Louisa's voice held a note of pride.

Evie tore her eyes from the vista before her to smile at her friend. "I can see why Arthur chose this spot to settle."

"It was David and Noah who found it first." She folded her arms across her chest and gave a satisfied nod. "My David is a man of vision."

Evie looked again at the panorama before her. No wonder Noah felt such a sense of responsibility for the success of this new town. He'd been one of the first white men to set foot on this shore. The idea stirred a sense of awe in her.

"This is the place." Miles cast a possessive glance around the clearing, as though he were personally responsible for its existence. "One day soon we shall own the first commercial building on this shore."

Evie scanned the area. This shoreline would one day become a busy port and be crowded with buildings. There was no doubt the view was lovely. But the way the ground sloped toward the water made her uneasy. And what about storms? This area of the bay was somewhat protected from harsh winds, but did the water ever rise enough to flood, as the river did back home?

"Behold our supplies, my dear." Miles pointed to a sheltered area down the beach where a canvas-covered pile rested.

"Mmm-hmm." Evie continued her survey of the area, turning in a half-circle to place the bay at her back. The path down which they'd just come was the only defined trail within sight. No doubt that would one day become the main thoroughfare from the port.

Louisa watched her closely. "You're thinking something—I can practically hear the wheels turning."

Evie tapped a finger thoughtfully against her lips. "I'm trying to picture where the town's center will end up being. I doubt it will be here, on the beach."

Louisa pointed toward a flat stretch of land a short distance down the shoreline. "The hope is to build a lumber mill there. That tributary just beyond is wide and deep enough to float logs from way up into the woods. The town will probably grow inland from the mill, I think."

That made sense. "So we'll want to be nearby, but not too close."

Evie began marching up the path in the direction they'd just come, the others following. As she walked, her eyes skimmed the landscape. They'd been walking some five minutes when she found what she was looking for. The ground flattened out, and was that a lightening of the shade just a short distance from the path? She turned to the right and plunged into the forest.

"Where are you going?" called Miles from behind.

"I'm looking for a place to build a restaurant," she shouted.

"I thought we were going to put it down there, near the dock. I'm sure that's what everyone expects." He pulled a large white handkerchief from his pocket and mopped his brow.

And that is one reason I don't want it there.

There was no trail here, but skirting the giant cedars wasn't difficult. A short distance from the trail the cedars grew sparse and the bushy fir trees became dense. The sounds from behind told her that the others were following, but falling behind as they struggled through the underbrush. She plowed further ahead and came alone to a place where the trees clustered so closely that they formed a wall of green branches. Instead of hesitating, she pushed her way through prickly needles and found herself in a clearing.

It wasn't an uncommonly beautiful place, like the one surrounding the Denny's cabin. There was no stream, though she could hear the sound of running water not far away. But the land was level here, and the trees were smaller, with wide grassy spaces between them. Tall cedars surrounded the glade, far enough apart to allow a good-sized building to be erected between them. She turned to the west, and a slow smile spread across her lips. The clearing rested atop a slight ridge with the land sloping gently downward, which gave her a glimpse of the bay below. When the land was cleared, which she had no doubt would happen as the town grew, she would have a stunning view.

Louisa emerged behind her, followed closely by Sarah and Lucy.

"This is it." Evie spread her arms wide as if to encompass the clearing. "This is where I shall build my restaurant."

Doubt showed on the sisters' faces, but Louisa turned in a circle and then nodded.

"It's a good location," she said.

Miles emerged, irritably batting a branch out of his face. He stopped beside Evie, settled his waistcoat with a tug, and cast a skeptical glance around. "Are you sure it wouldn't be wiser to be down by the shore? There would be less work involved in readying the area before building can begin."

With a certainty that she felt deep inside, Evie replied with no hesitation. "I'm sure."

He studied her for a moment and then shrugged. "This place is as good as any other, as far as I'm concerned. Besides, we still have time to scout around. We won't be able to hire the labor for at least another month."

With a glance in his direction, she assumed a casual tone, "Are there not extra tools in the camp? Axes and saws and so on?"

A frown gathered on his bearded face. "Why do you want to know?"

She folded her arms across her chest as she gazed at her clearing. "Because I don't intend to wait a month or longer. I'm not the weakling Noah seems to think I am."

Amusement danced in Louisa's eyes. "Are you saying you will build a restaurant by yourself?"

"Not at all. Miles will help."

"What?" He took a step backward, looking at her with alarm, and nearly stumbled over a sapling in the tall grass. "Me, wield an ax? My dear girl!"

She ignored him, and nodded toward the sisters. "And Sarah and Lucy and Ethel can help."

Sarah screwed her face in twisted angst. "I wouldn't know what to do with an ax."

"Then you can use a saw," Evie told her. "There aren't any huge trees in this area to give us trouble, only small ones. Between the five of us, we can get a good start. It's better than sitting around doing nothing."

Louisa leaned back her head and laughed. "Well, why not? I'll help too."

Her spirits high, Evie leaned over and pulled Louisa into a grateful hug. Noah thought she would go meekly into hiding until he was ready to deal with her. Ha! She could hardly wait to see his face when he discovered how wrong he was. She was an independent woman in charge of her own future, and she would not be tucked in a corner.

But clearing the land was only the first step of her plan. The rest would take some time to put in place.

"We-ell." Miles drew the word out and followed it with a loud sigh. "Every venture needs supervision. I suppose I can contribute something along those lines."

Evie turned a mock scowl on him and then put one arm around Lucy and the other around Sarah. "Think of how impressed all those loggers will be when they see how capable you are."

"Or how pitiful we are," moaned Lucy.

"Either way, you'll have their attention, won't you?"

That drew hesitant smiles from them both.

She squeezed their waists. "Now, let's go get some tea from our supplies and then we'll go back to Mary's and relax for the rest of the day. Tomorrow will be busy."

They trooped back down the trail together. Evie was well pleased with her morning's work. Finally, after two days of frustration and disappointment, she was in control again. And she fully intended to stay there.

Down at the landing site the muddy shore showed signs of drying out, but, like the trail, was still soggy in places. They skirted the edge of the open space, keeping to the firmer soil along the tree line. Evie's supplies had been unloaded from the ship and the crates stacked in a neat pile on a wooden platform in a small grassy area. The lot had been covered with a canvas tarp. Though she would prefer a sturdier shelter, especially for the heavy iron stove that had cost an astounding amount of money, at least the canvas would provide shelter from the rain and, if roped tightly, from wild animals. And the deck protected the crates from moisture on the ground. The sketch she had made of her restaurant included a large supply room, and as soon as the walls were up she would have Miles arrange to have these things moved.

The sight that greeted her as she neared halted her thoughts. The ties were in place on this side of the load, but at the back, the canvas flapped open. She broke into a run and reached the deck before the others. Lifting the loose tarp, she peered beneath it. A sob rose in her throat. The canvas covered only the large, heavy crate containing her stove and a few smaller ones which lay on their sides, pried open and empty. The sob nearly choked her as she straightened and her eyes searched the area. An object on the ground caught her attention, and she ran to the base of a nearby tree to pick it up. It was a linen napkin, trampled with mud. Not far away, an onion lay half-sunk in the wet soil as though it had been stepped on.

Tears blurred her vision. Her cargo had been ransacked. Her cookware, table linens, cutlery, all gone. The food and supplies for which she had paid so dearly had been stolen.

Nine

"Won't you please do something?"

Tears streaked down the reddened cheeks as the woman's pleading eyes fixed on him. Though Arthur stood in front of Evangeline, trying to extract details of the disaster she insisted had befallen her, the tearful plea was directed at Noah, and he found it impossible to steel himself against a surge of desire to answer the request. What was it about a crying female that stirred a man's insides?

Work had once again come to a halt when the ladies and Uncle Miles appeared at the trailhead and rushed into the cutting site. A handy log had been fetched and the distraught women now perched on it in a row, surrounded by men who twisted their hats and watched the tears, their expressions reflecting the same helpless urge to act as Noah felt. Three wore masks of misery, but only Evangeline wept openly. Uncle Miles hovered in the background, wringing his hands.

"We'll get to the bottom of this, Miss Lawrence." Arthur's promise held the ring of a vow. "I am sure the culprit is not among this company."

"It's them Indians." Big Dog stepped forward, his huge hands fisted. "Want me to go talk to them, boss?"

A chorus of male voices chimed in.

"Me too."

"Count me in."

Noah exchanged a glance with David. He was standing behind Louisa, a comforting hand resting on her shoulder. It was highly likely that a few curious Duwamish tribesmen had helped themselves to the supplies. They meant no mischief, but tended to think anything that wasn't in a person's direct possession was free for the taking. Shortly after the Denny party arrived, a whole load of clothing had disappeared from Mary Denny's clothesline. A few days later they'd spotted a brave wearing one of Arthur's purloined shirts. No doubt a huge pile of goods, unguarded and seemingly abandoned, had proven fascinating for them.

But judging by the fiercely protective glares on the men's faces, turning them loose on a mission of retribution would end in disaster.

Noah stepped forward. "No, I'll go. Uncle Miles and I were going to the Duwamish village tomorrow anyway. I'm sure this is an innocent mistake, and we can clear it up with Chief Seattle."

"Tomorrow?" Evangeline dabbed at her eyes with a handkerchief one of the men had given her. "I'll not have a peaceful moment until I know if my future is ruined." A sob broke her voice, and she drew in a shaky breath.

"Here, here, miss." Red made as if to pat her shoulder and then jerked his hand away with an awkward motion. "Don't you take on so. We'll get this settled today, one way or another." He turned a defiant stare on Noah, as though daring him to disagree.

Arthur caught Noah's eye and then dipped his head. "Go today." His expression grew stern. "But first, see that the ladies get home safely." Though he didn't continue, Noah read the rest of his message in the man's dark eyes. *And see that they stay there.*

As if he hadn't been trying to do that all along.

Steeling his jaw, Noah extended a hand toward Evangeline. "Come on. Let's go see if Cookee has any coffee back at the camp. It'll help settle you before we leave."

She hesitated, staring at his hand as if she didn't trust him. But then she took it and allowed him to help her to her feet. Men leaped forward to assist the other ladies.

Squinty stepped in front of them. "You sure you don't want some of us to go along? You might need help."

Noah was quick to shake his head. "I've got this under control. You and the others stay here and keep working. We've fallen far enough behind this morning as it is."

Evangeline gave him a sharp look, though he had taken care to filter any blame out of his words.

"He's right." Arthur's commanding voice was directed to the entire company. "We can't afford to waste another minute of this day. Let's get back to work."

With obvious reluctance, the men bade the ladies farewell. Noah kept Evangeline's hand tucked firmly in the crook of his arm as he walked her to the trailhead. Knowing her, she might decide to make another plea, and the men would swarm to answer her request.

As soon as they were out of earshot from the others, she leaned toward him and whispered in a voice that only he could hear. "I'm going with you, you know."

Noah took a deep breath and firmed his jaw. "No. Absolutely not."

She didn't answer, but from the set of her mouth, he knew he had yet another battle on his hands.

They stood outside Mary's cabin, having arrived moments before. Evie had conquered her tears, though uncomfortable warmth still hovered barely below the surface, ready to leap to her face if she allowed her thoughts to dwell on the hour past. She wanted to appear strong and independent, and what had she done? Wailed and sobbed like the weak female Noah obviously thought she was.

Evie folded her arms across her chest and faced him. "If you leave without me, I shall follow you."

He planted his feet in front of her, matching her glare for glare. "You can't keep up. You'll get turned around in a matter of minutes, and probably end up in the belly of a bear or something."

A gasp from inside the cabin told her Ethel stood watching with the others.

She lifted her chin. "If I do, then my death will be on your hands."

"That is the most—" His mouth snapped shut and he raked his fingers roughly through his hair. When he continued, it was with an obvious effort to maintain an even tone. "Would you please tell me what you hope to accomplish by visiting the Duwamish village?" She drew breath to answer, but he held up a finger to stop her. "And don't say you want to oversee the recovery of your supplies, because Uncle Miles and I are perfectly capable of doing that without you."

Evie matched his tone. "Perhaps it has not occurred to you that I prefer to manage my own affairs instead of relying on others, especially someone who has no sense of urgency for matters that concern me."

For that he had no answer, but his gaze fell upon something behind her. He strode past her and grabbed up one of the intricately decorated poles that still leaned against the cabin. Holding it aloft, he said, "You do realize that the braves who made these will be in the village." His eyelids narrowed. "Or perhaps that's your purpose. You want to get a look at your potential suitors."

From the tightness of his lips, Evie knew he was trying to provoke her. Instead of giving in to a flare of temper, the idea actually made her smile. If he had stooped to childish taunts, that meant he'd run out of arguments. She was close to winning this confrontation.

With a slight tilt of her head, she returned his gaze in silence. Let him wonder if perhaps there was a glimmer of truth in his jibe.

Miles had wandered away, apparently uninterested, and was now standing on the far side of the clearing, staring intently into the stream. Mary had taken the girls inside, and was no doubt doing her best to distract them from the adults' heated exchange. Ethel, Lucy, and Sarah looked as though they would like to slip away as well, and stood with their eyes downcast. Only Louisa seemed openly amused, as if she were witnessing a particularly entertaining diversion.

Her laugh broke the silence before it became awkward. "Oh, go on, Noah. Give in. You know you will eventually. In fact, I think I'll go along."

Noah refused to break eye contact with Evie. "Not a chance, Louisa! If anything happened to you David would skin me alive."

"What can happen? David is always saying how peaceful these particular Indians are, and that Chief Seattle is a man of integrity. If that is true, we shall be perfectly safe." She grinned at Evie. "Besides, I've been curious to see the Duwamish village for some time now. They're so interested in everything we do. Their lives must be drastically different from ours."

Evie returned her friend's grin with warmth. How blessed she was to have found a woman as supportive as Louisa. Though she'd become fond of the ladies who'd traveled with her from Tennessee, they were possessed of a timidity that she could not afford to adopt if she were to make a success of this venture. Louisa's sense of adventure and her undaunted spirit resonated deep inside Evie. Those were the qualities she admired, and the ones she would need to emulate if she were to survive on this unsettled frontier.

Noah's gaze switched between the two of them and then he threw up his empty hand. "What choice do I have? If I refuse, I wouldn't put it past the two of you to strike out on your own." He started to turn away, but then stopped to point a finger in Evie's direction. "You are not to say a word, do you understand? I do all the talking."

She agreed with a regal dip of her head. When Noah turned to gather the other two poles, Evie exchanged a grin with Louisa. A small victory, to be sure, but winning any battle that proved her independence was a positive step into the future she envisioned.

They struck out after a lunch of venison stew and thick slices of crusty bread that Mary and Ethel had baked that morning. Noah led the way, followed by Evangeline and Louisa, with Uncle Miles bringing up the rear. The sound of their travel echoed loudly in Noah's ears, but he maintained a sulky silence. The women had no business visiting the Duwamish village. True, the Duwamish were peace-loving people who welcomed the presence of white settlers in the area. But the only reason Evangeline wanted to go was because she knew he didn't want her to. The more he'd argued against it, the more determined she'd become. It was just pure stubbornness on her part, and that irked him to no end.

When he set off down the path they'd taken to the logging camp, Evangeline had given him a surprised look. Apparently she thought the village lay in another direction. He resisted the urge to point out that he would have to double back in order to see her and Louisa safely home, which would waste even more of his time.

They'd walked perhaps fifteen minutes when he left the trail and plunged into the forest, following a less defined footpath. The underbrush grew sparsely here in the deep shadows created by the trees, but had been disturbed in places. That must have been Uncle Miles yesterday, since the natives moved through the woods without leaving a single sign of their passing.

The sound of Uncle Miles clearing his throat attracted Noah's attention. "Before we arrive, there is something I should confess."

At the hesitancy in his uncle's voice, Noah experienced a prick of disquiet. He turned to find that his uncle had come to a halt and was watching him warily. "Something to do with the Duwamish?"

He toyed with the chain of his pocket watch and didn't quite meet Noah's eye. "Ah, we may merely be the victims of a misunderstanding rather than a theft."

Evangeline's shoulders went stiff. "What do you mean a misunderstanding?"

"As you know I visited Chief Seattle yesterday to discuss the purchase of salmon." He cleared his throat again and tilted his head back to inspect the treetops. "It turns out they are quite amenable to bartering for, ah, items rather than money."

The impact of his words struck Noah and Evangeline at the same moment. Her face went pasty and she wavered on her feet. Louisa slipped a supportive arm around her waist.

Noah strode back to face him. "Do you mean you *gave* them the supplies?"

"No!" Miles shook his head vehemently, and cast a quick glance at Evangeline. "Not *all* of them. Only certain food items. Cabbages and apples, and a few crates of potatoes."

"You traded our food?" Evangeline's words were no louder than a whisper, but so intense that she might as well have screamed them.

"Only a little," he rushed to say. "Fresh produce that will most likely go bad before we can open the restaurant anyway."

Now she did raise her voice. "Have you never heard of a root cellar?" If flames had lashed out from her eyes, Noah would not have been surprised. "Miles Coffinger! You must be out of your mind! Those items were vital to the success of our restaurant. They were not to be bartered." Tears shone in her eyes for the second time today, but these were different from before. These were fueled by a fury so intense she was visibly trembling. Noah wasn't sure if Louisa's arm around her waist was supporting her or stopping her from flying at Uncle Miles.

He stepped between them. "Let's all calm down. What exactly were the details of the bargain?"

Uncle Miles gave up fiddling with his watch chain and began smoothing the thick beard on his chin. "That's what I was trying to tell you earlier. The language barrier presented something of a problem when it came to details. I think I traded six crates of vegetables for a wagonload of salmon and three dozen barrels to store them in."

"You *think*?" Evangeline countered.

Wincing, Noah closed his eyes and formed a silent plea for wisdom. When he was a boy Mother had read an account from the Bible to him, of a king who asked the Almighty for wisdom. A story rose in his memory, and he had to swallow a burst of inappropriate laughter. If he mentioned Solomon to Evangeline at this moment, no doubt she would insist that they take the biblical king's advice and cut Uncle Miles in two.

With an effort to tame his thoughts, he opened his eyes. "Why didn't you mention this earlier?"

With a shamefaced duck of his head, he said, "I was going to mention it before we arrived." A quick glance up at the ladies. "When we were alone."

In other words, when no one except Noah would have to know of the arrangement. "Are you sure you agreed only to a few vegetables? None of the other items that have gone missing?"

Uncle Miles drew himself upright, and jerked at the bottom of his waistcoat. "I am not an imbecile, Noah." His posture flagged, and doubt colored his features. "I am fairly positive that's all I agreed to."

Before Evangeline could react, Noah turned to her, braced if she should lunge for him. "Chief Seattle is a reasonable man. I'm positive he will listen and act accordingly. But it is important that we all remain calm. If we give in to emotional outbursts we will only appear foolish before an extremely influential tribal chieftain. Do you understand?"

"We'll behave," Louisa assured him, tightening her arm around her friend's waist.

Still, Noah held Evangeline's gaze until, reluctantly, she nodded. When he had extracted a promise from Uncle Miles to remain silent and let him handle the conversation, he continued the trek toward the Duwamish village.

The smell of smoke and fish reached them before they caught their first glimpse of the Indian camp. Evie made a point of avoiding Miles, who straggled behind, but hung close to Louisa as they neared the edge of the primitive settlement. The trees grew sparsely here, similar to the clearing she had selected for her restaurant, only this clear area was much larger. Scattered between the wide-set trees stood a collection of small huts made out of split cedar, bound together by twine and mud and resting on mats of the same construction.

Louisa inspected one as they passed between it and its closest neighbor. "Their homes aren't nearly as sturdy as our log house."

She was right. Daylight clearly showed between the slats in the leaning walls of the hut nearest her, though the top was heavily coated with skins, presumably to keep out the rain.

Without slowing, Noah answered over his shoulder. "These are portable. The Duwamish travel all around the area, making camp for a season or so whenever they find a place they like. When they decide it's time to move on, they simply pack up their houses and go. It wouldn't make sense to spend the time and effort on anything sturdier, or more permanent."

Ribbons of smoke rose from small fires that were spaced around the camp. As they stepped past the first row of huts, Evie saw that each one was tended by small clusters of dark-skinned women, their hair black as night. Some sat cross-legged on the ground, working to scrape skins or grind a meal of some sort on large, flat rocks in front of them. Others focused their efforts on racks that had been erected beside or even over the fire pits. The racks were constructed of poles that resembled the ones that had been left at the Denny cabin last night, only without any design and with long strips of what appeared to be meat hanging from them.

The women stopped their work to stare with frankly curious gazes at the newcomers. Children appeared, seeming to come from all directions, chattering and rushing toward them. They greeted Noah as though they knew him, a few even running up to grab his hand. Smiling, he spoke a few words in their language, which clearly delighted them. Evie and Louisa found themselves surrounded as children fell into step beside them, peering up at their faces.

One little girl, probably only a year or so older than Margaret, reached a tentative hand out and ran it over the fabric of Evie's skirt. Liquid brown eyes gazed up at her and a set of perfect white teeth appeared when she smiled. Evie returned the smile, charmed by the child's frank fascination. Why, she might be the first white woman this girl had ever laid eyes upon. Though the men of the Duwamish tribe made regular visits to the logging camp and Denny cabin, no one had mentioned women or children accompanying them.

Encouraged, the little girl again fingered her skirt, this time running her hand down the length to touch the gathered ruffle at the hem, apparently fascinated by a garment she had probably never seen before.

With a quick motion, the child lifted the skirt high and peered curiously beneath it.

Emitting a little scream, Evie snatched her clothing out of the startled girl's hand. She quickly settled it properly in place, her face blazing.

Ahead of her, Noah turned with a frown. "What did I say about keeping quiet?"

Evie attempted to explain. "But she raised my…" The fire in her cheeks burned with new ferocity when his eyebrows arched. "Oh, never mind."

Noah resumed his forward march, and Louisa let loose with a

giggle. She pulled Evie's arm close, this time laughing. "They're only curious, you know."

Evie answered in a whisper. "I don't see you offering to show them *your* bloomers." But she smiled at the child to show she wasn't angry, and relief cleared the lines that had appeared in the girl's forehead.

They stepped between the last row of portable dwellings into a large circular area. The grass had been cleared and a fire pit dug in the center. On the far side stood a house that was longer and much sturdier looking than the rest, though still constructed of the same split cedar.

Apparently alerted by the sound of their approach, four men exited the narrow opening. These wore loose garments dangling around their waists, but little else. Their bodies were smeared with an oil of some kind, though from the smell it had long since gone rancid. When four pairs of intense dark eyes fixed on her and Louisa, Evie had another reason to be thankful for her long skirts. They hid the trembling of her legs.

Noah raised his voice and directed words she did not understand toward the empty doorway. A fifth person emerged from the dwelling. Without a doubt, here was Chief Seattle. An atmosphere of power emanated from this man. Hair fell to his shoulders from a part in the center of his scalp. Heavy brows covered prominent ridges above black eyes that sparked with intelligence. When those eyes turned her way, Evie's trembling ceased, not because she was no longer afraid, but because of a surge of paralysis that overtook her. Never had she seen such perception in a gaze, and she experienced an irrational fear that this man could read her thoughts simply by looking at her.

When he appeared, Miles surged forward from behind and approached the chief with the manner of one greeting an old friend.

"Chief Seattle, hello." He came forward to greet the chief with an outstretched hand. "I'm sure you didn't expect to see me again so soon."

Evie held her breath, sure that the chieftain would reject the familiarity. To her chagrin, he took the proffered hand in his, and gave it a firm shake. When he released it, he turned an expectant gaze on Noah.

A conversation followed that Evie found entirely impossible to follow. Not only because of the nonsensical words—hesitant on Noah's part, but flowing from the chief's tongue—but because she felt the increasing weight of the Indians' stares on her. Noah held the poles aloft, and, with a gesture in her direction, set them on the ground. With a long look at her, during which Evie's head went light from the effort of trying to appear unconcerned, Chief Seattle replied with a single nod. Was it her imagination, or did one of the stern-faced braves look disappointed?

Noah turned a smile her way. "I've explained that, though the newly arrived women are flattered by the offer, you prefer to accustom yourselves to the area before considering taking a mate. He has accepted the explanation."

That was true enough, at least by Evie's way of thinking. "Now ask him about the supplies."

Noah scowled at her impatience. "I'm getting to that."

Once again he faced the chief and resumed the conversation. Though Louisa appeared outwardly calm, she shifted her weight uncomfortably from one foot to the other and kept a firm grip on Evie's arm. At times Noah appeared to have trouble expressing himself, and communicated with hand gestures.

Louisa leaned close and whispered, "David should have come. He has nearly mastered their language."

Finally, after the chief called forward two of the half-clothed braves and conferred with them, the conversation drew to an end. He pulled in a long breath, extended his neck and opened his mouth. The bellow he emitted rang throughout the village, and struck terror straight through to Evie's heart. Louisa jumped, and began such a violent trembling that Evie thought she might faint. They clung to each other.

The area around them erupted with activity. People appeared from all directions, men and women, children and youth. Even a pack of dogs emerged from the forest and ran to join the gathering all around them.

The chief leveled a stern look on the assembled. He spoke several sentences in a harsh tone, his voice easily carrying to the distant edges of the crowd. When he finished, a good number of his people scurried away and returned a few moments later carrying familiar-looking burdens. Evie's restaurant supplies had returned, most of them still nestled securely in their unopened crates.

The crates and bundles were piled in front of Chief Seattle. As each person placed his burden with the others, he or she scurried away, avoiding the gaze of their leader. Evie watched, torn between desires to conduct an inventory and to shrink away after the culprits.

"My goodness," whispered Louisa in her ear. "You brought half of San Francisco with you."

When the last of the crates had been deposited, Chief Seattle folded his arms across his chest and spoke a single sentence to Miles.

Noah, who had stood watching the procedures with no expression, translated. "He apologizes for the actions of his people, and assures you that your belongings will be safe in the future."

Evie might have been offended that the man spoke to her partner, except for the fact that, while Noah translated, the chief's eyes rested on her. She was struck once again with the certainty that this man understood far more keenly than anyone knew. He may have chosen not to speak English, but she would not make the mistake of thinking him ignorant of the white settlers' language, or their activities.

In answer, she held his eyes while she nodded, and then lowered her head respectfully.

"As I thought," Miles was saying, "this was nothing more than a misunderstanding. I, ah, hope this won't have a negative effect on our agreement about the barrels and salmon?"

Noah shot him a warning glance, but then translated in his halting, broken manner. Chief Seattle answered, and Noah turned to his uncle.

"He says you are a fool, but a deal's a deal."

Miles looked startled and Evie and Louisa both joined Noah in a laugh. Even the chief's lips curved into a smile, further proof that he understood more of the conversation than anyone gave him credit for.

Noah faced her. Was it her imagination, or was that relief that lightened his features?

"He promises that these items will be returned to the landing site before the sun sets. I think we can trust him on that." He lowered his voice. "Are you satisfied with this arrangement, Evangeline?"

Evie experienced a surprising rush of warmth for the man she had come to think of as her primary tormenter. Though he had complained all the way, he had left his work behind in order to solve her problem. She awarded him a warm smile. "I am well satisfied." Then, in a spirit of shared accomplishment, added, "And you may call me Evie."

She didn't have time to react to his startled look, because at that moment she spied the item for which she had traveled to the landing site in the first place.

"My tea!" Rushing forward, she knelt before the crate. The top had been pried off and one of the burlap sacks inside opened. Apparently someone had helped themselves to her tea supply. No matter. The majority of it was still here.

An Indian woman stepped forward to stand next to her. Evie straightened and looked into her face as the woman said something she didn't understand, her expression earnest.

Laughing openly, Noah came to their side. "She says you should know that those tobacco leaves have spoiled. The taste was so foul they had to throw away their pipes and carve new ones."

Evie blinked at him. "They smoked my tea?"

The ridiculousness of the situation overtook her, and she too began to laugh. Proving her earlier suspicions about Chief Seattle's understanding of English, he joined her in laughter and without any further translation, spoke to his people. He brought a hand up to his face and imitated lifting a teacup to his mouth. Many of the tribe began to laugh, including the woman standing beside Evie. She covered her face with both hands, good-naturedly admitting her mistake.

In a gesture of camaraderie, Evie took the opened sack from the crate and thrust it into the woman's hands.

"Try pouring hot water over the tea and drinking it," she said, using the same motion as Chief Seattle. "I think you'll like it much better that way." The woman clutched the bag, smiling and nodding her thanks as she backed away.

When she turned back to her friends, she found Noah's gaze fixed on her. Was it her imagination, or did she see approval in his eyes? A rush of warmth flooded her, and her spirits soared higher than they had been since that fateful meeting in San Francisco.

Ten

The morning following her visit to the Duwamish camp, Evie awoke before sunrise. Moving quietly, she donned an old dress and slipped outside to greet the day. The air held the chill of night, but no clouds appeared in the predawn sky. Today promised to be as glorious as yesterday. She would take that as a sign of the Lord's blessing on her plans. They would have clear weather for their first day of work on the land that held so many of her hopes for the future.

Dawn broke with streaks of pink and purple in the eastern sky. The sight was so glorious that she stood for a long moment, drinking in the vistas of morning's first blush. A movement at the edge of the glade drew her attention. An animal. For one second, her heart leaped into her chest. Was it a cougar? Or perhaps a bear? In the next instant she recognized the shape, and her pulse calmed. A deer stepped out of the shadow of the trees. It stopped, its antlered head high and ears pricked to attention, alert to signs of danger. What a beautiful creature. Not daring to move, Evie held her breath. The deer seemed not to notice her presence and moved with slow, timid steps toward the stream. It drank quickly, muscles tensed and ready to dash to safety at the first sign of danger.

Only when the animal had disappeared inside the cover of the trees did Evie release her breath. Another sign. Yes, this would be a good day indeed.

When she entered the cabin, she found Mary stirring up the fire in the stove. "Good morning," she whispered.

Evie replied with a smile and stepped as quietly as possible around the cots where the other ladies still slept. She peeked behind the partition where baby Rolland lay in his parents' bed, his legs tucked beneath him and his diapered behind in the air. As she watched, he heaved a sigh and his lips moved in a sucking motion. Since she'd had no brothers or sisters, Evie hadn't had much opportunity to be around babies, either growing up or as an adult. Were they all as sweet and peaceful as Rolland?

The fire ready, Mary put water on the stove and measured tea from Evie's store into the teapot. Then she began pulling wrapped parcels off the shelves and placing them in a bag.

"Lunch," she explained quietly, and then gave Evie a shrewd glance. "If I understand correctly, you won't be journeying up to the cookhouse for a midday meal."

Though Evie had not specifically said so, Mary was perceptive enough to know that she preferred to keep her plans from the men, at least for now.

"We don't want to disrupt their work." A noble sentiment and at least partially true. The other half of the reason was that Evie didn't want the men, and particularly Noah, disrupting *her* work, or perhaps even putting a halt to it.

Though they spoke in hushed voices, the others began to stir and soon the entire cabin was awake. Over a breakfast of bread and porridge, Evie outlined her plans for the day.

"Miles is to meet us at the clearing with axes and saws and the other tools we'll need. Wear your oldest and dingiest dress, something you don't mind dirtying."

Sarah answered in a petulant tone, "I have no dingy dresses."

"You will before the day is over," Evie answered as she spread soft cheese on a piece of toasted bread.

Ethel, who had displayed more enthusiasm for the project than Evie would have thought possible, grinned over the table. "All of mine are old and dingy."

From her place near the stove, little Margaret piped up. "I have a dingy skirt. It even has a hole in the pocket." She looked hopefully at her mother. When Mary shook her head, the child drooped on her stool.

Evie turned a smile on her. "When you are older, you may come and help me in the restaurant if your papa says it's all right."

"I'm the eldest." Seven-year-old Louisa Catherine, seated next to her sister, clearly did not want to be left out of something fun like helping in a restaurant. "May I come too?"

Her eager expression, so like her mother's, made Evie laugh. "Of course you can."

When breakfast was over and the dishes rinsed in the stream, the ladies set out. They got an earlier start than Evie expected, and her mood was light. She carried the lunch bag by a strap over her shoulder and, with Louisa at her side, took the lead. The sisters followed and Ethel brought up the rear.

They'd barely stepped onto the trail when a loud *clang-clang-clang* pierced the air.

What in heaven's name?

Evie skidded to a halt and whirled around to find Ethel holding a spoon and a metal plate. "What are you doing?"

Ethel looked surprised that she had to explain. "I'm making a noise to frighten away the wild beasts, of course."

To demonstrate, she raised the plate above her head and beat another tattoo with the spoon. Wincing, Lucy covered her ears.

Sarah planted her hands on her hips. "What if they mistake that noise for a dinner bell?"

Ethel extended her neck and shouted in a voice that carried to the tops of the trees. "That's why we should talk loudly too."

Lucy dropped her hands from her ears and turned a pleading look on Evie. "Do we have to listen to that the whole way?"

A stubborn expression settled on Ethel's features. "I came to Oregon Territory to find a husband, not get eaten by bears." She aimed her voice at the sky and emitted a piercing cry. "Whoop! Whoop!"

Louisa erupted into peals of laughter. "That racket would certainly scare me off if I were a bear."

The deer Evie saw that morning had been attuned to any sound that might indicate danger. Loud voices or a metallic clamor would certainly have sent him scurrying away. Perhaps cougars and bears and coyotes were equally cautious.

She shrugged her shoulders. "I suppose it makes as much sense as anything."

They continued their trek down the now-familiar trail to the accompaniment of Ethel's clanging spoon. Every time she shouted, "Whoop! Whoop!" Louisa laughed in her infectious way, and before long they were all chuckling and giggling as they walked. At least the time went quickly and they saw no sign of animals, ferocious or otherwise.

◈

The afternoon temperatures rose higher than any since the Denny party first arrived at this camp. After lunch Noah joined the other men in peeling off his flannel shirt and working in his shirtsleeves. Around midday he stowed his ax with the rest of his tools and grabbed the cheat stick. In most logging camps the ink slinger might serve as a scaler also, splitting his time between record keeping and maintaining an accurate tally of the board feet of lumber the men produced. Rarely did the scaler or ink slinger pick up an ax and work as a lumberjack but on this job, with time pressing down on them, every man was needed logging.

An hour later he finished his measurements and sat down on a stump to do the calculations. Head bent over his ledger, he was so intent on his work that he didn't notice Arthur's presence until the sound of boots on ground alerted him. He looked up to find the boss peeling off his work gloves and watching him intently.

"Well?" Arthur's expression was almost fearful. "How are we doing?"

Noah shook his head. "It's going to be close. Our production's slowed down in the past few days."

He didn't finish the sentence, and a look at Arthur's face told him he didn't have to. Production had slowed since the ladies arrived. Not their physical presence, necessarily, though they obviously created a ruckus whenever they showed up at the cutting site. But even when they were out of view, the men worked slower and produced less than before.

"Hmm." Arthur slapped a glove against his thigh. "We've got to push harder. I hate to do it, but we might have to break out the suns."

Noah frowned. The suns were torches used for night work. "The men won't like that."

"I don't like it either." He shook his head. "Maybe if we tell them we're *considering* working at night, we won't need to."

If the threat of working nights would kick the loggers into motion, it was worth putting up with any amount of grumbling. But extra hours meant extra pay, something Noah knew Arthur would like to avoid if he could.

Truth be told, Noah couldn't place all the blame on the men's lack of motivation, or even on Evie and the others. "One thing that's slowing us down is we're getting farther away from Elliott Bay. It takes longer to haul logs to the skidway, and that ties up the bull-whackers' time when they could be logging."

"I've been thinking the same thing myself." Arthur's eyes scanned the area. "Maybe we ought to leave this cutting for later in the year and head back down toward the cutover where we started. The skid trail is shorter there and there's still some good lumber."

"Want me to go take a look around?" Noah gestured toward the logs he'd just measured. "I'm finished here."

Arthur nodded. "Good idea. Let me know what you think."

When the boss strode away, Noah gathered his ledger and tools and headed back down the work trail toward camp. He'd stow his things and then hike down to the bay on his way to checking out their original cutting site. He'd intended to check on Evie's supplies this morning before breakfast, but time slipped away from him. Though he felt sure Chief Seattle's people had kept their word, he'd like to be able to tell Evie he had checked.

⌇

Evie straightened, holding the heavy ax in one hand and pressing the other into the small of her back. Though she was no stranger to work, never had she felt such an ache. The pain crept from her back down her thighs until she thought her legs might give out from the strain. The weight of the ax dragged on her right arm, pulling at muscles already tortured with the unaccustomed exercise. She dropped the tool and lifted her heavy mane of hair to wipe perspiration from the back of her neck with a sleeve. Another item to add to her list for tomorrow—handkerchiefs. Or maybe a stack of linen napkins, since her dainty handkerchiefs were more for decoration than real work.

At a moan from behind, she turned to find Sarah resting in the shade of a bushy fir tree. Correction. She had collapsed on the ground, her arms thrown wide and her head obscured by the tall, thick grass. The girl had removed her shoes, and her bare feet showed beneath her skirt.

Evie crossed the glade to stand over her. A hot red flush stained her normally pale skin. Dirt smeared one cheek and her hair clung limply to her damp forehead.

Concerned, Evie knelt beside her. "Are you hurt?"

Sarah's eyes remained shut. "Yes."

She scanned the girl's body for signs of blood. "Where?"

"Everywhere." The word came out on a moan. "My shoulders, my arms, my legs, my feet. It all hurts." Her eyes fluttered open. "I can't cut down one more tree. I can't."

Lucy approached with a cup and the skin of water that Miles had refilled for them from a nearby stream. "Here. A drink will refresh you." She opened the cap and, filling the mug, held it out toward her sister.

Sarah did not move to take it but closed her eyes again. "The only way that will refresh me is if I can swim in it."

"All right, if you say so."

With a shrug and a wink at Evie, Lucy held the cup over her sister's supine figure and tilted it. Cool water splashed into Sarah's face and she shot off the ground, sputtering.

"Why did you do that?" she demanded, wiping water from her eyes.

Lucy smiled sweetly. "Because you looked so warm, dear, I thought it might cool you down." She thrust the skin and empty cup into Sarah's hands and flounced away, chuckling.

Her mouth dangling, Sarah stared after her sister. "I can't believe she did that."

Evie tried to control her mirth and failed. She slipped an arm around Sarah's waist and gave her a hug. "You do look cooler," she said, laughing.

Though she looked like she might voice a heated reply, Sarah held her tongue. Then she gave a reluctant smile. "Actually, I feel cooler." Then she turned a stern countenance on Evie. "But I can't use that saw anymore today. My hands are blistered."

She held one up for Evie's inspection. The tender skin between her thumb and forefinger was fiery red and a row of angry blisters had risen. They had realized early on that they needed to wear gloves and had sent Miles to scrounge some from the camp. He'd returned with several pairs of gloves that swallowed the ladies' dainty hands. Huge gloves were better than no gloves at all, but they did chafe. Evie's hands bore similar injuries.

"Maybe it is time to stop for the day."

She looked toward the sky. The sun had passed directly above the clearing several hours past, and was now nearly obscured by the tall fir trees that lined the western edge. She judged the time at around four o'clock, which meant they'd been working more than six hours. No wonder they were exhausted.

"But look what we've accomplished!"

The area where she envisioned her building was almost clear of trees. True, they had all been small, but that was one reason she selected this area. Stumps still protruded knee-high from the ground, shorn of their tops and looking like spikes planted around a battleground. On the far side of the glade, Louisa and Ethel were plying their saw to the last tree that stood in the way. Lucy was dragging a felled cedar from the center of the clearing.

When they'd begun that morning, Evie would never have dreamed they could accomplish so much in a single day. The achievement was in large part due to Ethel, who had given up her loud cries of "Whoop! Whoop!" hours past. She'd labored tirelessly and with an unending good cheer, and even seemed to enjoy the work. Evie had to admit that her sturdy build was more suited to this sort of industry than Sarah's stick-thin frame.

Tree limbs rustled and Miles's call preceded him into the clearing. "We've brought the last of it."

The man had proven absolutely worthless when it came to anything resembling physical labor. After a halfhearted attempt to fell a bush with a stalk no bigger around than Sarah's bony wrist, his feet became tangled in the tall grass and he fell. Claiming that he had injured his shoulder in the fall, he'd insisted on "resting" in the shade for an hour while the ladies worked. At that point Evie had realized he had no intention of actually doing any real work and began assigning him a series of tasks, such as fetching gloves and filling water skins. At least he accomplished those cheerfully enough.

Miles emerged from the trees, followed by a pair of Duwamish braves carrying crates of earthenware dishes. The natives had showed up shortly after lunch. For a while Evie hoped they would pitch in and help, but they seemed content to stand off to one side and watch the work with amused stares. She'd finally given Miles the task of engaging them to carry the restaurant supplies from the beach. Here the provisions would be far less visible, and therefore safer. At least that was her hope.

"There you go, my good fellows. Right over there." Miles, whose empty hands swung freely at his sides, nodded toward the pile of crates and bundles at the far end of the clearing, and the Indians good-naturedly followed his directions. Miles approached Evie. "The only thing left at the beach is the stove, which is far too heavy for two people to carry. We'll need to borrow the Dennys' mule before we attempt to move that."

"Here it goes," called Louisa.

Evie turned in time to see Ethel cup her hands around her mouth and shout, "Timber!" in an enthusiastic voice that filled the glade and rose into the sky. Grinning like a child, she said, "I just love doing that."

The tree stood around eight feet tall. Small by lumberjack standards, but it was one of the biggest the ladies had felled. They'd learned early in the day, by trial and error, to cut the smaller branches from the bottom of the trunk to save their faces being scratched, and to give them room to work around the trunk. Now Ethel jumped up and grabbed one of the remaining branches to tug it toward the ground while Louisa plied her saw to the last bit of wood attaching the tree to its stump. With a crack the trunk gave, and Ethel leaped out of the way as the tree fell to the grass. Evie let out a cheer that was echoed by the other ladies. Even the two Duwamish natives joined in with high-pitched victory cries.

"Good work, ladies." Miles pulled out his handkerchief and mopped at his forehead. "I think we've done enough for one day."

Evie turned a sour look his way, but chose to ignore the comment. "I have one more thing I want to do before we head back."

Sarah groaned aloud as Evie retrieved the lunch bag. From it she pulled a folded paper and a coil of thin, stiff rope—clothesline that she had borrowed from Mary that morning.

"I want to mark the boundaries of the building," she announced.

"Excellent idea." Miles smiled broadly. "I shall help."

From nearby she retrieved her ax and four straight branches she had cut earlier for this purpose. All day she'd been eyeing the exact spot she wanted, and now she marched across the grass to the first corner. Turning, she peered through the trees where sunlight shimmered off the clear waters of the bay. One day soon, she would see this same sight through the front window of her restaurant. With a satisfying sense of accomplishment, she placed the end of the first branch on the soil and, using the back of her ax, pounded it into the ground.

Louisa, Ethel, Sarah, and Lucy stood in a row nearby, watching. Evie looked at Miles. He might be untrustworthy when it came to money and supplies, and worthless when it came to work, but he *was* her business partner in the restaurant venture. And besides, without him she would be working as a housemaid back in Chattanooga, living in her rented room and waiting for James to determine when it was time to get married. She handed him the coil and smiled. "Tie it around that stake and follow me."

She made a show of unfolding the paper and examining her sketch, though she knew the dimensions by heart. With measured steps, she counted off five paces to the rear corner, where she drove the second stake. Then she turned to her left and counted ten paces for the third, and another five back to the fourth corner. Miles followed behind, securing the clothesline to each stake. He tied the last knot with a flourish and straightened.

A sense of triumph bloomed in her chest. With a grin she could not contain, she made a show of stepping across the line to stand in the exact center of the rectangle, accompanied by the cheers of her friends and the victory calls of the natives.

She had not nearly finished basking in the enjoyment of the moment when a man stepped between the fir branches and into the clearing. Startled, she turned to find Noah standing still, staring around the glade with a countenance of pure bemusement. Through most of the morning she had started at every noise, certain that he would show up and try to force them to stop working, but in the past hours she'd forgotten to be anxious. How perfect that he appeared now, when she finally had something worthwhile to show him.

"There you are, my boy," Miles said. "You're just in time to join in the celebration."

Noah spread his arms wide, his head shaking slowly back and forth. "What is this?"

Lifting her head high, Evie folded her arms across her chest with a contented grin. "This is the future site of my restaurant. We've worked all day and cleared it." She raised her eyebrows and added, "*Without* disturbing your lumberjacks."

"But…" Head still shaking, Noah walked slowly around the roped-off rectangle, examining the jagged stumps, the pile of brush in the far corner, and the mound of supplies with the two Indian braves standing in front of it. "Who did all the work?"

"We did." Louisa winked in Evie's direction and adopted a mock-simpering tone. "All by our sweet little selves."

"And we have the blisters to prove it," added Sarah, extending her hand for his examination.

He continued the circuit and came to a halt in front of Evie, just outside the boundary line. "So this is the place you've chosen for your restaurant?"

Irritation sparked in her. Did he have nothing else to say? No words of congratulations, or even acknowledgment of their accomplishment? How like him.

She raised her nose high. "This is the place."

"Really?" He made a show of looking around the clearing. "And have you filed a claim with the land management office in Portland?"

The words doused her irritation. She lowered her nose. "What?"

His lips formed a tight smile. "You didn't know you had to file a claim with the authorities? Have you bothered to check to see that no one else has claimed this particular plot of land?"

The blood drained from her face, leaving her cheeks cold and her head light. She cast a frantic look toward Miles, who stared at Noah with his hand covering his mouth. Eyes wide, he caught her eye and gave a slight shrug.

Her temper threatened to flare, but she held it in check. This was her fault as much as Miles's. After the fiasco with the financing, she should have known better than to rely on him to handle business details. What was she thinking to blithely assume the land she desired would be available for nothing? She looked back at Noah.

"Has—" Her voice wavered. She swallowed and tried again. "Do you know if this plot of land has been claimed?"

"Yes, it has."

She tried to read his expression, but could not look past the mockery in those steely eyes. "Wh—who owns it?"

He folded his arms across his chest in an imitation of her arrogant posture and planted his booted feet firmly in the grass. "Actually, I do."

Eleven

A few days before, Noah would have enjoyed this conversation immensely. But sitting across from Evie now, her features fluid as she struggled to control her emotions, he couldn't take pleasure in her discomfiture.

He'd refused to discuss the difficult situation of the land this afternoon. Not only did he have to inspect the former cutting site and report back to Arthur, but he also saw tears spring to Evie's eyes several times. If those tears had erupted into full-blown crying, he would be lost. He might as well have signed the land over to her on the spot. No, they both needed time to gather their thoughts and their composure before a sensible discussion could take place. So he'd promised to come to the Denny home when the day's work was completed, and the ladies had left. It had been hard to watch their drooping shoulders as they disappeared down the path. They really had done an amazing job.

Now Noah and Evie faced each other in the twilight, sitting near the stream where they could have some privacy for their discussion. At first they'd had a difficult time convincing the children to stay inside and Mary had been forced to speak sternly to the girls. Even now, two little faces peered over the half-door, staring intently in their direction.

Evie sat still, her hands clasped in her lap and her gaze fixed on the stream. "I thought Miles would come with you."

"He wanted to," Noah told her. "But after he followed me around all afternoon, reminding me that he is my mother's only brother and attempting to lecture me on the responsibilities of family bonds, I refused to let him. I needed the quiet of the trail."

That brought a faint smile which faded as quickly as it appeared.

The area's birds began to settle in the treetops before darkness overtook them, calling loudly to one another above their heads. Noah searched for something to say, something that would soothe the awkwardness between them. He would even welcome Evie's infuriating taunts over this gloomy silence.

"I'm sorry I disturbed your land." Her head ducked and she stared at her hands. "It was foolish of me not to realize I needed to inquire about ownership before we began the work."

Noah could have agreed, but he didn't have the heart to beat her down further. Instead, he shrugged. "Everyone makes mistakes. And at least now I have a head start on clearing that plot."

Her lips twisted, and she gave a silent nod.

"I'm curious about something. Why did you choose that place? Why not the landing area?"

She shook her head. "I don't want to be on the beach. I want a higher vantage point."

"But it seems to me that being near the dock, and hopefully soon the mill, would be an advantageous place for a restaurant. As this settlement grows, that will be the port of entry. When a ship docks, your restaurant would be one of the first buildings they see. You'd have sailors and visitors alike clamoring to eat there."

"I thought of that, but those aren't the customers I hope to have."

Noah furrowed his brow. "Seems to me that any customers are good. You don't agree?"

"I do, but sailors will eat there once or twice every few months, whenever they are in port. Visitors probably even less often." Finally, she met his gaze with a quick sideways flicker of her eyes. "What I want are regular customers. The men and women who will live here, and who will come back often. Eventually a town will grow here, and families will come to do their shopping and their banking and other business. And while they're in town, my restaurant will only be a few steps away."

Her logic began to make sense. "But why wouldn't the town be centered around the dock and the mill?"

"You know what sailors are. They get off the ship with their minds set on guzzling as much whiskey as they can hold, and finding"— she looked demurely away—"companionship."

Noah had to concede her point. He'd been on enough ships and known enough sailors to verify that.

She looked at him, a curious expression on her face. "Did you look at the area around the port in San Francisco?"

"Yes, of course. I've been there many…oh." His mind took him for a quick stroll down the port-side streets of San Francisco. The area was littered with dingy hotels, saloons, and houses of ill repute. The same was true of Portland. It was true, in fact, of every port town he'd ever visited. A new respect for Evie dawned. She'd spent time thinking of this, evaluating her future and planning for it.

Now she smiled. "You see? I have no doubt that this new town will be wholesome and upstanding, thanks to the Dennys' influence, but if growth is to come, so will those businesses. And I think they'll spring up around the docks."

"But why my land? What made you select that clearing?"

"It's close enough to the bay that supplies can be easily transported, and that's what most businesses will need. The trail is already well-defined and looked to me like it could become a main thoroughfare. The land all around that clearing slopes, but there's a long flat ridge right there that I thought would be the perfect place for a town to start. And besides." She lowered her eyes again and seemed almost embarrassed. "I loved it from the moment I saw it. When I stepped into it, I felt…"

Though she didn't finish the sentence, Noah knew what she was going to say. "It felt right."

The muscles in her throat moved as she swallowed, and she nodded without looking up.

He spoke in the softest whisper. "Me too. That's why I staked my claim there."

They shared a smile, and some of the strain seeped away. The air around them became lighter, easier to breathe, and somehow warmer even though the sun had disappeared from view and night's chill had begun to creep over the forest.

Evie broke the companionable feeling by straightening her spine and standing. "I suppose I'll have to start looking for a new place to build my restaurant." Her smile held a spark of her usual spunk. "Surely not all the land around here has been claimed."

"Now, wait a minute. We're not through here." Noah gestured toward the ground. Hesitantly, she lowered herself, but sat stiffly instead of settling back.

He could hardly believe what he was about to say. "What if we worked out some sort of business arrangement?"

Delicate eyebrows rose high on her forehead. "Like a lease for the land?"

"That's an option," he agreed.

She shook her head. "I don't have any money."

"Not yet. But once you're able to open, you will."

Her lips twisted into a sideways grimace. "And if you'll remember, I have a loan to repay, thanks to your uncle."

That was true. But the fact was Noah had paid nothing for the land beyond registering the claim. That had taken the last of his inheritance, what had been left him after the disastrous arrangement with Sallie.

Sallie. The thought sobered him. He'd forgotten for a moment that the last time he entered into a financial arrangement with a woman, it had cost him nearly every cent he owned. Even worse, the encounter left scars that no one could see, but which haunted his dreams.

On the other hand, this venture wouldn't cost him anything. If Evie was right in her analysis of the town's future—and he felt a growing confidence in her predictions—he stood to gain a lot when her restaurant became profitable.

Plus, she would be indebted to him in the meantime. He'd have the right to insist that she abide by the rules he had already outlined. No contact with the logging crew until their contract was fulfilled.

He became aware that she watched him as though attempting to read his thoughts. Straightening, he cleared his expression. "What if I agreed to defer lease payments until after your loan is repaid?"

She narrowed her eyes. "Why would you do that?"

"Because I think you have a real chance of success," he told her frankly. He then added with a smile, "And because I'll want a percentage of your profits in lieu of a set rental amount. If you make nothing, then you pay nothing. But when you make money, so do I."

Her head tilted sideways and she fixed him with a suspicious look. "And?"

Drawing a breath, he spoke calmly. "And I insist on having equal say in decisions concerning the management of the establishment."

She straightened, her features contorted. "That's…that's outrageous."

"I think it's quite fair." He held her gaze. "Regardless, those are my conditions."

A struggle played across her face, and the corners of her lips drew down into a frown. Her eyes narrowed and opened and narrowed again. Noah returned her glare without blinking and held his placid smile in place.

Then her shoulders sagged. She drew in a long, loud breath and expelled it before speaking. "Fine." The familiar stubborn spark appeared in her eyes. "But your percentage is coming out of your uncle's share. And you can tell him I said so."

❦

When Noah headed back to camp, Evie returned to the cabin to find five women waiting for news. The girls had already been put to bed, but when they heard the door close they scrambled down, demanding to know where Uncle Noah had gone and why he didn't come in to say goodnight. Evie climbed the loft to settle them for the night, glad for a few moments to think about the arrangement she'd just made.

After a bedtime story that she'd pulled from the recesses of childhood memories, she climbed back down the ladder to discover that the cots had been laid out and her friends had changed into their nightdresses. Sarah and Lucy sat cross-legged on their cots while the others had taken seats at the small table in the corner, sipping mugs of tea in the candlelight. Mary rose and went to the stove to pour from her teapot into a sixth mug that sat in readiness on the surface.

"Well?" Louisa asked. "What did he say?"

Ethel set down her mug. "Was he very angry?"

"No." Evie picked up the cotton nightdress that someone had thoughtfully laid across the bottom of her cot and began to unbutton her blouse. "Not angry at all. He was quite calm."

Mary set the steaming mug on a stool near Evie's cot before returning to her chair. "Noah is always a gentleman."

"I suppose we'll have to look for another location for the restaurant." Louisa rubbed at her right shoulder with her left hand. "Though I hate to think all our work today was for naught."

"Look on the bright side," said Ethel. "At least now we know what we're doing. The next time the work will go faster."

Sarah let out a loud moan and threw herself back on her cot. "I can't do that again. If I'd known I would be forced to cut down trees I would have stayed in Tennessee."

Her melodramatic outburst would normally have irritated Evie, but tonight she was too busy thinking. "Oh, we won't have to clear another place. Tomorrow we'll continue our work there." She stepped behind the partition to remove her clothing.

"Do you mean Noah is giving you the land?" Mary's voice held a note of surprise.

"Not giving it to me." Evie spoke in a whisper that would carry around the partition but hopefully not disturb Rolland, who slept soundly in his parents' bed. "Leasing it to me. We're going to be partners." She slipped the nightdress over her head and returned to the main room to find Louisa grinning widely.

"Partners?" She clapped her hands. "This is wonderful. You'll have your restaurant *and* a handsome man hanging around every day."

The implication was clear. Evie settled the last button, bent to pick up her tea, and fixed a stern look on Louisa over the rim of her cup. "We will be *business* partners, nothing else. He will be more like a landlord than anything, and not in evidence on a day-to-day basis."

Though his insistence that he have equal say in management decisions worried her. She wouldn't have agreed to that condition except that she felt she had no choice. No doubt they would clash over many issues once the restaurant was up and running, but if he thought he would dictate to her, he would soon learn otherwise. She could hold her own, and intended to.

"So this means we're finished working?" A hopeful note sounded in Lucy's question.

Evie shook her head. "Of course not. We've cut down a few trees, but there's no restaurant in place. We have a lot of work still to do."

"Evie." Louisa set down her cup, for once her ready humor not in evidence. "Surely you don't expect us to build the restaurant by ourselves. We simply don't have the skill."

"I'd hate to step inside any building we put up," agreed Ethel, "for fear it would collapse on my head the first time the wind blows."

"We won't have to." Evie settled herself on her cot. "In fact, you don't even have to go back if you don't want." She extended her leg and nudged Sarah's still-prone form. "Tomorrow I intend to put the next phase of my plan into place. I shall hire men to build the restaurant for me."

Worry lines creased Mary's brow. "Arthur won't like that."

"He won't mind." She smiled to dispel the woman's concern. "I don't intend to hire his men. I shall hire Indians."

Louisa's mouth dropped open. "Surely you aren't going back to the Duwamish camp."

Truthfully, that had been her original plan, and the reason she had insisted on accompanying Noah yesterday—to discover the location of the camp. But one visit had been enough. She could not see herself marching into the village alone, or even with Miles at her side, and trying to converse with Chief Seattle. Not with an entire tribe of half-clothed natives circled around her.

"No, I'm not." She took another sip from her mug and set it on the stool. "I'm going back to the clearing tomorrow to continue work. But first I'll pay a visit to the logging camp and assign that task to my new business partner."

Sarah sat up on her cot. "To the logging camp? I'll go with you."

Ethel let out a sardonic snort.

"What? We can't let her go alone. It's not safe." Sarah cast a wide-eyed glance around the room. "Well, can we?"

Evie exchanged a grin with Louisa. Sarah was the most man-hungry girl she'd ever known.

She slipped beneath the blanket and settled it around her feet. "Then you'd better get to sleep. We'll leave at first light."

Noah plied his ax with a newfound energy. Once again the sun shone in a clear blue sky. Maybe they had seen the last of the rain for a while. In the light of a beautiful day, with his lungs full of clear, fresh air and the sounds of busy men ringing in his ears, the future looked brighter than it had for a long time.

On his walk back to the camp last night, he had a lot of time to think. This logging contract had kept him so busy he hadn't spent much effort planning what he would do afterward. He was committed to this venture, and to Arthur Denny's plans for the new town. The plentiful resource the Oregon Territory offered—lumber—was the key to his success. Of that he was certain, and he fully intended to capitalize on it. But the past few months had taught him something. He did not want to be a lumberjack, not even to work his own land. The deal with Evie was a perfect opportunity. He had every confidence in her ability to make a success of her restaurant, and that would give him some breathing space to figure out his next venture.

And besides, he enjoyed the unaccustomed feeling of finally being in accord with her. It felt good.

Arthur strode into view around a tree blind, his head moving as he scanned the area. When he caught sight of Noah he tromped forward, his work boots covered with mud almost to the knee. Straightening, Noah put down his ax and waited.

"I've just come from the original cutting. You're right. The access is better, and there's enough lumber in the area to fill this order and hopefully several more." In a rare display of joviality, he slapped Noah on the shoulder. "We'll start there tomorrow."

A fresh wave of enthusiasm sent a confident smile to Noah's face. "We're going to get it done, Arthur."

An answering smile started to form, but then Arthur's eyes focused on something behind Noah and a scowl appeared instead. "What are they doing here?" His gaze lowered and Noah found himself the full focus of the glare. "Again."

Whirling, he saw the last thing he expected. Five ladies strolled up the work trail, their skirts swishing and their smiles wide. In the lead, Evie strode beside Uncle Miles.

Noah slapped a hand over his eyes. That woman was determined to plague him.

"I'll take care of it," he told Arthur and moved toward them, determined to shoo them away quickly.

An eager call sounded from the trees. "It's the women!"

Behind him, Arthur's voice boomed through the site. "Do not stop work. Palmer, don't you dare come down out of that tree. You either, Mills. Any man who stops working will be docked a day's pay."

Grumbles sounded from the treetops, and ahead of Noah the ladies' faces fell. All except Evie's. She didn't even slow, but kept up her determined pace, her gaze fixed on him.

Noah planted his feet in front of them, blocking their way. Behind Evie, Sarah rose on her tiptoes to see past him, wagging her fingers in the air.

Noah glared at Miles. "Didn't I ask you not to let them come here again?"

"But, my boy, they have an idea you must hear."

David approached from one side and Louisa rushed toward him. Noah almost snapped at the young man to get back to work, but stopped himself. David was a Denny and had more at stake in this contract than he. Besides, being the boss's brother had its benefits.

Instead, he turned his scowl on Evie. "I thought we had an understanding. You are not to interfere with the men's work."

David, with Louisa's arms still around his neck, said reluctantly, "He's right, Sweetbriar. Whenever you ladies show up, we lose work time."

Evie showed no signs of contrition. "We won't be here long. I need you to do something."

Miles interrupted. "Evangeline has the most splendid idea. We're going to hire Duwamish villagers to build the restaurant. Isn't that brilliant?"

Noah frowned. "Duwamish? I don't know. I need time to think about it."

"There's nothing to think about," Evie insisted. "It's the perfect solution. My restaurant"—she corrected herself with a quick smile—"*our* restaurant will be built, and your work won't be disrupted."

David gave him a skeptical look, and then spoke to Evie. "You've seen the Duwamish camp. Do you really want to erect that kind of building?"

"Not the portable ones, no. But we know they can make sturdier ones. They did for Chief Seattle." Evie switched her gaze from David back to Noah. "We need you to talk to him for us."

"I don't have time." Noah spoke in a stern tone that left no room for argument. "Uncle Miles, you do it."

But Evie shook her head. "I won't agree to that. He doesn't know the language like you do. We need someone who can be specific about what we want. I can't afford to lose another thing."

The sound of boots approaching alerted Noah to Arthur's presence. A similar pounding began behind his eyes.

At least when Arthur greeted the ladies he wore a civil smile, which disappeared when he turned to Noah. "What's going on here?"

Briefly, Noah explained the situation, though he could not manage to look the man in the eye. He'd intended to tell Arthur about his arrangement with Evie, but there had been no time.

Arthur's immediate answer surprised him. "Go. Do it now."

Noah jerked his head toward the man. "What? But what about—"

With a chopping motion, Arthur cut him off. "We can't afford any more interruptions. The quicker you get this resolved, the quicker you can get back to work." He turned a pointed look on Evie. "May I assume once this is settled, we won't have the pleasure of your company here at the cutting site anymore?"

She had the grace to look embarrassed, and lowered her eyes. "Yes, sir."

"Good." With a hard stare at his brother, he stomped off, shouting orders at the men to keep working.

Noah heaved a sigh. Just when he thought things were looking up. He ignored the triumphant grin Evie awarded Louisa, but the familiar irritation erupted, like an itch that he couldn't scratch. Even when that woman was getting what she wanted she wasn't content, but insisted on pushing him. Maybe this partnership wasn't such a good idea after all.

Twelve

$\mathcal{E}$vie paced the length of the log boundary that had been laid across the front of the building site. The six Duwamish tribesmen who had worked industriously for the past three days stood in a row to one side, watching. They had removed every stump the ladies left, along with every blade of grass. The soil beneath what would soon become her restaurant's floor was flat and clear of foliage.

In the corner of the clearing, Ethel, Louisa, and Lucy knelt in the grass beside two Indian women, who were telling them with many gestures and demonstrations how to weave the wooden mats that would cover the dirt floor once the walls were in place. Sarah sat nearby, busy with a needle and thread. Finally, Evie had found work that the girl not only enjoyed, but at which she excelled. They might not be able to afford glass, but the restaurant would have nice curtains fluttering in the windows—when it didn't rain.

She reached the end of the log. Nine and a half paces only. Facing her workmen, she pointed to the log. "It's too short."

They returned her stare with blank ones. A quick glance in Miles's direction showed her he had fallen asleep in the shade. Apparently his "supervising" duties were proving too taxing for him. She considered stepping over to wake him with a kick to the boots so he could attempt to make them understand, but decided not to. Some tasks were easier to handle without him.

She pointed again to the log. "Too short." Holding her hands far apart, she nodded as though satisfied. Then she moved one hand inward to shorten the space between them, frowned, and shook her head.

The Duwamish were masters at concealing their thoughts behind blank expressions. She was never sure what they thought, except when they broke their normal reserve and laughed, usually when watching her attempt a task at which she was inept.

"It needs to be longer." With an exaggerated step, she planted her foot a half-pace beyond the edge of the log and pointed at the ground.

They exchanged glances between them, and then two came to her side. They stooped and grabbed the end of the log and pulled it to the place she pointed.

"Oh." Evie walked to the gap in the center, where the log had been cut in half. The opening, which would become the front door, was wider than most doors to which she was accustomed, but not extraordinarily so. In fact, she liked having a bigger door. It would give her restaurant a more welcoming feel.

She lifted a smile to the pair, and nodded happily. "That works."

At a sound from behind, she turned. One of the first tasks she had assigned was the clearing of a path from the main trail. Though she regretted the loss of one of the bushy fir trees that had stood guard over this clearing, an open path would be necessary for her customers to find her restaurant. In the meantime it gave her a clear view of any visitors who approached from that side. There hadn't been many, mostly curious Indians who came to watch their fellow tribesmen at work. Occasionally Noah had appeared, ostensibly to check on their progress, though she suspected his visits were pre-emptive in nature, designed to keep her and the others away from the logging camp.

Since he had not yet checked in today, she half-expected to see him enter the clearing and was therefore surprised when she recognized the visitor.

"Chief Seattle."

Miles proved that he had only been pretending to sleep by leaping up from the ground and rushing toward the newcomer. "Welcome, my friend. Come to check on the work? Here, let me show you what we've done."

Evie caught Louisa's eye and rolled hers toward the sky, which made her friend giggle. The chief joined Miles and together they strolled across the grass. He awarded her a nod of acknowledgment and then completed a slow circuit of the cleared area, with Miles chattering the entire time.

"Here we've left plenty of room for storage, and back there we'll put a wood shed so we can always be certain of dry fuel for the stove." He raised his hands and sketched a pitched roof in the air. "And above, we'll have a second floor where the ladies will live."

They completed their circuit and arrived back at Evie's side.

"Evangeline, show him your drawing," Miles instructed.

Evie pulled a folded paper from her apron pocket and handed it to the chief. He inspected the rough illustration she had drawn with interest.

"See there?" Miles pointed at the sketch. "That's the upper floor I was telling you about."

Seattle nodded sagely at Miles, but when he handed the drawing back to Evie there was an indulgent twinkle in his eyes that let her know the man was well aware of the work, and who had accomplished it.

He exchanged words with his tribesmen and then walked over to watch the ladies work for a few minutes. When he returned to the building site, Evie fancied she glimpsed approval in the look he turned on her. With another nod, this one deeper, he clasped his hands behind his back and strode toward the path, apparently satisfied with his quick visit.

Miles scurried after him. "I'll accompany you a short ways, if you don't mind. I'd like to have a word about my salmon." His voice trailed behind him long after they'd disappeared down the path.

Louisa approached to stand beside Evie. "I wonder what that was all about."

"I don't know." She looked up at her friend. "But I think we've just been given his stamp of approval."

❦

The walls were starting to rise. Every evening when Evie left the clearing she stood for a moment gazing at her restaurant, a fiercely possessive feeling deep in her stomach. The clothesline was gone, replaced by a frame made of logs and walls of the thick cedar slats the Duwamish cut and attached. At this rate they would be ready for the roof within a matter of days.

Truth be told, she wasn't entirely satisfied with the walls. Though they were certainly sturdier than the portable huts she'd seen in the Indian camp, she couldn't help comparing them to those of the Denny cabin where she spent every night. When she voiced a tentative comment to Miles about the fact that she could see cracks of light through them in places, he brushed aside her concerns.

"That's because the mud hasn't been applied yet." He'd given her a paternalistic smile and a pat on the arm. "Don't worry, my dear. Once it's finished, you'll love it."

Evie hoped so. And besides, what option did she have?

Six days after the work had begun in earnest, Evie and Ethel arrived at the clearing mid-morning, as had become their custom. Since the floor mats were finished and laying in readiness, the other ladies had stayed behind to help Mary with the washing and other household chores.

When they arrived at the end of the path, they stopped short in surprise. The clearing was full of men. At second glance, Evie realized there were only four in addition to the regular Duwamish braves, and that the newcomers' faces were known to her. Four lumberjacks from the Denny crew stood at one corner of the building, one kneeling to inspect the support log while the others stood over him.

"What's this?" Evie asked, her voice sharp. Had Noah sent them? If not, he would be furious that she had once again disrupted the men's work. Only this time it was not her fault.

They turned and, with suspicious glares directed at the watching Indians, strode across the glade toward her.

Big Dog, who towered a full head above the others, pointed behind him. "What is that supposed to be?"

Evie tilted her head to see around his massive frame, but saw nothing out of place. "That is my restaurant. Or will be soon."

"Ain't no restaurant." Squinty proved his nickname by fixing a cross-eyed stare on her. "Ain't nothing but a bunch of sticks piled on top of each other."

"That is not a proper building, ma'am." Red glanced over his shoulder at the watching braves, and then leaned toward her to whisper. "That's an Indian wigwam. You can't open a restaurant in a wigwam."

Ethel drew herself upright. "And what choice do we have, I ask you? We had all we could do in clearing the land ourselves."

Red's mouth fell open. "You females cleared the land?"

"Certainly we did." She jerked her head in a nod. "We're not as helpless as all that. But neither are we stupid enough to attempt to finish a job on our own we weren't trained to do."

Evie set a confident smile in place. "When it's fully done it will be perfectly fine. You'll see."

Big Dog snatched a wool cap off his head. "Ma'am, if you needed something built, we'd've done it for you. All you had to do was say so."

What a predicament. The urge to tell the men she'd desperately wanted to do exactly that was almost overpowering. But if she did, they would certainly blame Noah and Arthur. She had agreed not to disrupt their work any further, and a conflict of this nature would definitely do so. Instead she must try and smooth things over, and rush them back to their logging camp.

"I appreciate that, truly I do, but you've plenty of work to do already." She swallowed and schooled any hint of doubt from her tone. "And besides, I'm quite happy with the work our Duwamish friends have done for us." There. She'd bent the truth in order to keep her promise to Noah. And she intended to make sure he knew it too. "Now, you gentlemen run along. We appreciate you stopping by. And we do hope to see you often after the restaurant opens."

Doubt showed clearly on their faces and they would have lingered, but Ethel grabbed Red by the arm and gave him a firm shove toward the path. "You heard her. Go on now. Shoo!"

The others followed him, though not without many backward glances.

When they had gone, Ethel stood staring at the place where they'd disappeared, hands planted on her hips. "We haven't heard the last of this."

"I have a feeling you're right," Evie said.

No matter what, she would not let Noah blame her. Not this time.

❧

Noah was sitting in the command tent, rechecking his calculations and feeling guilty that he wasn't at the cutting site lending a hand, when the light from the doorway dimmed. He looked up to find Big Dog's massive form filling the entrance.

Caution zipped through Noah when he caught sight of the glower on the man's face. "Is something wrong?"

Big Dog stepped inside, followed by Red, Squinty, and Mills. The confines of the tent shrank alarmingly, filled as it was with mountains of lumberjack muscle, all of them wearing scowls. With slow movements Noah laid his pencil down and closed the ledger, gathering his composure around him as he did so. When he spoke, he was able to do so in an even tone.

"What seems to be the problem, gentlemen?"

"It's them females," said Squinty.

Noah suppressed a shudder. What had Evie done now?

Big Dog placed a ham-sized fist on the surface of the plank that served as a desk and leaned over it toward Noah. "Did you know they've hired themselves some o' them natives to put up a building for them?"

Judging from the stern look on the man's face, the wisest course of action would be to deny any knowledge. But Noah had always followed a policy of honesty. Lies always caught a man out eventually.

"Yes." He held the man's eyes as he answered. "I took their request to Chief Seattle and negotiated the arrangement."

Mills swore under his breath while Big Dog threw his hand in the air in disgust. "You're letting that gal *pay* them Indians? You know we'd've done it for free."

"I know you would have." Noah tried to be unobtrusive about leaning back on the stump that served him as a stool, out of arm's reach. "But she's paying in foodstuffs, not money. Besides, I tried to convince her to wait until we finished this contract, but she's as stubborn a woman as any I've ever met."

Red grinned. "I love a spitfire woman."

Noah could contribute a few comments about working with a spitfire like Evie, but deemed it wiser to hold his tongue.

Squinty pounded on the board. "We outta be the ones to build that restaurant. Who ever heard of women clearing land themselves and hiring Indians to do work when there's able-bodied men like us willing to do it for them? 'Sides, we could do a better job."

"Yeah," agreed Mills. "Have you seen that hovel they're putting up?"

"Not in a few days," admitted Noah. "But I'm sure they're doing a fine job. Have they started on the second level yet?"

"Second level?" Big Dog's eyes bulged. "That building can't support any second level. It's flimsy, I tell you. It'll cave in for sure."

"We can't let that happen," said Squinty.

Noah rubbed a hand across his chin, noting absently that he needed to shave sometime soon. "I've never seen a hut in the Duwamish village with a second floor," he admitted. "Maybe that's stretching their abilities a little. If I could think of a way to convince Evie to wait until after we've finished this contract…"

The men exchanged a look, and Noah had the uncomfortable idea that a silent agreement had just been reached.

Sure enough, Big Dog caught his gaze with a stern look. "We're gonna build that restaurant for them, and we're gonna do it now."

Alarm zipped through Noah's frame with a shudder and sent him to his feet. "No, you can't. You have a job to do."

"So dock our pay," said Red with a shrug. "We don't care."

The others nodded.

"But you committed. Arthur will have my hide if he finds out you're skipping out to work on Evie's restaurant."

"Look here. Relax. " Mills stepped around the side of the desk and, placing hands on Noah's shoulders, forced him to be seated on the stump. "We can do both. First of all, it won't take but a few days to put up that building, and that's with only us four working on it."

Big Dog and the others nodded.

The man continued, his voice pitched to a reasonable tone. "And when we finish, we'll get back to logging like you ain't ever seen before. There's almost three weeks before the *Leonesa*'s due to transport those piles. Plenty of time to put up a building and fill that shipment. We won't be found short."

Squinty added with a grin, "And we'll get to see them purty women all the while."

Noah looked at each of the other three men, and each of them nodded in agreement with Mills's words.

Hope flickered to life. They seemed certain they could do both. And besides, what choice did he have? If he disagreed, they might very well walk off the job. The draw of a pretty woman in this male-dominated country was stronger than he could battle.

"All right," he finally agreed, and then straightened and delivered his own stern glare to each of the four. "But you'll have to work with the Duwamish. We can't afford to offend them."

They conferred silently, and then Big Dog nodded. "If we hafta, we will."

Noah sagged on the stump. Somehow he would have to convince Arthur that this was the best course of action.

～

The next morning, the sight that met Evie when she stepped off the path into her clearing brought her to an abrupt halt. This time the area was filled with lumberjacks. Not only that, but the carefully constructed walls of which she was so fiercely proud were gone. Gone!

"What happened?" Louisa's face reflected the same shock that Evie felt. "Two days ago there was a building here."

Ethel's mouth fell open, but no sound came out.

A shout went up in a strong male voice. "They're here!"

A moment later the three ladies were surrounded by smiling men.

Evie fixed a pleading look on Big Dog's face. "Where's my restaurant?"

"Gone." He flashed a wide grin around the circle, and the men all nodded. "We tore it down this morning."

Her vision blurred as tears sprang to her eyes. What had she done to upset them to the point they would do such a horrible thing? "But why? Why would you do this to me?"

"Aw, ma'am, don't take on so." George, the one they called Pig Face, patted her awkwardly on the shoulder. "We're gonna build you a new one, and it'll be better than that old lean-to you had before."

Hope flickered in the darkness of her thoughts and she looked up into Big Dog's face. "You are?"

He laid a hand over his chest. "On my honor. You're gonna have the finest restaurant in all of the Oregon Territory, you wait and see."

Deep lines carved into Louisa's smooth forehead. "Arthur won't like this at all."

"Nah, he don't mind none." Perkins cocked his head and corrected himself. "At least, not much. Noah done cleared it with him."

Evie couldn't believe her ears. "*Noah* spoke to Arthur about this?"

"That's right." Big Dog nodded. "And don't you worry any about your Indian friends, either. David talked to that chief and they're all right with us taking over for a while, and they're even gonna work with us. They already helped us pull down the old stuff this morning."

Louisa's eyes went wide. "My David did that?"

"Yes, ma'am. If you don't believe us, you can ask him yourself. He's right over there."

The wall of men parted and Big Dog pointed to a place on the other side of the clearing where David and Noah stood beside Miles, examining a paper. Louisa's face lit and, gathering her skirts, she took off toward him at a run. Still unable to make sense of what was happening, Evie followed at a more subdued pace.

"There you are, my dear." Miles snatched the paper out of Noah's hands and wadded it in a ball. "Would you be so kind as to let us examine your excellent sketch? I'm afraid my skills with a pen are reserved to letters, not drawings."

Numbly, Evie pulled the sketch from her apron pocket and handed it to Noah.

"I don't understand." She peered into his face, trying to make sense of this confusing turn of events. "What about the lumber shipment?"

"They took a vow." His eyes fixed on the men behind her, shaking his head. "After they finish here they'll work days and nights both if that's what it takes, but they insist we'll be ready by the time the brig arrives." He turned his gaze on her, and a tender smile softened his lips. "You've made quite an impression on them." The smile disappeared and he straightened, resuming a businesslike manner. "And the other ladies too, of course."

Evie didn't dare speak, but merely nodded and turned to watch the men, white and Indian alike, begin work on her new restaurant. Her emotions rode high, too close to the surface to trust to words. Not only because of the men, but also because of the gentle look she had seen in Noah's eyes a moment before. Was it her imagination, or was some of that tenderness meant for her alone?

Thirteen

O h, Lester!"

Sarah's voice, pitched even higher than usual, drew Evie's attention away from counting. She looked up from her list to see the girl holding a pitcher and a cup, her head thrown back and her gaze fixed on a trio of men up on the roof. Once Sarah heard the men were working on the building, she'd once again begun accompanying Evie and the others on their daily treks to the clearing. In fact, she was usually the first up in the morning, urging the others to hurry with breakfast so they could go.

"Are you thirsty, hon?" With a flirty tilt to her head she lifted the cup toward him. Lester descended the ladder faster than a cat chasing a mouse, grinning like an idiot.

A few days ago Evie would have spoken sternly to Sarah and the others about distracting the men from their work. It amused her to realize she had stepped into Noah's role. Now, however, she didn't feel she had any reason. The restaurant was almost finished, and the jacks had only begun four days ago.

She surveyed the building with more than a little satisfaction. Four sturdy log walls, their surfaces stripped of bark to display smooth red wood, stood in the center of the glade where Mary's clothesline had once marked the boundaries. Lester and his partners were busy applying tight cedar shakes to half of the second floor roof, while a handful of men, both lumberjacks and Duwamish, completed the walls of the other half. The wooden slats the Indians had used initially had not been wasted, but were deemed by Big Dog and his men to be plenty sturdy for the second floor, where Evie and the other ladies would live. Men's voices floated through the first floor windows, where they worked inside laying stone for the hearth. At the rate the men were going, they would be finished enough tomorrow that Evie could move in.

"Hey, Noah, how's the count today?"

The call from the roof drew Evie's attention from her musings. She looked up to see Noah striding across the path toward her.

"Improving, but we're still down," he called back. "We need you."

Evie busied herself with her inventory. Since the morning he and the others had showed up and announced their intention to build her restaurant, she'd felt shy around him. Since the moment they met, their relationship had consisted of one clash of wills after another. She'd grown accustomed to that. Now that they were in accord, she wasn't sure how to proceed. Nor was she sure of her feelings concerning Noah, or his for her. He treated her with the same courtesy he accorded Louisa and Ethel and the Burrows sisters, but she sensed something different in his dealings with her. Restraint, maybe?

Of course, they were not merely acquaintances. They were business partners. Their relationship *should* have a tone of formality, the same as with Miles.

So why did most conversations with Noah leave her feeling slightly dissatisfied?

"It's looking good," he observed as he came to a stop and turned to survey the building.

"Yes, it is," she agreed. "I knew they would be quick, but I had no idea how quick. If they had started a week before, I could be open for business by now."

When he gave her a sharp sideways look, she realized what she'd said. Given their previous clashes, the comment sounded very close to *I told you so.* Warmth crept up her neck toward her cheeks. "I'm sorry. I didn't mean that the way it sounded."

He shoved his hands in his pocket and shuffled his feet in the grass. "Actually, that's something I need to talk to you about."

His manner, the way he did not meet her eye, said he was wary about her reaction to whatever he wanted to discuss.

Studying him carefully, she said, "Go on."

"There's some grumbling in the camp. The men who have returned to the cutting site are jealous of those still here."

"Are they not doing the work they promised to do?"

"Oh, yes." He gave a quick nod. "They're working like mules, every one of them. But Arthur and I were trying to think of a way to keep their spirits up, so they'll stop grumbling, and maybe even work faster."

What did that have to do with her? She kept her silence, waiting for him to explain.

With the heel of his boot he ground grass into a mashed circle. "So we were thinking if the men could see you and the other ladies on a regular basis, they'd be happier. Like maybe at breakfast and supper."

Wait. Was this the total reversal it sounded like? "Are you saying you want me to go ahead and open my restaurant now?" She shook her head. "Because that's not possible. I have no tables, no benches." She fixed an acerbic look on him. "No tomatoes."

He stared at her for a moment, his expression incredulous, and then threw back his head. Laughter from deep in his chest filled the glade, drawing stares from the workers.

She frowned. "What's so funny?"

"Do you realize we've switched positions? All along I've been insisting that the men would be distracted by the presence of ladies in the logging camp, and you've been insisting that you open your restaurant as soon as possible."

The ludicrousness of the situation struck her, and she joined in with a chuckle.

He pulled a handkerchief from his pocket and wiped tears from his eyes. "Maybe we can meet in the middle this time. What I propose is to hire you and the other ladies to work with Cookee, preparing and serving meals for the men." She started to interrupt, but he rushed on. "Only for the next two weeks, until the *Leonesa* arrives and we send this shipment on its way."

"You mean in the cookhouse?" At his nod, she narrowed her eyes. "Have you spoken to Cookee about this? He doesn't strike me as the kind of man who would tolerate anyone interfering with his cooking."

"I have, and you're right." Again he failed to meet her eye. "He wants me to make sure you understand you'll be taking orders from him and not the other way around."

Not surprising. She could picture the little man stiffening and demanding that Noah make sure they understood he would be the boss.

She stepped in front of him and forced him to look her in the face. "Why the change of heart? I thought you were determined to keep us out of sight."

"This happened." He waved toward the building. "I've never seen men work like they've done, and they're doing it because of you and the other ladies. I figured if they know they'll see you a couple of times a day, that'll keep them happy, at least for the time being. A happy man works harder than a grumbling one."

His reasoning made perfect sense. Evie chewed on her lip, considering the proposal. The reality was she couldn't open her restaurant until after this shipment was gone anyway. She'd already decided she owed her support to Arthur and Noah and the rest of the men in gratitude for the good turn they'd done her, and that meant staying out of their way until their job was finished. Besides, the alternative was to spend the next two weeks helping Miles capture and pickle salmon, a task for which she could not generate any enthusiasm.

Another thought occurred to her.

"How much will we get paid?"

"Not as much as Cookee." He grinned. "But more than you're making now."

She had to laugh at that. Anything would be better than nothing. She could put her pay toward her first loan payment.

She extended a hand. "We'll do it. Or at least I will, and I'll speak to the others. I feel certain Ethel, Lucy, and Sarah will agree, but I don't know about Louisa."

When he clasped her hand, warmth enveloped her. A flutter started in her stomach. Releasing him after a quick shake, she turned away lest he see the emotions in her face.

"Oh, I doubt if Louisa will want to. She's about to get some news that will keep her occupied for the next two weeks as well."

Evie jerked back toward him and inspected the secretive grin on his face. "Oh?"

His head turned as he did a quick check of the area around them, and then he leaned toward her to speak in a low voice. "Can you keep a secret?"

"I am excellent at keeping secrets," she assured him.

"A visitor arrived at the camp a little while ago. He came from Alki Point with a message for David. The *Leonesa* is bringing someone with her. A minister."

Evie gave him a look full of questions, and then the meaning dawned. "A minister that can perform weddings?"

His grin broke free. "He and Louisa will finally be able to be married."

Delight flooded her, and erupted on a giggle. Quickly, she covered her mouth with her hands and glanced around to make sure she hadn't been heard. This would be a hard secret to keep. Hopefully David wouldn't wait too long.

She caught sight of Sarah and her water pitcher. She was giving a drink to Big Dog while one of the Duwamish workers waited his turn. On the other side of the clearing Lucy loaded cedar shakes into a barrel, her eyes constantly straying to the men on the roof who watched her just as closely.

"Well, at least this arrangement at the cookhouse will solve one of the problems I've been worried about," she told Noah.

"What's that?"

With a sardonic laugh, she pointed. "I've been wondering how in the world I was going to keep the girls away from the men."

≈

"I'm getting married!"

Louisa's eyes sparkled with a joy that went soul-deep. Watching her dance around the cabin, her skirts twirling and her hair flying out behind her, Evie's eyes filled with tears on her friend's behalf. Thank goodness she didn't need to keep her secret for long. David had arrived at the cabin shortly after supper and asked Louisa to take a walk with him. She'd returned floating on a cloud.

The two little girls danced with their aunt, giggling and spinning with glee. Lucy and Ethel wore giant grins, and Sarah could not contain herself, but jumped in place, clapping her hands.

Only Mary seemed unruffled by the news. "Long past time, if you ask me." But her lips twitched and she bounced baby Rolland on her knee with enthusiasm.

Louisa's delighted laugh filled the cabin. "True enough, but that was hardly David's fault. After all, there's been no minister to perform the ceremony." She clasped her hands beneath her chin, eyes shining. "Just think. In only two weeks I'll no longer only be David's Sweetbriar girl. I'll be his Sweetbriar bride."

Mary stood up and went to the stove to stir the stew. Evie took baby Rolland and settled him on her hip. "I've heard him call you Sweetbriar and wondered where the name came from."

"I'll show you."

She climbed the ladder to the loft, reappearing a moment later with a small pouch. Opening the drawstring, she carefully poured some of the contents into her hand. The others crowded around to look.

"They're seeds," said Evie.

Louisa nodded. "Sweetbriar seeds. Back in Cherry Grove, my dearest friend from childhood had a beautiful flower garden full of sweetbriar. When we left, we gathered these seeds together, and I told her I would plant them in my own garden one day." She carefully poured the seeds back into the pouch and cinched the string closed. "David promised me that one day he would build me a home with a garden where I could plant them. That's when he started calling me his Sweetbriar girl."

Sarah heaved a sentimental sigh. "I hope someday a handsome man will have a sweet name like that for me."

Ethel turned a sour look her way. "The way you've behaved around those men the past week, it'll be something *tart* instead."

Evie hid a smile by placing a kiss on Rolland's soft baby head.

"I just thought of something." Lucy rushed to grab her sister's hands. "If there's going to be a preacher here, maybe he can marry more than one couple."

At the stove, Mary turned. "Picked out a husband so quickly, have you?"

"Not yet," Lucy informed her. "But we have two whole weeks."

This time Evie didn't bother hiding her amusement, but laughed openly. "You do seem to have plenty to choose from, I'll say that. But I'd be careful if I were you."

"She's right," Louisa advised. "You don't want to end up married to a man you don't know. Why, he might turn out to be horrid, and then where would you be?"

Neither Lucy nor Sarah seemed convinced. They exchanged secretive smiles and said nothing. Evie hoped the men would have more sense than these two, or else they might have a disaster on their hands.

"In the meantime, we have a wedding to plan." Evie switched the baby to her other hip. "Maybe we could have it at the restaurant. I expect everyone will want to come, and there's plenty of room there."

Louisa turned a grateful smile on her, and then jerked upright. "Oh. I nearly forgot. David gave me a message for you. Chief Seattle came to the cutting site today and asked him to make sure everyone who worked on the building is there the day after tomorrow at sunset."

Evie had not seen the chief since his visit the previous week. "I wonder why?"

"Apparently he has some sort of speech to make." She shrugged. "Like a dedication, maybe?"

Evie hadn't considered a dedication ceremony, especially not before the restaurant opened. But if Chief Seattle wanted to make a speech, he was certainly entitled. His people had worked as hard as the lumberjacks, and friendships had developed between the Duwamish and the white settlers.

"I think the men will finish with the shakes on the second floor roof tomorrow, so we'll be able to move in." She included Ethel and the sisters with a glance. "It will be a dedication of our new home as well as the restaurant."

Margaret ran over to tug at Mary's skirt. "Can we go, Mama?"

Louisa Catherine added, "Please?"

Mary looked at Evie with a silent question.

"We'll have plenty of room, if you don't mind cots and pallets on the floor," she said.

Mary smiled at her girls. "I think we can manage that for one night."

Their excited cheers pierced the air, startling baby Rolland and making him cry. Mary hurried over to take him from Evie and soothe him. When she spoke to her girls, she was once again all business, a trait that reminded Evie strongly of her husband. "That's enough now. Go up and get your nightdresses on. It's time for bed."

As the girls scampered up the ladder, Evie realized she was looking forward to Chief Seattle's visit. It was a fitting way to end the construction phase and move on to the next. The following morning, she and the other ladies would begin working with Cookee.

≈

Evie smoothed the blanket over her cot and gave it a final pat. Standing back, she examined her new bedroom. The cot looked pathetically small, and the room ridiculously huge and empty. The only other furnishing was her trunk, which Big Dog had hauled up the ladder for her. She'd positioned it beside her cot to use as a nightstand until she could commission one to be made, along with a proper bed.

A memory rose in her mind. Not too long ago she had stood looking at her room in Mrs. Browning's boardinghouse. That morning she'd been saying goodbye, and not only to an empty room. She'd bid farewell to Chattanooga, the town of her birth and childhood. To James and the life they'd planned. But this evening she was greeting a new life, one she could never have imagined. One with a lot of empty places still yet to be filled. If she were to make a list entitled *Things I Will Accomplish in My Life*, there would be many blank lines. Evie did not like blank lines on her lists.

Ethel appeared in the doorway. "Now, that looks just fine for the time being."

Thrusting away her disturbing thoughts, Evie dusted her hands on her apron. "It will do for now. Are you girls settled in?"

"Not much settling to do, but what there is, is done."

Chuckling, she led Evie through the doorway into the outer room where three cots had been set up. This room would one day be her main living area, but without furnishings there was no use for it. Ethel had insisted that the three sleep there and leave the bedroom for Evie, since it would be hers permanently.

"Where are the others?" Evie asked.

She waved a hand vaguely toward the window. "Some men fetched down cots for Mary and Louisa and the kids to use tonight, and you know Sarah and Lucy." Her thick eyebrows waggled. "If there are men around, that's where you'll find them."

"Tonight they can flirt to their hearts' content. This is a celebration, after all. The work starts tomorrow."

"You think they won't flirt then too?" Ethel blew a rude noise through her lips.

Laughing, Evie descended the ladder and went outside. The area around the restaurant was already alive with activity. Men had clustered around Lucy and Sarah, who were holding court like princesses and looked completely happy to do so. Margaret and Louisa Catherine ran around the area, watched closely by Mary. Evie noted with surprise that Arthur stood near his wife, holding baby Rolland. He'd taken time to attend the celebration. On the far end of the glade Louisa and David strolled arm in arm, their heads together. The sight of the happy couple brought a smile to her face.

"Good evening, Miss Lawrence," said a familiar voice close to her ear.

She whirled to find Noah standing behind her. Flustered, she took a backward step. "You startled me."

"I'm sorry." He grinned, belying his words. "The men have something for you."

She realized that every lumberjack in the area had begun to converge on her. They gathered before her, grins on every face.

"For me?" She put a hand self-consciously to her collarbone. "Why?"

George answered. "On account of we want to celebrate your new digs here."

"But you did all the work." She held her hands out to encompass the entire group. "I should be giving you gifts, not the other way around."

Squinty stepped forward, his hat in his hands and his balding head looking like it had been recently scrubbed. "Ma'am, you and the other ladies gave us a gift jest by comin' here."

"This is sort of a welcomin' present," added George, and then raised his head and shouted. "Bring it here, boys."

Big Dog and Mills came around the corner of the cabin, each holding one end of a long, sturdy table. On the surface rested a metal pitcher she recognized from the cookhouse, filled with wildflowers. Evie stared, speechless, as they carried the table toward her and set it down carefully so as not to unbalance the pitcher.

Squinty gave the surface a proprietary pat. "We all had a go at it, building and sanding and such. Been working on it nights."

"It's not as nice as the ones you'll want for your restaurant, but we figured every kitchen needs a work table." Big Dog slapped a huge hand on the surface. "You won't find one sturdier than this."

Evie moved toward it slowly, hardly able to believe her eyes. True, it did not gleam like the highly polished table in the Coffinger's dining room back in Tennessee, but the surface was wide and sanded smooth. The swirling design in the wood was lovelier than any she had ever seen. The legs were solid blocks of wood, also smoothed and leveled. That was all she could see, because her vision blurred and her eyes swam with tears.

"I…" She choked, and then turned a tearful gaze on all the men. "I don't know how to thank you. I've never seen anything more perfect in my life."

Her reward was grins all the way around as the men slapped each other on the back and congratulated one another on a job well done.

The sound of a beating drum rose above their voices, and Noah, who'd been standing to one side while the men presented their gift, said, "Sounds like Chief Seattle has arrived." He looked toward the western horizon, where the sun had sunk behind the trees a moment before. "Exactly on time."

Evie ran her hand over the beautiful table once more, and then hastily dried her eyes and turned to watch the path in time to see the chief's entrance.

He wore a headdress of leather and bark, decorated with feathers that trailed down his back. Miles strode along beside him, his chest puffed with self-importance. They were accompanied by six Duwamish men, five carrying stone tools and one beating on a large drum.

"Over there." Miles pointed at an open area on one side of the glade and the natives proceeded to that spot. He searched the assembled faces, smiling when he caught sight of Arthur. With a hand, he waved him over. "We'll be seated beside Seattle, you, and David and Noah." His gaze fell on Evie. "You too, my dear. And the rest of you can gather round."

Noah slid a hand beneath Evie's arm and guided her toward the area where four of the Duwamish men had begun to clear a wide circle of grass.

"What is going on?" she whispered.

Eyebrows arched high, Noah shook his head. "I have no idea. All David told us was that the Chief wanted to present us with a gift and say a few words." He grinned. "That's why the men wanted to give you the table they've been working on tonight. They didn't want to be outdone."

"Gift?" Evie gave him a worried look. "We should give them gifts in return, don't you think?"

"He said not to worry about it," Noah whispered, but then they arrived beside Miles and Seattle.

The circle was completed quickly, and the chief lowered himself gracefully to the ground. Miles indicated that the others should do the same, and took a place on Seattle's right. Evie and Noah shared a quick glance, full of humor. Miles had certainly endeared himself to the Duwamish leader.

Noah helped her to the ground. Modesty demanded that she not sit cross-legged, as the men did, so she folded her legs to the side as she would at a picnic. When Evie had settled her skirts around her legs, she looked up to find Chief Seattle watching her. His perpetually solemn expression softened with a brief smile and he dipped his head. Feeling as though she had been honored, Evie nodded in return.

More natives entered the clearing, carrying wood that they piled on the circle of soil. Ah, now she understood. They'd created a fire pit. As the assembled watched, another man appeared on the path, this one with a burning torch held straight out in front of him. He moved with slow, measured steps, his face solemn, obviously following some sort of prearranged ceremony. All the while, the drummer pounded a steady beat that filled the air and rang in Evie's ears. In moments, the wood blazed high. The torchbearer tossed his torch on the top of the bonfire and stepped back to sink to the ground between two lumberjacks.

Chief Seattle lifted his arms and spread them wide in a request for silence. The drum ceased and though no one had been speaking before, an attentive hush came over everyone around the fire. The chief said something in his language to David.

David nodded and spoke in a voice pitched to reach everyone present. "Chief *Si'ahl* asks me to speak his words in our white man's tongue so all can understand."

The chief lowered his arms and lifted his head. His deep voice projected past those circled around the crackling fire, far into the forest. The words he spoke had the now-familiar sound of their language, but took on a grace Evie had never noticed when spoken in Seattle's fluid baritone. After a few sentences he paused and waited for David to translate.

"My people have lived on this land for many years. Every part is familiar to us. We know the sap that courses through the trees as we know the blood that courses through our veins. We are part of the earth and it is part of us. The perfumed flowers are our sisters. The bear and the great eagle are our brothers. The rocky crests, the dew in the meadow, and man, all belong to the same family."

Seattle spoke again, his words falling with an exotic but oddly calming resonance on Evie's ears.

"Then white men came. Your ways are a mystery to us. You take more trees than you need, and send them away in big canoes. You offer payment for what is as freely yours as it is ours."

The chief fixed a look on Miles, who seemed oblivious that the comment might have been directed at him and his recent salmon purchases.

"You crash through the forest shouting like wounded elk instead of listening to the earth's voice."

Evie searched the faces around the circle and exchanged a grin with Ethel, who was trying not to laugh. Flickering firelight illuminated the faces of the Denny girls, one seated on each side of the stocky woman, their eyes round and mouths dangling open.

"But some of your ways are common to ours. I have seen awe in your faces as you gaze over our land, our waters. I have seen the respect you accord one another. I have seen you labor together to meet the needs of another."

Now Evie found those eyes, darker than the night, fixed on her.

"These are also the ways of my people. When I consider them, I am comforted. Though our ways differ, perhaps we are not so different. As we are part of the land, you are part of the land. This earth is precious to us. It is also precious to you. I have hope that we can learn to live side by side, to share with one another. And so I, Chief Si'ahl, and my people, welcome you."

The chief folded his arms over his chest and lowered his head when the echo of David's final words faded. For the space of a breath, silence reigned. Then someone—she thought it might be Big Dog—let out a cheer and began to clap. Every white settler joined in. Tears filled Evie's eyes for the second time this evening as she clapped until her palms ached.

The chief once more lifted his arms and the drum started again. This time the rhythm was fast and lively, and Evie's heartbeat skipped along with the cadence. More Duwamish tribesmen stepped into the clearing, eight men carrying a huge log. Instead of approaching the circle, they marched past on silent feet, heading toward a place in the center of the glade. Evie and Noah both turned to watch their progress, and she was surprised to see that a deep, narrow hole had been dug in the ground while their attention was focused elsewhere, apparently by those who had cleared the ground for the fire. The newcomers placed the end of the log in the hole and then, working together, slowly raised it up. It settled with a thud, and two men knelt to pack soil around the edges while the others held it in place.

As she looked, Evie realized she had been wrong. This was not merely a log. The surface had been carved and painted with the same vivid colors she'd admired on the courtship poles—only these designs were much larger.

She leaned toward Noah to whisper in his ear. "It's not another marriage proposal, is it?"

His eyes were wide as Cookee's flapjacks. "If it is, you might want to consider accepting this one. It's huge."

Suppressing a laugh, she answered by jabbing an elbow in his ribs.

He grinned, rubbing his side. "I'm joking. I've heard of these. They're called totem poles. This must be the gift they told David about."

When the Indians stepped back, the totem pole stood tall and straight. Evie realized its top was on level with the window in her bedroom. If she positioned her cot just right, she would be able to see it in the morning when she woke.

The chief said something and stood, and David leaped to his feet. "He says we can look at it if we want."

The drum kept up its rapid tempo while they gathered in front of the pole to admire it. Evie saw that instead of one design, the pole actually consisted of many individual carvings, one on top of another, all intricate and colorfully detailed. Some she recognized right away, like the bear head and, at the top, an eagle with its wings spread wide. The words of the chief's speech came back to her. These symbols held special significance for the Duwamish people.

"Look." David pointed halfway up. "That's a lumberjack."

Sure enough, the carved scene depicted a beefy man wielding an ax and standing before a tall tree.

"And there we are again," said Arthur.

Below the picture of the lumberjack another carving showed two men shaking hands. One was obviously Indian, wearing a headdress very similar to the one Chief Seattle wore tonight. The other had a bare head and wore white man's clothing. "That must be when we first met."

Chief Seattle had joined them, and he dipped his head at Arthur's comment. Evie studied the scene, a sense of awe rising in her. This totem pole was meant not to commemorate her restaurant only, but the entire settlement. It was a symbol of the Duwamish people's acceptance of the white men and women who had settled here.

"Evie, look." Noah's face held a grin so wide she saw his back molars. "That's you."

"What?" She followed his gaze to a carving near the top. Night had fallen in the clearing and darkness obscured the details, but she could see the shoulders, neck, and head of a woman. "No, it can't be me."

The chief said something, and Noah laughed. "He says the carving is you, though not nearly as pretty as it should be. You're meant to represent this place, where his people and ours worked together toward a common goal for the first time."

Overcome, Evie covered her mouth with a hand. A lump of emotion had gathered in her throat. If she wasn't careful she would cry. When she was certain she could speak, she faced the chief. "Thank you."

Her reward was another of his rare smiles, and then he turned away, leaving her and Noah standing side by side.

His head tilted as he gazed up at the top of the pole, where the eagle's bright eye looked out toward Elliott Bay, wings spread wide as if to embrace all the land it saw.

"Will you be all right with this here, in front of your restaurant?" He spoke in a low voice that couldn't be overheard. "I mean, it's rather primitive."

Definitely primitive. What would Ethel think of that snarling bear's head? And the carved woman who was supposed to be Evie... How strange would it feel to see that every time she walked in or out of her restaurant?

But she didn't care. This totem pole was a gift that she would treasure not only for the beauty of its design, but for the significance it symbolized.

"I love it," she told him. "It's perfect."

Fourteen

Cookee stabbed at Evie and Ethel with a crooked finger. "I told ye time and again, it don't matter if they's a feather or two left. Jest get the big 'uns off and start them birds to roastin'."

While Evie examined the bird carcass in her lap for big feathers, Ethel drew herself up and snapped, "Don't tell me how to pluck a chicken. I've been doing it since before I could talk." The effect of her severe retort was somewhat spoiled by the fact that an assortment of soft, downy feathers had collected in her hair.

"That ain't no chicken, missy. It's a wild turkey."

She met his glare. "No difference, only bigger."

Cookee planted his bowed legs in front of them and glared down the not-inconsiderable length of his nose, taking advantage of the fact that they were seated. "Ain't neither, and that there jest shows how ignor'nt you Tennessee girlies are."

Ethel sucked in a breath, ready to deliver a scathing reply, but Evie gave her a warning look. She let it out slowly, and, with obvious restraint, kept her silence.

"We're almost finished," Evie told the man. "Only two more and then you can show us how to roast them."

Her conciliatory tone seemed to calm him. "Well, see that you hurry. In a few hours this place'll be swarming hungry men expecting to be fed, and I ain't gonna be the one to tell them they gotta eat raw turkeys." He gave Ethel one more glare before stomping off to the kitchen.

The woman followed his exit with a black look. "I know the difference between a turkey and a chicken, but the plucking is the same. That's all I meant."

"I'm sure you do." Evie reached up and picked the feathers from her hair. "Only one more week and then you can tell Cookee anything you like. In the meantime, we promised to keep the peace."

"Hmph." With a vicious jerk she ripped a handful of feathers from the huge bird in her lap. "Right after the boat sets sail with that load of wood, I'm going to march right into that cookhouse and give him what for."

Evie chuckled. Truth be told, the ill-tempered cook had grown on her in the week since they'd begun helping him cook and serve the lumberjacks. At first he felt threatened by having women assistants in his cookhouse, and she'd had to steel herself against surly comments about females who wanted to do jobs that ought to be left to men. Her timid suggestions about new seasonings for beans or sweeter pie crusts were not only soundly rebuffed, but treated as personal attacks on his abilities. Finally, Evie adopted an attitude of restraint. When given a task, she did it cheerfully and without comment, even though at times she had to clamp her teeth together to keep from snapping a reply.

Besides, she'd learned a few things in the past week. Cookee had worked as a trail cook on cattle drives before coming here, and he knew a thing or two about feeding a group of tired, hungry men. He could turn a sack of flour into a mountain of flapjacks that stretched out over a whole week, cheaper and better than anything Evie had ever made. The men devoured them every morning. And his venison stew was hands-down better than any stew she'd ever produced. She'd taught him a better way to make shoepack pie and he'd had to admit it was downright finger-lickin' good. After carefully observing Cookee this past week, she had dozens of new ideas for her restaurant.

"There." Ethel tossed the last de-feathered turkey on top of the other five. "Now I suppose he'll want to hover over us and make sure we know what we're doing when we gut and spit them." She glared toward the cookhouse door, and then stood with a resolute sigh. "I'll go tell him we're finished."

"Be nice," Evie warned.

The grim smile Ethel pasted on would have scared away a starving grizzly.

❦

Despite Cookee's dire predictions, the turkeys were roasted in plenty of time for the men's return to camp. Evie and the other ladies delivered platters piled high with the succulent meat to the tables, along with roasted potatoes, onions, early carrots harvested from Cookee's garden, loaves of bread, and dozens of pies. The men devoured every bite of the feast. Evie was thankful she'd set some aside for Noah, who rarely joined the others for supper.

One other benefit from the past week was that she'd had the opportunity to observe her restaurant employees in action. She had come to expect that Ethel would be a hard worker, and was not disappointed. The woman's strength and stamina outlasted the other girls time and again. Lucy surprised her by working almost as hard as Ethel and maintaining a cheerful attitude besides. Sarah, on the other hand, tended toward laziness except when the men were present. No surprise there. When the company returned from the cutting site for supper she became the model of helpfulness, though she frequently flitted from one table to the other, leaving tasks unfinished as she went in search of someone else's attention.

While the men flirted tirelessly with Lucy and Sarah, they at first ignored Ethel. But after a week they seemed to accept and even appreciate her brusque manner.

Evie herself they treated with respect and admiration, though also a touch of reserve. Their attitudes amused her. Was it because she held the role of employer over the others? Regardless, she was secretly relieved that she was not called to constantly fend off unwanted attention.

When the last of the food platters had been set on the make-shift tables in the cookhouse and her employees were occupied with keeping the lumberjacks' cups full while they ate, Evie picked up the plate she'd fixed for Noah, covered it with a napkin, and slipped through the doorway. As she expected, the glow of candlelight shined from inside the command tent. For the past week Noah had worked at the cutting site all day and spent his evenings hunched over his ledgers. Oftentimes the candle still burned after the supper dishes had been washed up and Evie and the ladies were ready to be escorted down the trail to the restaurant for the night.

Dark had fallen over the camp when she carried Noah's supper plate to him. Night in this vast forest always filled her with a sense of smallness. She tiptoed as she walked, unwilling to intrude on the natural sounds that surrounded the camp.

The low thrum of a male voice reached her ears. Evie decided the voice was coming from ahead, from around the corner of the cook-house. A few of the men must not have gone in to supper yet. She walked on, intending to inform them that they would miss out on a treat of roasted turkey if they didn't hurry. But the moment before she rounded the corner, she heard something that brought her to a quick halt.

"This one is for Miss Ethel."

She recognized the voice as belonging to Randall Miller, one of the lumberjacks who had helped to build her restaurant. Was he spearheading a tribute for Ethel, then? How sweet.

Moving with stealth, she crept toward the end of the building and peered around the corner. Four men crouched in a circle, each one staring at the ground between them. She knew them all. Besides Randall there was Big Dog, Squinty, and George. What were they doing?

Randall's arm shook back and forth and then he released something from his hand. Four heads crowded together to peer at the ground.

"Aw, no!" George reared up, throwing his hands toward heaven. "I don't want the ugly one. I want Miss Evie, or maybe Miss Lucy. Put my name back in for the next roll."

In a rush, Evie realized what was happening. These four men—she took note again of which ones were present—were tossing dice to determine who would court which of her ladies. As if they were cattle, to be won in a game of chance! Why, this was absolutely barbaric.

A series of possible actions flashed into her mind. Option one, she could storm into the midst of them now, confiscate their dice, and give them a piece of her mind. Possible, though she wasn't sure that would bring about a change of attitude, except maybe they would think twice about pursuing *her.* Option two, she could whirl around and march back into the cookhouse to inform Ethel, Lucy, and Sarah of the insulting drama upon which she had just stumbled. Again possible. Lucy and Ethel were sure to be as outraged as she, but Sarah would probably be upset that she hadn't waited to see who won the right to court her.

Option three seemed the only logical solution. Setting her spine as stiff as a cedar log, Evie marched toward the command tent. She burst through the tent's opening with no ceremony and did not bother to filter the outrage from her voice.

"What kind of camp are you running here?"

Noah looked up from the ledger over which he had been bent, his expression blank. "Huh?"

"Do you know what I saw just now?" She allowed anger to blaze in her eyes. "*Your* men rolling dice for *my* women!"

He looked at her a moment, then set his pen down and

straightened slowly. "Last time I checked, I don't own any men. And you don't own any women."

His response only fed the fire of her irritation. "You know what I mean," she snapped. "They're my friends and my employees. I won't stand by while they're auctioned off like heads of cattle." She drew herself up with renewed outrage. "And me along with them."

A grin tugged at the corners of his lips. "Really? Which of the men won you?"

For a moment, Evie battled between further outrage and humor. She held herself stiffly upright, but then the twitch in his lips won her over. This could not possibly be his fault. To hold him accountable for the men's actions would be the same as holding her accountable for Sarah's. Though she intended to allow only a brief smile, she ended up chuckling.

"Truthfully, I was afraid to stay and find out." She leaned forward and spoke in a conspiratorial whisper. "It might have been Pig Face."

He threw back his head and laughed. "Heaven forbid!"

When the laughter died, they were left gazing at each other fondly.

"I'm sorry I shouted at you," she said finally. "This isn't your fault."

"I will speak to the men," he promised. Then he extended his neck toward the plate she held. "Is that my supper?"

Smiling, she set the plate before him and lifted the napkin. "I set some aside before the swarm devoured it all."

If he had been truly hungry, he would have fallen on the food as she expected him to. Instead, his gaze barely flickered over the plate. He seemed far more content to give her his full attention.

"So," she said, mostly to fill the silence before it became awkward, "what are you doing here?" She gestured toward the ledger in front of him.

He shrugged. "Calculations. I keep tally of the men's work, their pay, and the number of trees felled every day along with the measurements and calculations of the feet of lumber each will yield."

"Is that all?" She attempted a light laugh, though the weight of his gaze bore down on her. "I could do that for you."

He straightened. "You could?"

"Of course. I'll be happy to. It would free your time up to chop down trees." She battled the warmth that threatened to rise in her cheeks at the ravenous look in his eyes.

"Thank you."

The words seemed to hold more meaning than they implied, and she didn't know how to answer. So she took a backward step and said nothing.

Noah's eyes bored into hers. "Evie, I…"

He seemed to be on the verge of something big, something of import. Evie's heart fluttered inside her ribcage, and her breath came shallow. She could not hold his gaze, and instead looked away.

Leaving the plate untouched, Noah rose and rounded the rough cedar log that served him as a desk. He came to her side and stood close, though he did not touch her. The silence inside the tent grew heavy. There were only a few inches between them, but those inches were charged with energy. Evie fought to keep herself erect. Every fiber of her being wanted to lean into him.

He cleared his voice, though when he spoke it was with a husky tone. "I want you to know how grateful I am."

Was he going to kiss her? An almost magnetic pull on her lips had Evie leaning toward Noah, her face turned up to his. Her heart seemed to have stopped beating. She answered without really knowing what she said. "Whatever I can do to help."

One inch of empty air stood between their lips. That air felt warm, hot even, as she gazed into Noah's eyes. She inhaled his breath, and her insides tickled at its warmth deep inside her lungs. As if pushed by an unseen force, she felt herself being pulled forward…

"Hey, ink slinger!"

A voice from outside the tent sliced through the air like a cold blade through hot bread. Evie jerked backward and busied herself with settling her collar high on her neck. Noah too leaped back-ward as if burned.

"Yeah," he answered in a loud voice, his gaze averted from hers. "I'm here."

A man appeared in the tent's opening. "The pusher wants to see you." When he caught sight of Evie, he jerked upright and snatched the hat off his head. "Evening, ma'am."

Wordlessly, she smiled and nodded a greeting at him while Noah rounded the desk and snatched up his ledger. "Probably wants to see the day's counts. Samuel, see Miss Lawrence gets home safely, would you?"

Mumbling something about seeing her later, Noah hurried out of the building, leaving Evie in charge of the eager messenger, her emotions in turmoil.

～

The last week before the *Leonesa's* scheduled arrival passed in a blur. Evie rose at three every morning for the trek up to the logging camp, where the ladies worked to get breakfast ready for the lum-berjacks by four thirty. Her days were spent transcribing the produc-tion records that Noah scrawled down at the cutting site and gave to her at night. She calculated the men's work time and pay, keep-ing tallies to give to Arthur at night when the loggers dragged them-selves back to camp. Supper was a silent meal, the lumberjacks too tired even to flirt.

And then the last log was cut.

The men's pace became feverish as they corded the floating logs down the streams and tributaries to the mouth of the Duwamish River, where they would stay until they were loaded onto the *Leonesa*. This work was completed a full day before the brig was scheduled to arrive, and the exhausted men gave a weak cheer and then stumbled to their cots for the first long sleep they'd had in weeks.

Evie spent that day at the restaurant with Louisa, seeing to the last arrangements before the wedding.

"I can't believe it." Louisa ran a hand down the soft white mull of the wedding gown she had brought all the way from Illinois. It had been spread out on Evie's trunk. "In two days I'll be married."

Seated on one of the stumps that the men had given her to use as temporary stools, Evie tugged her needle through the soft fabric of another skirt. The unaccustomed work since coming to this settlement had stripped an inch or two from Evie's waist, but the excess weight seemed to have crept onto Ethel's, requiring that the seams be let out of her nicest dress before she could wear it to the wedding. Since Sarah could not be found—she was probably off flirting with one of the men—Evie had volunteered.

She smiled at her friend. "You will be a lovely bride. Lucy has staked out a patch of wildflowers not far from here to weave into your hair the morning of the wedding. They're not sweetbriar, but they are very pretty."

Louisa sank onto the edge of the cot, her eyes brimming. "You and the others have done so much to make sure our wedding day is perfect. Thank you."

"You deserve it." Smiling, she bit off the thread. "I'm still not sure about the tent, though. You're more than welcome to stay here. The girls and I will be happy to stay with Mary."

"Oh, no. I'm looking forward to the tent. David has worked so hard on it." She peered out the back window with a faraway gaze, toward the land that David had claimed as theirs. "The tent stands where we will one day build our home, which is a fitting place to spend one's wedding night." A distant smile hovered around her lips. "David says the one thing he regrets is that he has worked so hard on this lumber contract that he hasn't had time to build a proper home for me. But I don't care." Her gaze focused on Evie, and the smile widened. "As long as we're together, I don't care if we have to live in a tent forever."

"Evangeline!"

The call filtered through the window, and Evie turned around to peer outside. Miles stood beside the totem pole, staring up at her.

"There you are, my dear." He held up a paper and flapped it in her direction. "We must consult on these supplies you've requested."

"I'll be right there." She turned back to Louisa with a sardonic roll of her eyes. "If you weren't going along, I wouldn't trust that man to purchase a single bag of flour. I hate to ask you to keep watch on Miles while you're on your wedding trip, but you will check to be sure he has my supplies before you return, won't you?"

"Don't worry about a thing."

Evie almost reminded her that it was *Miles* she spoke of, but merely shook her head. Setting her needle and thread aside, she folded Ethel's dress and left it on her cot on her way downstairs.

Outside, Miles studied her list with a creased forehead. "It says here you need twenty-five pounds of wheat flour. Are you sure that will be sufficient?"

"Perfectly," she answered. "We still have plenty from our original supplies."

"Only ten pounds of coffee? Surely we'll need twice that." He leveled a scowl on her above the top of the paper. "The quantities you've listed here seem far from sufficient."

As if he knew anything about the supply levels they would require. She drew in a breath and forced herself to speak calmly. After all, he was finally showing an interest. "I'm trying to keep our costs down. Since many of the men are leaving with the *Leonesa*, we won't need the vast quantities of food Cookee has been producing. At least not until they return."

He dismissed her logic with a scowl. "You must aim higher, my dear. I shall double your list."

Now she did snap. "Don't be ridiculous. We can't afford it, and we don't need that much."

He folded the list, slipped it in his pocket, and patted it. "Leave the finances to me."

She planted her hands on her hips and frowned up at him. "Because that has worked so well up until now?"

Instead of being offended by her sarcasm, he merely smiled. "With the money I shall make on my salmon, we'll have plenty for these supplies and I'll still be able to pay the bank."

"Well…" As long as he paid the first installment of their loan, let him bring all the supplies he wanted. "See that you bring the tomatoes. And salt, since you've used all of mine to pickle your salmon."

"I didn't use it all. You've still some left." He turned and began strolling away toward the trail.

"I do?" Puzzled, Evie did a quick calculation. "Didn't you say you packed a hundred barrels of salmon? The brine—"

With a wave of his hand he cut her off, speaking over his shoulder. "Don't worry, my dear. I have everything well in hand."

Evie stood shaking her head, staring at the trail after he disappeared. Knowing Miles, he would return with ten barrels of brandy and no tomatoes. If Louisa and David hadn't promised to keep an eye on him in San Francisco, she would have to go herself. That man needed close watching.

❦

"Ship's in the bay!"

The shout rang through the forest and was picked up and repeated until Evie heard the announcement from at least four male voices. With a grin at Ethel and Lucy, they tossed the potatoes they'd been scrubbing into Cookee's giant pot, dried their hands on their aprons, and joined the stream of men running from camp to the dock.

"Where's Sarah?" Evie asked as they hurried down the trail at a rapid but appropriately dignified pace.

Lucy frowned, shaking her head. "She's gone off with Lester again. I expect they'll turn up down at the dock."

Ethel caught Evie's eye behind the girl's back, one eyebrow arched high. Evie knew exactly what the look meant. She only prayed that Sarah would exercise more restraint when alone with a man than she did in public.

By the time they arrived at the landing site, a crowd had gathered on the shore. Not only the entire complement of the Denny logging camp, but a good representative of Duwamish people as well. Chief Seattle stood off to one side of the group on a patch of grass that lay slightly higher than the half-moon shaped beach. A handful of his tribesmen stood with him. As Evie had come to expect, Miles hovered at the chief's side, not far from a massive pile of barrels.

"Look at all those barrels of salmon." Ethel shook her head. "To be honest, I never thought he'd do it."

"Neither did I. I guess he proved us both wrong."

"You want to know the best thing about it?" Lucy gave a prim nod. "We didn't have to catch a single fish. He did it all himself."

"With the help of the Duwamish," Evie reminded her.

"There's Louisa and David," said Ethel. "And Mary's come too."

Evie followed her gaze to the opposite side of the beach where her friend stood beside David and Arthur. Mary carried the baby on one hip and held Margaret firmly by the other hand, with Louisa Catherine close to her side. A flutter erupted in her stomach when she saw Noah beside them. She and Noah had not been alone for a single moment since the night a week past, when he'd almost kissed her in the command tent. A good thing too. Until she could manage to control the bothersome giddiness that overcame her every time she thought of his breath warm upon her lips, she preferred to steer clear of him. If not she might end up flirting or fawning on him like Sarah. The last thing she wanted to do was make a fool of herself by mooning after one of her business partners.

Lucy's head turned in the opposite direction. "There's Sarah and Lester." She marched toward them. From the determined set of her jaw, Evie deduced that the girl intended to insert herself between her sister and disaster. Judging by the cloying way Sarah clung to Lester's arm, it wasn't a moment too soon.

"Let's go down where the children are." Ethel didn't wait for a response but took off in that direction.

Evie hesitated a moment before trailing after her. After all, it wasn't as if she would be alone with Noah. There were several dozen people gathered around. No need to be nervous.

When Louisa caught sight of her, she rushed toward her and grabbed her arm. "There you are, Evie. Isn't this exciting?"

She mumbled an affirmative reply and allowed herself to be pulled forward, unable to stop herself from looking toward Noah. When their gazes met, his mouth curved in a smile that held special warmth just for her. The flutter in her stomach returned with new energy.

The *Leonesa's* approach slowed as she neared the dock. Her crew worked on the deck, climbing in the riggings and manning ropes. Evie glimpsed the captain on the bridge, standing tall and keeping a watchful eye on his men. Then the sails were backed and the ship drifted to starboard a short distance until she was even with the dock. Then, at a shout from the captain, the anchor plunged into the water as the sails were lowered.

"Why isn't he bringing the boat to the dock?"

Evie was glad Ethel asked because she wondered the same thing, but Noah had moved to her side and she couldn't concentrate on forming the question.

"The *Leonesa's* bigger than the *Commodore* that brought you here," explained David.

"I'm sure she'd be fine," said Noah. "We selected this place because of the deep harbor. But Captain Howard isn't a man to take chances."

Three men were lowered to the water in a boat and one of them took up oars. Arthur hopped up on the dock and turned to help Mary up. She handed the baby to Ethel before joining him.

Louisa turned excitedly to her. "I recognize Captain Howard from the last time he was here. That other man must be the minister." Then she allowed David to assist her in climbing onto the dock.

Thank goodness Noah made no move to join them. If he did, Evie feared he might take her hand and pull her along with him, and she wasn't sure she could handle his touch. Instead, she knelt and held out her arms to Margaret, glad when the little girl ran to her. There. Her hands were full and out of danger of being touched.

When the rowboat arrived at the dock, Arthur caught the rope the oarsman tossed him and secured it. David did the same with the stern line thrown by one of the passengers. The captain, perhaps? That man lifted a hand and allowed David to haul him out of the boat.

Once he stood securely on the dock, he extended that hand to Arthur. "Mr. Denny. I see you've got a full shipment ready for me." He aimed a huge grin past Arthur toward the boom at the mouth of the river where the logs had been corralled.

Arthur stood tall and answered proudly, "Every last pile you ordered."

An impromptu cheer rose from the throats of the lumberjacks gathered around the landing area.

The captain nodded toward them. "You're to be congratulated. And well-paid besides. This lumber will bring top dollar down in California."

At that, a louder cheer nearly deafened Evie. Noah turned a wide grin on her that she found impossible not to return.

The second man in the rowboat was helped onto the dock. When both of his boots were planted securely, Captain Howard gestured for him to come forward.

"Here's someone you'll be happy to meet," he told Arthur. "This is Henry Yesler from Maryland. Henry, this is Arthur Denny and his lovely wife, Mrs. Denny."

The man shook hands with Arthur and nodded to Mary.

"Is it Reverend Yesler?" she asked politely.

A startled expression settled over his face. "I've been called a lot of things in my day, ma'am, but reverend isn't one them."

The first stab of caution struck Evie then. If this wasn't the minister, then where was he?

"Oh! I almost forgot." Captain Howard pulled a letter from his inside jacket pocket and handed it to Arthur. "They told me to hand this to you personally. It's about Reverend Mitchell."

Up on the dock, Louisa grabbed hold of David's arm. Evie heard Ethel suck in a loud breath.

Arthur opened the letter and glanced at the contents. When he lifted his face, he looked directly at his brother. "Reverend Mitchell died of malarial fever three days before the *Leonesa* left port in San Francisco."

The breath that Louisa drew sounded like the gasp of a wounded woman. Indeed it was, for the look she turned on Evie held as much pain as if her heart had been shattered.

Fifteen

The atmosphere in the little group clustered to one side of the landing area was gloomier than a thick fog on a sunless morning. Noah stood beside David, trying to decide if he should come up with comforting words or remain silent. Evie stood with an arm around Louisa and looked almost as miserable as her friend.

"No, it's all right," Louisa insisted, though she did not lift her face to meet anyone's gaze. "The Lord must have a purpose in this. Who am I to thwart Him?"

David strode forward to stand close to her. "Sweetbriar, we can still be married. Captain Howard can perform the ceremony."

Swallowing hard, she shook her head. "We've discussed this before. I want to be married by someone who is officially appointed by the laws of the Oregon Territory, not by maritime laws." She lifted tear-filled eyes to him. "Our marriage is to be the first of this settlement. I want it to be performed by a lawfully licensed official of the territory." Her lips trembled for a moment before arranging themselves into a smile. "The delay will give you a chance to build a proper home for us."

She ducked her head and rested it on Evie's shoulder. Wrapping her arms around her sorrowful friend, Evie's eye caught Noah's.

Though she didn't say a word, her command was as clear as if she had shouted it. *Do something!*

But what could he do? He wasn't in charge of finding a minister.

"Come on, love," Evie muttered, pulling Louisa toward the trail. "We'll go find a cup of tea to settle us."

They wandered away, leaving Noah and David staring after them. Chief Seattle and Uncle Miles approached from one side.

"What seems to be the problem, my boy?" the old gentleman asked.

Noah let out a loud breath. "The minister died, and that means there won't be a wedding."

The chief's expression grew curious. He said something in his language, and Noah was pleased that he recognized the question.

"Why does the *klootchman* cry and cast her face to the ground?"

David stirred from his misery to answer. "We were to be married tomorrow, and now we can't be."

An idea struck Noah. Louisa said she wanted an official of the Oregon Territory to perform the ceremony. There was no one more qualified than Chief Seattle. He caught the chief's eye. "Can you marry them?" he asked in his language.

Seattle jerked back as if stung, then spoke shortly. Noah and David both laughed. "He says he has a wife already," David translated.

"No, that's not what I mean. We have a man." Noah pointed to David. "We need someone to marry him."

Now a highly offended expression stole over the chief's face. "You want to buy *klootchman* for David Denny?" he asked as Noah translated. He drew himself up. "We no sell our *klootchmen* to each other, or to white men."

While Uncle Miles laughed, Noah rushed to explain. He wasn't sure the chief actually understood, but at least when the man left he no longer wore the look of outrage.

David clapped him on the shoulder. "Thanks, Noah. I appreciate it, but I think Louisa has her heart set on a minister, or at least a justice of the peace. I don't blame her. That'll be at the top of my list when I get to San Francisco, or failing that, when we put in at Portland on the return trip." He stared after his intended, a look of longing in his eyes. "I won't come back without a duly licensed official from the Oregon Territory who can marry us."

Their conversation was interrupted when Arthur walked up, waving a letter in the air. "Have you seen this?" He slapped the letter at Noah's chest. "It's addressed to me at Duwamps, Oregon. I tell you, we must have a better name for our city than Duwamps." He fixed Noah with a narrow-eyed stare. "What have you come up with, Hughes?"

In his practically nonexistent spare time, Noah had put some thought into possible names. "What about Bayside?" He nodded toward the bay.

Arthur curled his nose. "Too predictable. What else?"

That had been Noah's favorite, but he had a list of alternatives. "Bayshore? Loggerston? Dennysburg?"

David scowled deeply at the last suggestion. "Absolutely not."

Uncle Miles had been standing silently beside Noah. Now he spoke up. "I rather fancy the name Seattle."

Noah turned a sour face toward him. How like Uncle Miles to want to curry favor with the chief by naming their new city after him. Arthur was sure to dismiss the suggestion immediately.

But the man paused and cocked his head sideways. "Seattle." He spoke the word slowly, as though testing the taste on his tongue. He straightened, one side of his mouth lifted in a smile. "I like it. What do you think, David?"

Jerked out of his silent scrutiny of the trail down which Louisa and Evie had disappeared, David focused on his brother. "Seattle?" He tilted his head, considering. "Yes, I like it."

Noah had to admit, the name had a nice ring to it. Seattle. The chief would no doubt be honored, which wasn't a bad thing either.

"Seattle it is!" Arthur slapped the letter against his thigh, satisfaction settling over his features. "And a thousand times better than Duwamps. I'll draw up the paperwork. When you dock in Portland, you can file it with the land management office."

With a final clap on his brother's shoulder, Arthur strode off, his knee-high boots pounding on the packed soil.

Uncle Miles stood in place a few seconds, and then said, "I expect the loading will start soon. I must see to my salmon." He followed in Arthur's footsteps.

Noah stood beside David in silence. There should be something he could say, something to convey the depth of his sorrow to this young man he'd come to respect.

"Do you want me to go in your stead?" he finally asked. "You can stay here and work on your cabin. I promise I'll find a minister willing to come back with me."

David gave him a grateful look, but shook his head. "Thanks, but you had to go last time. Besides, it's better if I do it. I think we need a little time to let the emotions calm down."

With a final sad smile David followed his brother, though his stride was slower and more ponderous, and not nearly so commanding.

❧

On the morning the *Leonesa* was to sail, Evie rose early and climbed silently down the ladder, leaving her friends asleep. She lit a candle on her beautiful worktable and turned, a sense of satisfaction settling deep inside as she gazed at the main room of her restaurant. The long room was still mostly empty, but when she looked at the open space her mind supplied the furnishings. One day tables would be placed this way and that, with plenty of chairs. Not rough benches like those in the logging camp's cookhouse, but real chairs. She would put tablecloths on every table and fresh flowers in the center. Now that the lumber contract had been fulfilled, the men would have time to work on the furnishings for her.

A noise drew her attention and she turned to find Louisa descending the ladder. She had stayed with Evie for the past four days while the *Leonesa* was loaded with wood and salmon. She wanted to see as much of her beloved as possible in the days before he left.

"Did I wake you?" Evie whispered. "I tried to be quiet."

Louisa reached the ground. "I was awake. My mind was too full to sleep last night."

"I'm sorry." Evie laid a comforting hand on her arm. This morning David would set sail alone on the trip that was supposed to be their wedding journey. "You could still go, you know. The rooming house in San Francisco where we stayed on the way here was inexpensive and nice enough. Take Mary along to chaperone. The ladies and I would love to keep the children for the few weeks you'd be gone."

Louisa shook her head. "Thank you, but it would not be the same. No, I'll stay here." She gave Evie a smile that held a hint of her former good humor. "Who knows? Maybe you and the other girls can help me clear some land so David can start on our home as soon as he returns."

Laughing, Evie knelt to build up the fire in her fine new stove. "Don't mention that to Sarah or we'll have to put up with a fit."

"I'll tell you what she's going to pitch a fit about." Louisa glanced toward the ceiling where the girls slept in the upper floor. "David told me when Lester Perkins collected his pay yesterday, he said he'd be leaving and didn't plan to return."

"Hmm." Evie held a hand above the stove, testing the heat, and then set the teakettle on. "The way that girl has been hanging on him, it might not be a bad thing."

"A lot of the men are leaving." Louisa dropped onto another of the stumps Big Dog had provided. "David says most will blow all their money on drink and wild pursuits in San Francisco and then come back here to make more. Some will be seduced by the man-catchers for more money. That's what he and Arthur expect will happen, anyway."

"Man-catcher?"

"Recuiters for the logging camps. It happens all the time."

"What does David say about Mr. Yesler?" Evie measured tea into the pot and then rummaged in one of the crates piled against the back wall for cups. Something else she needed as soon as possible was a proper pantry and shelves. Hopefully some of the men would stay behind so she could hire the work done.

"Oh, he likes Mr. Yesler. So does David. He has grand plans to build a steam-powered mill, the first of its kind in this area."

"I thought Arthur wanted to build a mill. Wouldn't Mr. Yesler's mill spoil his plans?"

"I thought so too." Louisa lifted a shoulder. "David says Arthur is willing to discuss the idea, but he won't agree to anything quickly." A dimple appeared in her cheek. "Arthur will do what's best for Seattle, but he'll make sure it's also what's best for the Dennys."

"Seattle." Evie let the name roll off her tongue. "I like the sound of that." She smiled at her friend. "And one day soon, you will be the first bride of the city of Seattle."

The look Louisa turned on her was full of gratitude.

The kettle started to sing and Evie picked it up, speaking over her shoulder. "Would you wake the others? The captain said he intends to sail with the morning tide. We don't want to miss the big send-off."

⁊

The sun had been up an hour when the *Leonesa*'s captain signaled for the smaller craft to begin ferrying passengers from shore to ship. The Duwamish had been prevailed upon to assist with the disembarkation, and four dugout canoes paddled alongside the ship's dingy. Evie, Lucy, and Ethel situated themselves near the small dock so they could bid farewell and safe voyage to the lumberjacks, some of whom had become friends in the month since their arrival. Louisa and David stood off to one side, their heads close together. Evie was glad to see that her friend's cheerful smile had returned, though she suspected Louisa was putting forth an effort to make sure David had a happy fiancée to remember on his two-week trip.

Noah and Miles stood opposite the dock, talking, and every so often Evie looked over to find Noah's gaze fixed on her. She battled breathlessness and determined to keep her eyes turned away.

"Where is Sarah?" Ethel craned her head, searching the crowd.

Lucy shook her head, a look of disgust on her face. "She ran off to meet Lester earlier."

"Telling him goodbye?" Evie asked.

Lucy shrugged, but did not reply.

"Here come George and Randall, their faces scrubbed and wearing clean clothes." Ethel pitched her voice low enough to be heard by only the ladies. "I heard the others threatened to douse George in the bay and scrub him with pine cones if he didn't bathe before getting on the ship."

The man the others called Pig Face approached, and Evie noted that he did, indeed, smell much cleaner than in recent days. She gave him a big smile. "All ready to leave these fair shores, I see."

He ducked his head. "Yes, ma'am. I wanted to tell you it's been a pleasure knowing you." His head circled to include the others. "All of you."

"Will you return to Seattle?" Lucy asked.

"I reckon not. Jacking is good work, for sure, but I hear tell there's been gold found near Placerville. Think I might try my luck there for a while."

Evie bit back her true opinion of those who rushed to California at the whisper of the world. "Well, I wish you the best."

"I'm coming back," Randall said. "If that Yesler fella builds a mill here, like he's been thinking about, there's gonna be plenty of work."

"We'll look forward to seeing you again soon."

Evie extended her hand and George gave it a shake. The other ladies followed her example, and soon the departing lumberjacks all lined up to shake their hands before they climbed up on the dock and stowed their gear in the boats. She lost count of the number of men to whom she bid farewell. Would anyone be left in Seattle after the *Leonesa* sailed?

Miles approached, dressed in his shirt and waistcoat, a gold watch chain dangling from a pocket. Noah walked by his side, carrying his travel bag.

"Now, my dear, don't worry about a thing. I shall handle everything. When I return, I expect to receive a good report."

"Don't forget my tomatoes," Evie told him sternly, but then smiled. "Take care, Miles. I hope your pickled salmon becomes the talk of San Francisco."

"Ah, yes." He beamed, and then leaned close. "I've considered branching out to trout next time."

Noah handed his bag into the canoe, and with a final smile for Evie, Miles lowered himself into the center. The ship's dingy had already reached the *Leonesa's* starboard side, and men were climbing the ladders to board her while three canoes waited their turn.

Louisa joined Evie and the others, her gaze fixed on David as he shook hands with Noah and then joined Miles in the dugout.

Noah straightened, his gaze scanning the beach. "Is that it?"

No more than a handful of people stood on the shore. Big Dog had remained, Evie was glad to see. He had promised to make the tables for her restaurant in return for free meals while the work was being done. Red, the fiery-headed lumberjack, also remained, along with a few others who had helped with the building.

"Where is Lester?" asked Ethel. "I thought he was going."

Lucy's expression darkened. "And where is Sarah? That's what I'd like to know."

A shout from the trail reached them. "Wait! Wait for us!"

The missing couple appeared, Sarah waving while Lester struggled beneath the weight of a trunk. Sarah wore her travel cloak and dragged a bulging pack behind her.

"Don't leave us!" she shouted. "We're going too!"

Lucy's mouth fell open, her eyes round as ripe apples. A couple of the men on the shore came to their aid and took the heavy bag from Sarah. They helped Lester carry the trunk, which Evie now recognized as Sarah's, to the dock.

Lucy ran forward, Evie right behind her.

"What do you mean, you're going?" Lucy clutched Sarah's forearms. "You can't leave Seattle."

"I can, and I am." Sarah grinned over her shoulder. "Lester and me's getting married!"

"Married? But you just met." Lucy wavered on her feet.

Sarah lifted her chin. "I know what I want, and I want him." A wide grin stretched across her face. "And he wants me too."

Evie placed a steadying hand on Lucy's back. "When will you return, Sarah?"

"We're not coming back. Soon as we get to California we're going to hook up with a wagon train heading back east. Lester says there's a lot of logging going on up in Michigan. White pine." Her gaze softened when she looked into her sister's face. "You can come with us, Lucy. Maybe not right now, on account of the boat's getting ready to leave, but you can catch the next one. We'll wait for you in San Francisco."

Lucy's hands dropped to her sides and she shook her head. "No. I'm staying here. In Seattle."

A long look passed between the sisters. Evie lowered her head, not wanting to intrude.

"Are you sure?" Lucy said.

Her sister nodded. "Sure as a gal can be. Are you?"

Lucy's head turned as she scanned the area. Evie followed her gaze beyond the landing place, to the tops of dense forest. Cedar trees, taller than any building, stretched into a deep blue sky, and in the distance majestic, white-capped mountains pointed toward heaven.

Lucy took a deep breath and released it slowly. "I'm sure."

"We got to get going, Sugarplum," Lester called from the dock.

Giggling, Sarah leaned toward her sister. "He calls me Sugarplum."

Evie exchanged a glance with Ethel and tried not to laugh when the woman rolled her eyes expansively.

The sisters embraced, and then Sarah dashed to the dock, where Lester helped her into the canoe. She cupped her hands around her mouth and shouted that she would write when they got settled. Ethel came to stand on Lucy's other side to watch the canoe shove off and paddle toward the *Leonesa*.

"Well," said Ethel, "she got herself a husband. That's what she wanted."

"Yes, it is."

Lucy sounded so forlorn that Evie squeezed her shoulders. "I'll pray she has a good life. And us too."

"Amen to that," chorused Louisa, who joined them.

They turned and headed for the trail. Before they left the shore, Evie looked over her shoulder, ostensibly at the ship. But her attention was fixed on the man standing on the dock, watching the sails unfurl. As though aware of her gaze, Noah turned his head. Their eyes met, and though the length of the shore lay between them, the familiar tickle returned to her stomach.

Sixteen

*E*vie glanced up from the bubbling pot on the stove to see another table being carried through the restaurant doorway. Wiping her hands on her apron, she hurried over to examine it. Though not nearly as beautiful as her worktable, this one was sturdy and smooth, everything she wanted in a dining table.

"Jacob, it's perfect. Just like the others." She pointed out the place where she wanted him to place it, resting an admiring hand on the smooth surface as he carried it inside.

"I keep telling you to call me Big Dog, ma'am," he said, walking backward. "Every time I hear Jacob I want to look around for my old mama."

"I'm sorry. I forgot."

Her promise to remember from now on went unspoken when the person carrying the other end of the table entered the room. A blush heated her cheeks when she caught sight of Noah, and she couldn't hold back a smile. He'd become a regular visitor at the restaurant in the weeks since the *Leonesa* left.

"Good evening." The spark in his eyes deepened, and his smile took on the special curve she'd come to recognize as being especially for her. "Thought I'd come a little early tonight and see if there's anything you need me to do."

From the grin Big Dog didn't bother hiding, the offer of help didn't fool him. Noah spent more and more time at the restaurant, working with Big Dog on the new furniture, stacking firewood, or even carrying water from the nearby stream. Or sometimes merely sitting on a stool, talking to the ladies as they cooked. Evie liked those times best, though her stomach was in a constant state of flutter whenever he turned that special smile her way. Like now.

When the table had been set in place, the three of them stood back to admire the room. Four identical tables had already been placed around the room, each of them covered with a linen tablecloth. Candles with glass chimneys rested on each surface, and when the sun's light failed they cast a soft yellow glow around the room. Curtains hung at the windows, waving gently in a slight breeze and giving the restaurant the homey atmosphere she had hoped to achieve. There were no chairs yet, but Big Dog promised to start on those as soon as he finished the last table. In the meantime, she had agreed to borrow a few benches from the camp since the cookhouse had been unused since the men left on the *Leonesa*. Though she disliked the clunky things, her customers needed a place to sit while they ate supper.

The restaurant was not yet officially open, but Evie already enjoyed a nightly custom. Big Dog ate breakfast, lunch, and supper there every day as reimbursement for his work on the furnishings. Randall, who had decided to try his hand at trapping until the logging crew started up again, usually showed up around suppertime with an offering of rabbit, turkey, or the occasional brace of pheasant. Even Arthur and Mary and Louisa had joined them once or twice, and it was always a pleasant evening when the children were present.

Then there was Mr. Yesler, who had taken up lodging in one of the camp tents and spent his days either in conversation with Noah and Arthur or scouting the land near the shoreline for a likely place to build his mill. Initially Lucy had made a point of serving him personally, ensuring that his coffee mug was never empty or his plate never in need of an extra helping. That stopped when he mentioned his wife, who planned to join him when he decided where to settle.

Evie bent over one of the crates and retrieved another tablecloth, which she tossed to Noah. "Would you put this on, please, and smooth out the wrinkles as best you can? I'll ask Lucy to heat the iron later."

"Mmm." Big Dog extended his neck over the bubbling pot, inhaling with obvious pleasure. "What's for supper tonight?"

"Pheasant stew with dumplings." She gave the pot a stir and then turned to the big bowl on her worktable where a soft, flavorful dough waited to be turned into dumplings. "Would you please ask Ethel when the rest of the birds will be ready? She and Cookee are out back tending the spit."

Left without any work to occupy his time until the return of the lumberjacks, Cookee had taken to hanging around the restaurant all day, mostly making a nuisance of himself to Ethel. The stalwart woman had given up any pretense at cooperation the moment the ladies were no longer in his employ, as promised, and seemed to take a great deal of pleasure in giving back as much torment as she got.

"Yes, ma'am."

The room felt almost cavernous when the big man ducked out the back door, leaving Evie alone with Noah. A pleasant silence settled between them while he spread the linen over the new table—a silence broken only by the soft bubbling of the stew and occasional crackle of burning wood from inside the firebox.

When he finished, Noah sat on the stump nearest the stove, the seat that she had come to think of as his since he occupied it so often. She added a pinch of salt to the stew from her dwindling supply and slid the pot half-off the cooking plate to reduce the boiling liquid to a simmer.

Noah broke the silence. "I was hoping you and I could talk tonight."

She glanced at him while placing a pot of marmalade—orange, thanks to Cookee's grudging gift of the remainder of the oranges—on the table nearest the stove. "About what?"

"About us."

The words struck her like a muffled blow. How could her heart stop and her pulse race at the same time? That was what it felt like. Her fingers lingered on the marmalade pot while her mind grasped for a response.

He cleared his throat. "About our partnership, I mean."

Ah. A professional conversation concerning the lease of his land. Relieved, though also oddly disappointed, Evie straightened and turned a pleasant expression his way. "We can talk now, if you like."

He shook his head. "I don't want to be interrupted. I thought maybe after supper I could help you carry the dishes to the stream, and that would give us an opportunity to speak privately. Would that be all right?"

Gathering her composure, she nodded.

❦

Throughout the meal, Evie could not concentrate. Was it her imagination, or did tonight's supper last longer than normal? The conversation around the table was lengthier than her patience, with talk of politics and the possibility of a war in the east. Though she typically enjoyed the nightly exchange of opinions, tonight she barely spoke more than one-word answers. What did Noah want to speak to her about? Did he regret his hasty decision to let her build the restaurant here? Or perhaps he was unhappy with something she had done, something involving the business operation which was unfair?

Finally, the moment arrived when the last bite was taken and the plates had been stacked. Lucy and Ethel made as though to pick them up, but Noah stopped them.

"Tonight Evie and I will do the washing up." He flashed a smile full of charm on each of them. "You ladies relax. Have another cup of tea."

When Ethel handed the wash bucket to Evie, she waggled her eyebrows. Ignoring her, Evie took the pail and marched out of the restaurant, aware that several speculative stares followed her.

The sun was no longer visible, though the western sky was still aglow with evidence of its passage. A bright moon shone in the east and a single star twinkled brightly. Evie led the way, following what had become a well-defined path to the shallow stream they frequented.

"Someday soon we should dig a well," commented Noah from behind. "Just think. We could have Seattle's first well. Only we should hurry before someone else thinks of it and claims the honor."

Was that a note of nervousness in his voice? Evie glanced behind and caught him chewing on his lower lip. She looked quickly away. Somehow seeing evidence of his nerves calmed her.

"I've intended to ask about Chief Seattle." The bucket swung from her hands and bumped against her knees. "Have you spoken to him? What did he think about having the city named after him?"

"Believe it or not, he wasn't happy."

She looked back at him, surprised. "Why not? I would have thought he would be honored."

"Seems there's a legend among his people that the dead awaken from their slumber whenever their names are spoken by the living. He said since the city will be discussed many times every day, he fears he will turn over restlessly in his grave for all eternity."

Evie turned on the path. "Oh, no! Has he forbidden it, then?"

Noah shook his head. "I thought he might for a while, which would have been bad since David has no doubt already filed the papers with the land management office. The chief finally relented, though reluctantly." Noah smiled. "Turns out he converted to Christianity a few years ago."

Her jaw dropped. "Chief Seattle is a Christian?"

"Hard to believe, huh? Anyway, he still isn't happy about it, but he decided he wasn't going to make a fuss about an old superstition."

They reached the stream and Evie knelt down on the wide, level bank and indicated that Noah should set the stack of dirty dishes beside her. Plunging the bucket into the stream, she scooped up fresh, cold water and then rubbed the cloth over the sliver of lye soap inside before reaching for a plate.

When it seemed as though he was content with silence, she spoke. "You said you had something to discuss? Something about the restaurant?"

He took the clean plate from her and leaned over to rinse it in the stream. "Not about the restaurant. About our partnership."

So he wasn't planning to complain about something she'd done. She let out a deep breath she wasn't aware she'd been holding. "We've never defined the exact terms. I suppose we need to do that before we officially open."

"Mmm-hmm."

He took an inordinately long time rinsing the plate. Evie nudged his sleeve with another soapy one. He flashed an apologetic smile as he took it.

"You're right, but it isn't the terms of our partnership I want to discuss. It's our relationship."

Though the word rang in her ears, Evie forced her hands to keep moving, to keep scrubbing the plate with her cloth. "I'm not sure what you mean."

He didn't respond at first, and for a moment she thought she might have to ask him outright to explain himself. When he did speak, his words surprised her.

"I had a woman partner once before."

What was it Louisa had told her shortly after they arrived in Seattle? Noah had been hurt by a lady in California. Could this be the woman? Careful to keep her expression impassive, she waited for him to continue.

"Her name was Sallie Harper. I met her the first day I arrived at Coloma."

Coloma, California, the location of the now-famous Sutter's Mill. Though she had determined to remain silent, surprise got the best of her. "You went to California looking for gold?"

"Sure did." A silent laugh shook his shoulders. "What a fool. When my mother died there was nothing to keep me in Tennessee except Uncle Miles and Aunt Letitia." He gave her a knowing look. "My aunt is a hard woman to feel close to."

Yes, Evie was well aware of that. "So you decided to go west."

"I had a little money left from my father's inheritance, and I decided, why not? I could try my hand at gold mining, and if that didn't work out I'd still have something to fall back on. Surely there were opportunities in California for a young man with some money in his pocket and a willingness to work."

That sounded very much like Evie's own thoughts when she made the decision to come to Oregon Territory, only the money in her pocket had belonged mostly to Miles. Or so she thought.

His head dropped forward, and he continued while watching spring water run over the plate in his hands. "Sallie worked in a saloon in Coloma." Before Evie had a chance to react, he looked up. "She was a nice girl, not one of those fancy women you usually find in saloons. Or"—his shoulders slumped—"so I thought. She'd come west with her family, but they died of the ague shortly after they arrived. Her papa planned to stake a claim, buy a herd of cattle, and settle down with his family. That's what Sallie wanted to do, find a place to settle down. Build a home. Have a family. It sounded so good."

The last was whispered as Noah stared across the stream, into the rapidly deepening darkness that blanketed the forest. The note of longing in his eyes plucked a string in Evie's heart, and the telltale sting of tears burned her eyes. A home and family were what she had wanted too, long ago in Tennessee.

"What happened?" she asked quietly.

He gave his head a quick shake, as though banishing thoughts that had drawn him back in time. "She was lying. I fell for her, started making plans, looking around for a likely place to settle. I even asked about buying cattle because I thought it would make her happy. I told her we'd go into the cattle business together, and she could teach me everything she learned from her father. What a fool I was."

Pain and derision showed so clearly on his face that Evie's heart ached for him. She wiped her soapy hand on her apron and laid it on his arm. "She left you for someone else, didn't she?"

"I'll say. I was living in a tent on the outskirts of town, like a lot of would-be prospectors from back East. I got there one day to find Sallie and another man there going through my stuff. Turns out she already had a business. It wasn't in cattle, and I wasn't the first dupe to come along. She'd find a chump flashing money around, some-body young and stupid like me, and charm him with a sad story. Then she and her husband would clean him out and move on to the next guy."

"Her husband?"

"Yeah." He rubbed a hand across his jaw. "Guy about the size of Big Dog, only not nearly so easygoing. Took every cent I had, beat me within an inch of my life, and left me for dead."

A righteous anger ballooned in Evie's ribcage. "Did you call the sheriff? Go after them to get your money back?"

"Yeah, but by the time I was conscious that pair was long gone. I had nothing left, not a cent to my name, so I hired on with a ship heading to Portland, meaning to make enough money to get me back to Tennessee. That's where I met Arthur and David." He spread his hands to indicate the forest, and then smiled at her. "And that's how I ended up here."

Evie retrieved the cloth and continued scrubbing the plates, her mind busy trying to process what she'd learned. No wonder Noah had been so cross with her when they met at the greengrocer's in San Francisco. She had introduced herself as a businesswoman, and the only experience he had with women in business had left him beaten, penniless, and with a broken heart.

"I'm surprised you agreed to let me build my restaurant on your land."

His hand reached into the bucket and grasped hers. Startled, she looked up and found him gazing intently at her. He lifted their hands, heedless of the soapy water that dripped off of them, and entwined his fingers with her nervous ones. The nighttime noises of the forest dimmed until the only thing Evie could hear was her own breath and her blood surging in her ears.

"I believe in you, Evie. You work hard, and you plan, and I believe you'll accomplish whatever you set out to do."

It was back, the magnetic force that had drawn them together in the command tent that night. Evie felt herself being pulled toward him. Or was she leaning toward him willingly? A thick fog of emotion had descended on her, and she couldn't think.

"You—you do?"

Moving slowly and without releasing her gaze from his, he climbed slowly to his feet, pulling her with him. The soapy water, the dirty plates, the cloth were all forgotten in an instant, shoved away by the intensity in Noah's eyes.

"I told you about Sallie because I want there to be nothing between us. No secrets. No mistakes of the past to rise up and cause trouble in our future."

Our future. The words rang like bells, vibrating through her mind and down her spine.

This was why I came west. The idea sliced through her whirling thoughts like a beacon in the darkest night. She'd come looking for a future, and somehow she had found it. Right here, in Seattle. Right here, in Noah's arms.

His gaze never left her face as he raised her hand and planted a gentle kiss on her palm. A delicious shiver zipped up her arm and down her spine, robbing her of breath. Her lips ached, desperate for the feel of his. Almost of its own accord, her free hand crept up his neck and she rose on her toes. She pulled his head down.

"Evie."

The sound of her name in his husky whisper resonated in her ears. The moment their lips touched, her eyes fluttered shut and with a swell of love that threatened to overwhelm her, she gave herself over to his kiss.

Seventeen

Noah topped a rise in the land, pulling Evie along behind him. He loved the way her hand felt in his, small and dainty and warm with more than exertion from their walk, and the way color rose high on her cheeks when she caught him watching her. In fact, he loved everything about this amazing woman. In the week since their kiss by the stream, he had spent nearly every minute he could near her, dreaming up the flimsiest excuses to stop in the restaurant. The others no longer bothered to hide their indulgent smiles, and even Arthur had taken to making sly comments about how the food at Evie's restaurant must be extra special good for him to go back so often.

"Slow down. Your legs are longer than mine." Though slightly out of breath, her eyes sparkled with good humor. "I have to take two steps to your one."

"It will be worth the effort, I promise." He slowed his pace though. "We're almost there."

She cast a backward glance over her shoulder. "We've come a long way from the restaurant. Are you sure you want to live this far from town?"

"Not at first, of course. We have a business to run, and soon more than one, I hope."

They spent their evenings sharing their plans for the future. It appeared as though Henry Yesler and Arthur were close to an agreement about the location of the new mill. Though Arthur had always planned to build a mill himself, Yesler possessed something neither he nor any of the other Seattle settlers did—a letter of credit for thirty thousand dollars. Arthur refused to finalize any arrangements without discussing them first with his brother, but he told Noah he would consider adjusting the boundaries of his claim to accommodate the new mill, because the move was definitely in the best interests of the fledgling town.

If the mill became a reality, and Noah suspected it would, he and Evie had planned their next move. Men and women would flock to the area, and only the loggers would stay in the work camp. The others would need lodging. As soon as the restaurant showed a profit, they would begin building a boardinghouse next door.

He climbed a ridge and came to a stop. Panting with exertion, Evie came up beside him.

"There." He gazed at the area before them, pride swelling in his chest. "What do you think?"

The admiration on her face was everything he hoped it would be. They stood atop a hill, looking down on a lush and fertile valley covered in grass so deeply green it almost looked blue. A wide stream ran the length of the vale to one side, the water sparkling in the afternoon sun. Towering above the distant trees stood the imposing figure of Mount Rainier, its snow-covered ridges in stark contrast to the blue sky. The highest peak was veiled behind a fluffy white cloud, like a mystery waiting to be discovered.

"It's the most beautiful place I've ever seen." Awe turned her voice into a barely more than a whisper.

"The moment I saw this valley, I knew one day I would live here. In all the acres of land I've walked since we arrived here, that clearing is the only one that felt to me like home. How can anyone look at that mountain and doubt that God exists?" Noah slipped his arms around Evie's waist and pulled her close, her back pressed against his chest and the heady scent of her hair filling his nose. "One day I'll live here. My wife and I will raise our children in the shadow of the mountain."

She went still. Though they had talked of building a boarding-house together, and of their plans to be a part of Seattle's future, he had never broached the subject of marriage. He wanted to wait for the special moment when he could bring her here and share with her the place that had drawn him from the moment he first saw it.

He pointed to a level area in the valley. "I know it will be a while before we can live here, but I always pictured that would be the per-fect place for a garden. We could go ahead and start now, and grow vegetables for the restaurant."

Still she said nothing, but continued to gaze over the land, barely breathing.

"I know it seems like a long way from town, but you mark my words. Seattle will grow quickly. Before you know it, the town will come all the way up here." He drew in a satisfied breath and tight-ened his arms around her waist. "But not here. This valley I intend to keep for us."

"Noah." She stepped away from him, turning as she did so. "We need to talk."

Were those tears filling her eyes? A sense of apprehension descended on him, and his enthusiasm of a moment before evapo-rated like a mist. Had he misjudged her affections for him?

He took a backward step. "What's wrong?"

"Nothing," she said hurriedly, "only I have—"

A distant shout interrupted her, a man's deep voice echoing through the forest. The call was picked up by another, this one closer and louder. "Ship in the bay!"

"They've returned." Evie looked through the forest toward the bay, as though by looking she could glimpse the ship. "We should go and meet them."

"Wait." He stopped her with a hand on each of her forearms, and forced her to look up at him. "What do we need to talk about?"

Her features softened when her eyes met his, and her lips formed the sweet smile that haunted his dreams. She placed a hand on his cheek, and her touch was warm.

"Later. When we have more time."

She rose onto her tiptoes and brushed her lips against his in the softest kiss.

Noah's fears were only partially stilled as he followed her through the forest toward the landing area.

The ship that sailed toward the dock was not the *Commodore,* as Evie and the other settlers had expected. This vessel was smaller, with sleek sides and crisp white sails not yet dingy from years of exposure to saltwater and storms. When she drew near enough to read the letters painted on her bow, Lucy read the name aloud.

"Olympia." She said the word as though testing its taste on her tongue. "Never heard of her."

"I know her." Cookee stood apart from the others who gathered at the landing area to welcome the ship. "Sails out of Portland. Short trips only and not much room for cargo."

That was certainly true, judging by the look of her.

"David and Miles were going to Portland before returning." Evie shielded her eyes with a hand, scanning the figures that lined the ship's deck. "Perhaps they hired a different ship."

She was painfully aware of Noah's tall form beside her, close enough that she could reach out and touch him if she wished. And she did wish to, if only to feel the comforting warmth of his skin. Their conversation battered her thoughts, threatening to distract her from the here and now. His wife. He spoke of his wife as though he took it for granted that it would be her.

And Evie wanted to be his wife. She'd known that ever since their kiss beside the stream, when her hands dripped soap from the washtub and her heart pounded crazily inside her ribcage. He had opened his past to her that night, had shared the devastating circumstances that brought him to Seattle. To her.

She owed it to him to do the same, and yet every time she started to tell him about James, about her reasons for coming to Seattle, something clogged the words in her throat. This place was new, and fresh, and untainted. The same could be said of their love. Of course she would eventually tell him about her former life as his aunt's servant and as fiancée to a river dock worker. But for now she reveled in his image of her as a smart, competent business owner, proudly independent and confident of her future.

As the ship neared the small platform that served as Seattle's dock, Randall and Big Dog took up stances on the edge, ready to catch the ropes. They pulled the ship forward and secured her to the posts that had been put in place for that purpose.

Evie scanned the ship's deck, looking for Miles's familiar waistcoat or David's trim form. A dozen or more men stood at the railing, their heads held high as they scanned the tall cedars and thick, bushy fir trees that surrounded the landing area. Not a single familiar face caught her eye, until...

With an alarming stutter, her heart thudded. One figure stood out among the others. A female surrounded by men, stout and with a ridiculous feathered hat on her head. Evie blinked to clear her eyes. From this angle, with the sun slanted just so, the woman almost looked like Letitia Coffinger.

The man standing next to her bent down and said something in her ear, drawing Evie's attention to him. Now her heart really did stop, and her lungs emptied of breath. Was it her imagination? Had thoughts of him tricked her mind into conjuring his likeness? Surely that could not be James standing on the deck of the ship that was being tied up at the dock.

The man scanned the small crowd, and then his eyes fell on her. His expression brightened, and a smile evident to all on shore lit his face.

"Evangeline, my darling fiancée! I've found you at last."

Stunned, Evie could only stare. At a choking sound beside her, she turned to find Noah's stare leveled on her. He held her gaze for a long moment and then, shaking his head slowly, whirled and walked away.

In her whole life, Evie didn't think she would ever be rid of the memory of the betrayal in his eyes.

Eighteen

The man's words, shouted from the deck of the *Olympia,* struck Noah like a fist to the gut. He called Evie his fiancée. She was engaged to be married?

Questions battered at his mind, but he couldn't focus on them. One thought overrode all others. He had to get out of there. Escape the pitying looks his friends turned on him. Mostly, though, escape the guilt in Evie's eyes. What he needed was a place to think, to pray, someplace where he could be alone. Whirling, he began to stalk into the forest when a shout stopped him. This was what she had wanted to talk to him about. A little late for conversation now.

"Noah! There you are. Go and fetch your uncle at once. I have plenty to say to my worthless wretch of a husband."

The voice, sharp enough to carry throughout the entire clearing and a good distance beyond, stopped him short. Aunt Letitia. And judging by the demanding tone, she had not changed much since the last time he saw her.

Schooling his features, he turned.

Evie breathlessly caught up to grab his arm. "Noah, I can explain. It's not what you think."

Her words stabbed at his heart, opening a wound that he'd thought had healed months ago. He couldn't talk to her. Not now, in front of all these people. With a stone-faced grimace, he pulled his arm from her grasp, gently but firmly, and climbed onto the dock.

The ship's crew fixed a ramp in place. Aunt Letitia approached first, blue feathers standing tall atop a ridiculous little hat. The young man who had called Evie his fiancée held her arm and assisted her onto the ramp. Noah could barely look at him, but focused instead on helping his aunt down the ramp and onto the wooden dock.

"This is where you live?" She inspected the landing area, her nose wrinkled with distaste. "Where is the town?" He didn't have a chance to answer before she continued. "Never mind that. More importantly, where is my husband?"

Evie's fiancé stepped off the ramp and immediately strode toward Evie, his arms thrown wide. Noah could not look in that direction.

He swallowed, and faced his aunt. "Uncle Miles isn't here. He's in San Francisco arranging some business. But we expect him within the week."

"A week?" Her features pulled themselves into a frown, an arrangement with which they seemed familiar. "I should have known. That man is most tiresome. I suppose it can't be helped. Noah, see to my bags." She waved a gloved hand vaguely toward the ship behind her. "Have them delivered to the cleanest boardinghouse in town." She sniffed through a curled nose, her gaze roving the shore. "I only hope there is something decent to be had."

Noah kept silent. Drat Uncle Miles anyway. He should be here to deal with his wife.

A familiar voice behind him stirred a fresh pain inside his chest.

"There is no boardinghouse, Mrs. Coffinger." Evie spoke from the beach near the dock. Noah could not force himself to turn and look at her. Not with *her fiancé* standing beside her.

Aunt Letitia sniffed. "Noah, is this true?"

"Yes, ma'am, I'm afraid so."

"I run the only business in Seattle," Evie said. "You're welcome to stay with me."

Aunt Letitia drew herself up, her arrogance in full evidence. She fixed Noah with a piercing glare, and her voice carried to every ear in the area. "I would rather sleep on the hard ground than under the same roof with the little tart that ran off with my husband and left me penniless."

The words battered Noah's ears, and his mouth fell open. Now he did whirl toward Evie. Her face had gone pasty. She wavered where she stood, and for a moment he thought she might faint. Before he could leap off of the dock and come to her aid, her fiancé slipped a supportive arm around her waist.

His stomach threatened to revolt. How could he stand here and watch Evie in the arms of another man? He couldn't. Without a second thought, he hopped down from the dock and strode across the beach toward the solitude of the forest.

❦

"Noah. Wait!"

Evie watched his retreating back. He increased his long-legged pace until he appeared to be practically running. Running away from her.

With a jerk, she threw James's arm aside. "Don't touch me. I am not your fiancée."

James took a backward step, surprise etched on his face. "Evangeline, how can you say that? Of course you are. We're to be married."

Though those crowded around did not openly stare, she felt the heavy regard of at least a dozen pairs of ears. Ethel and Lucy stood three feet away, their eyes round as wagon wheels, trying to look everywhere but at her.

"We are not going to be married." She turned the full force of her rage on James and stood her ground. "Our relationship ended months ago in Chattanooga."

"Now, darling, you were upset and not thinking properly. I knew you didn't mean it." He tried to place a comforting hand on her arm, but she jerked away from him. "And then you disappeared before we could patch things up."

"I most certainly did mean it!" She whirled on Mrs. Coffinger. "And I did not run off with your husband." She stopped, the words stumbling from her mouth. "At least, not the way you think. We had a business arrangement."

Mrs. Coffinger jerked her nose toward the air and refused to look at Evie, and James, his expression hurt, said in a pouty voice, "What sort of *business*, darling? That's what we'd both like to understand."

Replies crowded Evie's brain, elbowing for space and making no sense. Her pulse throbbed loudly in her ears, and she felt as though her eyes would explode from her head if she were forced to look at James or her former employer one second longer. Unable to find words to fit her fury, she settled on a satisfyingly piercing screech.

James jerked back, stunned, but Evie didn't pause. She ran toward the forest after Noah.

~

Noah had disappeared. Evie searched everywhere, but to no avail. No doubt he didn't want to be found, at least not by her. She wandered the timber alone, calling for him in a voice choked with tears. If only he would give her a chance to explain.

Then anger stirred. Why should she have to plead? If he loved her, he would know she would never behave like the tart Mrs. Coffinger accused her of being. An association of that sort with Miles? The very idea made her shudder.

As for James…Tears once again blurred her eyes. James's appearance must have been like a knife to Noah's heart. Why hadn't she told him about James before? If only he would listen to her, let her explain.

And so her thoughts circled round and round, even as she wandered round and round in the forest. She could not force herself to return to the restaurant and face her friends there. Not yet, not with her emotions so raw and her hopes in shreds. When she stumbled across a familiar trail, she realized that she had not truly been circling, but had been all the while heading steadily toward the place where she knew she would find a sympathetic ear. Drawing a shuddering breath, she quickened her pace to the Denny cabin.

The girls saw her from the cabin doorway when she entered the clearing. "Evie! Evie!"

They raced toward her, giggling with delight at her unexpected appearance. Evie tried to smile, but when they neared, she couldn't maintain the pretense. Her face crumpled, and the tears she tried to hold back poured forth.

The girls stopped their little faces full of distress.

"Evie, what's wrong?" Margaret asked. "Did you hurt yourself?"

Louisa Catherine turned and ran toward the cabin, shouting for her mama and aunt, while Evie gulped in air and tried to compose herself for the little girl's sake.

"No, sweetheart, I'm not hurt. Just sad."

The child took her hand gently in one of her small ones and patted it. "Don't be sad. Mama made apple pie for supper. Papa says things always look better after a cup of tea and some pie."

Laughing through her tears, Evie stooped and gathered Margaret into a hug. "Thank you. I'll remember that."

By then Louisa Catherine had alerted everyone, and they piled outside. Evie was embarrassed to see Arthur hurry toward her, concern etched in the heavy creases between his eyebrows.

"What's wrong?" He searched her face. "Has there been an accident? Is someone hurt?"

Evie shook her head. "No, nothing like that. It's just…" She swallowed, mastering a sob. "A ship has arrived."

Louisa's eyes lit up. "David is home?"

"No not his ship. Another one. My…my…" She could hardly

bear to speak the words. "My former fiancé has arrived. And Noah saw him. And Mrs. Coffinger said…" Her throat squeezed. "She said…"

She couldn't finish, but covered her face with her hands and gave in to a fresh wave of tears. Louisa's arms were around her in an instant, and she found herself being guided toward the cabin.

"There, there. Don't cry. Come inside and tell us about it."

❧

Noah heard Evie's voice echo through the forest. Fresh pain wrenched his heart at the tears he heard plainly, but he ignored it. What right had she to cry? Did being caught in a lie justify tears? He forced his legs to move faster and faster, dodging around cedar trees and plunging through fir branches until he was running. Running away from her. Only when her voice had faded behind him did he slow, his breath coming heavy and his heart pounding like an Indian drum.

But then the other voices echoed in his mind.

I would rather sleep on the hard ground than under the same roof with the little tart who ran off with my husband and left me penniless.

What was that all about? Though he knew without a doubt that there was nothing between Uncle Miles and Evie, what about the other accusation? Had Evie stolen something from Aunt Letitia? He snatched at a branch and came away with a fistful of pine needles. No, he could not believe that. Would not believe it.

Far more disturbing was the other voice.

Evangeline, my darling fiancée!

No man would greet a woman that way unless it was true. Evie, engaged to be married to that man on the boat. Had she run off and left him heartbroken? Why else would he cross the country to find her? Obviously he still loved her, still wanted to marry her. How could she do that to someone who loved her?

And why hadn't she told him?

It's like Sallie all over again.

He came upon the stream suddenly, and realized he'd been wandering without being aware of his surroundings. If he turned right, he would come to the place where he and Evie had washed dishes, where they shared their first kiss. Turning his back toward that painful spot, he hurried away. The more distance he could put between himself and that area, the better.

Thoughts circled in his mind as his feet carried him of their own accord. How could he have been such a fool twice?

When he topped the ridge, he realized he had come once again to his valley. Before him stretched the fertile land fed by the shimmering stream. Mount Rainier stood tall and majestic, looking down on him. What had he said just this morning? That no man could look on that mountain and doubt the existence of God. Nor did he.

Why is this happening again?

The cry rose toward heaven from a soul in turmoil. He sank to his knees, his gaze fixed on the imposing form that sat like a crown on the valley. The valley that had come to represent his future, the fulfillment of his dreams.

But he had shared this valley with Evie, and now a shadow lay across it. And like his future, the pinnacle of Mount Rainier was hidden from view, shrouded in clouds.

❦

By the time Arthur escorted Evie back to the restaurant, she had regained a measure of composure. This was a horrible misunderstanding. No, she had not told Noah about James, but she'd planned to. She would have done so that very day, except she was interrupted by the untimely arrival of the *Olympia*. If only he would give her a chance, she could make him understand. She must.

When they reached the totem pole, the curtains fluttered at the restaurant window. The next moment, the door opened and Ethel hurried outside.

"Thank goodness you've come." She cast a look over her shoulder, and then lowered her voice. "I'm in danger of becoming Seattle's first murderer."

No question concerning the identity of the murder victim. "Mrs. Coffinger?"

Ethel rolled her eyes. "That woman would find fault with the pearly gates themselves, and wouldn't mind telling St. Peter about it, either."

"So she's decided to bed down here, has she?" Arthur looked toward the restaurant. "I'm to convey Mary's invitation to stay with us if she wants."

"Trust me, Mr. Denny." Ethel shook her head. "You don't want to inflict that woman on your poor wife and children." She tilted her head, an idea stealing over her face. "Maybe we could send her in that direction, though, and don't tell her about making noise to keep the bears away."

Evie stared at the building, trying to see through the opening in the curtains. "Is...anyone else here?"

"No one. Once that woman started complaining, everyone left. They're all up at the logging camp." She scowled. "Where it's quiet."

"That's where I'm going, then." Arthur turned a kind smile on Evie. "You'll let me know if you need anything?"

If she still possessed any unshed tears, they would have appeared then. Arthur had been unexpectedly compassionate when she sobbed the details of the encounter at the dock. While Louisa and Mary took turns hugging her and forcing honeyed tea on her in tangible offerings of comfort, he stood silently nearby, his expression kind and without a hint of judgment. After the tears ceased and she felt able to face the others, he offered to see her safely home. On the trail, he spoke only one piece of advice.

"Noah is a good man, and he values the truth. Give him that, and I think all will be well."

She turned to him now. "Thank you for everything." She hesitated. "If you happen to see him…"

Smiling gently, Arthur shook his head. "I know better than to meddle in affairs of the heart. I have all I can do to handle my own. Some things you must do yourself."

With a nod toward Ethel and a final smile for Evie, he left.

When they were alone, Ethel peered into Evie's face. "Are you all right, then? We've been worried about you."

She drew in a long breath and let it out slowly. "I'll be all right. One way or another." She linked her arm through her friend's. "Let's get this over with."

When they entered the restaurant they found Mrs. Coffinger standing stiffly in front of Lucy, who appeared ready to cry. "I tell you, it's impossible. You must make other arrangements immediately."

"That's what I keep telling you, ma'am. There are no other arrangements." The girl cast a silent plea for help toward Evie. "Tell her. She won't believe me."

The sturdy woman turned and, when she caught sight of Evie, seemed to gain six inches in height. Perhaps it was just her neck, which stretched to its limit, her nose pointed skyward.

"What doesn't she believe, Lucy?" Evie was proud of her calm tone.

"That the only bedrooms are up there." She pointed toward the opening in the ceiling, where the ladder led to the second floor.

"I will not climb that contraption like a baboon. Besides being undignified, it is most certainly unsafe." Her generous bosom inflated, the very picture of offended dignity.

Ethel folded her arms across her chest and matched her tone. "Then you can sleep on the hard ground, like you said in the first place."

"This is outrageous, I tell you." She looked down her long nose at Evie just as one would inspect an insect. "And being forced to stay with a woman of tarnished reputation besides."

Had her emotions not exhausted themselves with tears, Evie's temper might have flared. As it was, she was too tired to do more than shake her head. "I don't know what you think, Mrs. Coffinger, but I assure you I do not, nor have I ever, entertained romantic notions about your husband. He and I have become business partners. That is why we came to Seattle."

"And we came with them." Lucy stepped hastily across the floor to stand beside Evie and Ethel. "All the way from Chattanooga."

"Nothing inappropriate occurred on the entire journey," Ethel said. "As we already told you."

"Hmm." The woman's eyes narrowed. "What about my money?"

Evie held the woman's eye without flinching. "I don't know anything about that. Miles's part of the bargain was to finance the venture. When we reached San Francisco, I discovered that he did not bring the necessary finances after all, and was forced to take a loan at the bank."

Ethel's glare deepened. "And none of us have been paid a penny of what we were promised, either."

Mrs. Coffinger considered the explanation, her tightly twisted lips forming an almost invisible straight line. Evie wasn't sure whether she believed them or not, and at the moment she found it hard to care. Where was Noah? Would he join the rest of them for dinner tonight?

The woman broke her silence with a sniff and a question. "What is the nature of this business venture you mentioned?"

Evie spread her hands. "This restaurant."

Generous gray brows arched over scornful eyes as Mrs. Coffinger examined the room. She reached out a finger and touched the table beside her, and then tilted her head sideways to see the rough bench beneath it. "If I'm to be the owner of this establishment, there are a lot of changes to be made."

Ethel's mouth opened, and judging by her outraged expression she was about to voice her opinion of Mrs. Coffinger having any part of the restaurant. Evie stopped her with a raised hand. She had not the energy for an argument right now. Besides, her business partners needed to be present for a discussion involving ownership.

Noah, where are you? Please let me explain.

"Time enough for that when Miles returns. In the meantime, I can assure you that Lucy and Ethel have told the truth. Unless you want to sleep outdoors or in a tent in the logging camp, this is the only place to stay." She nodded toward the ladder. "And that is the only way to get to the bedrooms."

Mrs. Coffinger's sigh could have blown the curtains off the windows. "Very well. I suppose one must make do when one is penniless." She marched to the ladder with a swish of her voluminous skirts and, with a look of pure distaste, began to climb.

The back door opened as she disappeared through the opening in the ceiling. Evie's hopes rose. Noah? They deflated when Cookee entered.

"All I got to say is you gals better have a mighty good supper planned for tonight." He threw himself onto a bench. "I ain't feedin' no visitors. Cookhouse's closed till the logging starts up again."

"Visitors?" Evie looked to Ethel for an explanation.

"A dozen or so of them came in on the ship. Men looking for logging work, mostly."

Lucy added, "Big Dog took them up to the camp, on account of we sure don't have room for them."

A dozen men. They'd need to be fed, of course. And there was only one restaurant in town.

She shook her head. "But we're not even open for business yet."

Cookee planted an elbow on the table and dropped his chin into it. "I guess you are now."

Stomping from overhead drew her gaze toward the ceiling. Mrs. Coffinger's face, full of outraged disbelief, appeared at the top of the ladder. "A cot? You can't be serious. I won't stand for it."

Evie sank onto a stump next to the door. No matter what Ethel said, she would not have the privilege of becoming Seattle's first murderer. Evie intended to claim that title the moment Miles Coffinger set a boot onto that dock.

Nineteen

vangeline, we really should talk about the future," James said. "Won't you walk with me after breakfast?"

"Must I say it again?" Evie set a platter of flapjacks on the table with a clatter that caused eyebrows to rise all over the restaurant. "We have no future."

At supper last night James tried repeatedly to get her alone, insisting that she speak with him. Evie had neither the patience nor the strength to put up with him, either then or this morning after a sleepless night on Sarah's cot, Mrs. Coffinger having claimed her bedroom. Noah did not come to supper, and no one knew where he'd gone. The *where* didn't matter to Evie. It was the *why* that kept her awake—that and the ache in her heart.

She plopped down a pot of warm molasses and turned away from James to return to the stove, but he stopped her by grasping her arm. "Your future, then."

With a pointed look at his hand, she asked, "Shall I call Big Dog?"

So insistent had James been last night that Evie prevailed upon the giant lumberjack to "escort" him back to the logging camp.

James removed his hand with haste. "You've certainly grown stubborn since leaving Tennessee."

Evie sniffed.

Lucy, having finished her task of feeding the chickens, entered the restaurant through the back door. "You'd better get out there," she told Evie. "*She's* giving orders again."

Evie glanced at her breakfast customers. The restaurant was satisfyingly full this morning with hungry men who were eager to explore the area.

"We'll take care of things in here." Ethel gave her a gentle shove. "You go make sure that woman doesn't cause any harm."

With a grateful glance, Evie hurried out the back door. The sun was hidden behind clouds this morning, which cast a pallor over the grass and trees surrounding the glade. It seemed her gloom had spread to the sky.

"That's the ideal place." Mrs. Coffinger pointed toward Evie's bedroom window. "There's plenty of room if you remove part of the wall."

"What?" Evie hurried over to where she and Big Dog stood, both gazing at the restaurant's second floor. "Why would we need to remove a wall?"

Mrs. Coffinger looked surprised that she would ask. "For the staircase, of course. You can't expect me to continue to use that archaic ladder."

What Evie expected was for Mrs. Coffinger to go home to Tennessee shortly after Miles returned. Preferably in his company, and with James as well.

Without waiting for an answer, the woman tapped Big Dog on the arm. "Now, Mr. Dog, if you begin today, how long do you think it will take?"

Big Dog cast a questioning glance toward Evie, who gave her head a very subtle shake.

He screwed up his face and made a show of examining the area in question. "Well, ma'am, first I gotta cut and split the wood, and that'll take several days. Then I'll have to take out part of that wall, like you said. Have to shore up the roof so it don't collapse. Then

building the steps." He scratched his scalp. "I'd say three weeks
ought to see the job done."

"Weeks?" Clearly, she had not expected that.

"You don't want the stairs to break down first time you walk up
'em, do you? We gotta do it right. And I can't do it by myself. I'll
need to hire help, and that takes money—a lot of money."

Hiding a smile, Evie turned away. The matter could be safely left
in Big Dog's hands.

Louisa stepped through the restaurant door. When she caught
sight of Evie, she hurried forward with a hug.

Evie returned the embrace. "I didn't know you were coming
today."

"When Arthur returned last night he was full of excitement about
the shipload of men who want to move to Seattle. He was eager to
show them around this morning, and I decided to come with him.
I thought you might need help feeding them all."

More likely she wanted to check on her friend after the emotional
scene of yesterday. Touched, Evie covered her hand and squeezed.
"Thank you. Between Ethel, Lucy, and me, we've managed. But I'm
always glad to see you. How about a cup of tea?"

Louisa nodded, but when Evie moved toward the restaurant,
stopped her. "I brought other news." The eyes that looked into Evie's
were full of meaning.

She held her breath. "About Noah?"

"An Indian came to the cabin with a note from him last night.
He's staying in the Duwamish camp for a few days and says no one
should worry about him."

Relief struck Evie a moment before anger displaced it. "A note
to Arthur? How kind of him."

Louisa answered gently. "The note was not addressed to anyone.
He knew Mary or I would tell you. I'm sure it was your mind he
wanted to set at ease."

"Then why did he not send the messenger here?" Evie's tone came out more bitter than she expected. She smiled to take away the sting. "I'm sorry. At least we know he is safe."

"Give him time." Louisa hugged her again. "It will all come out all right in the end. You'll see."

Evie was about to reply that she had no faith in a happy ending for her and Noah, but a shout reached them. "Ship in the bay!"

Louisa clasped her hands beneath her chin, her eyes shining. "David has returned!"

Another voice, this one heavy with a different meaning, answered. "And Miles with him."

Evie turned to see Mrs. Coffinger glaring in the direction of the dock. Judging from her searing expression, Miles would not enjoy as pleasant a welcome as David. Well, if the woman wished to do harm to her husband, she would have to stand in line behind Evie.

~

The announcement of the ship's arrival echoed through the Duwamish camp. Noah crawled out of the hut Chief Seattle had been kind enough to assign him to find the camp astir. Not the excitement the settlers exhibited at the same news, but the call was noted. A handful of braves gathered in the central area, preparing to go to the dock to observe the arrival of yet another of the white men's ships.

The chieftain exited his longhouse, his expression placid as he nodded permission. The men left, several with curious glances in Noah's direction. Seattle watched their departure, and then approached Noah.

"You do not welcome your friends on the ship?" he asked in his language.

Noah did the translation in his mind. Though he wanted to hear David's news of the lumber shipment, and would love to see the moment when Uncle Miles first saw Aunt Letitia, he knew Evie would be there. Maybe even with her fiancé at her side. He shook his head. "I will see them soon enough."

For a long moment the chief studied him. "I wish to see this ship. Come."

Without waiting for Noah's reply, he strode through the camp. Had he followed his men in the direction of the dock, Noah might have refused to accompany him. But Seattle took a path in the opposite direction. He glided through the forest, his deerskin shoes making no sound and leaving no sign of his passage. Though Noah tried to so the same, the sound of his boots crunching through the leaf-covered ground were nearly as loud in his ears as Ethel's tin plate and spoon.

In five minutes' time they reached a place where the land ended abruptly. The forest grew right up to the edge of a grassy overhang that looked down on Elliott Bay. Ten minutes' hike to the left lay the settlement that bore the chief's name, though outcroppings in the land hid the dock from view. The water today looked dark and murky in the absence of direct sunlight. To Noah's right, a ship sailed in the bay, its bow pointed toward the unseen dock.

Chief Seattle advanced to the very edge of the bluff, where he stood with his arms folded over his chest, watching the ship's progress. Noah hung back, not confident of his balance on what might turn out to be soft soil. Or maybe he didn't wish to be seen from the ship's deck.

It was the *Commodore*. Noah recognized her familiar lines and spotted David at the railing as she glided past. A few other men stood beside him, though no one that looked like Uncle Miles.

The chief remained silent until her stern had passed. Then he spoke without turning. "Why are you sleeping in my village?"

"I will leave if you want."

He did not reply, but waited for an answer to his question.

Noah dislodged a half-buried twig with the toe of his boot. "I need a place to think. Sometimes white men talk so much we can't hear our own thoughts. Your people aren't like that."

The chief's shoulders lifted with a silent laugh.

"I guess I need guidance, and I can't seem to get it there." The words came from Noah's aching heart, from deep within the confusion of his thoughts. Would the Duwamish chief offer him wise advice? Noah sure didn't have any of his own right now.

Chief Seattle's answer, when it came, surprised him. "Our God is your God."

"I know that," he said quietly.

"Then why do you think you will hear Him here, when you don't listen to Him there?"

Before Noah could come up with a response, the chief turned. Though his expression was as impassive as ever, kindness showed in the dark depths of his eyes. "You are welcome to stay as long as you need."

He left, moving as silently as before, but his words resonated in Noah's soul long after he was gone.

⁂

Evie and Louisa maneuvered themselves to the front of the group assembled on the beach as the *Commodore* put in to port. Mrs. Coffinger stood beside them with a glower dark enough to frighten away a pack of prowling wolves.

"There he is." Louisa bounced, her hand waving in the air. "David! Over here!"

While the ropes were secured, Evie scanned the ship's deck. No sign of Miles. How curious. Had he somehow gotten wind of his wife's arrival in Seattle and decided not to return? If that were the case, she would personally assist Mrs. Coffinger in tracking him down so she could exact her revenge.

David leaped from the ship before the gangway was secured and gathered Louisa in his arms. Then he turned to Arthur, who stood waiting nearby, and announced in a voice loud enough to be heard by all, "Success! We've been offered a standing contract for as much timber as we can produce."

A cheer went up from the watchers.

Mrs. Coffinger surged forward and spoke in a voice that cut through the joyful shouts. "Young man, where is my husband?"

While Louisa performed a hasty introduction, Evie joined them on the dock.

"Yes, where is Miles?" she asked. "Did he arrange for my supplies? Did he pay the bank?"

David gave them both an uncomfortable look. "Miles encountered a bit of trouble with his pickled salmon."

Oh, no.

Wincing, Evie braced herself. "He couldn't find a buyer?"

"Oh, yes. He found buyers aplenty. So many they were trying to outbid each other right there on the pier in San Francisco. But when he opened the first barrel to give them a sample, the fish was spoiled."

"Spoiled?"

David wrinkled his nose. "The stench was horrible. He insisted there must be something wrong with that barrel, and opened another." He shook his head. "They were all the same."

In an instant, Evie knew what happened. "The salt. I suspected he didn't use enough, but he insisted he had everything in hand." If Miles was unable to sell his salmon, then that meant he had no money. "Was he able to purchase any of my supplies?"

"A few." He gave her a sorrowful look. "Not many, I'm afraid."

Evie closed her eyes, the reality of her situation striking her like a fist. Customers she had aplenty, but with no supplies and no food to cook, how could she repay the bank loan? What would they do to her when she couldn't make the payments? Send someone to take control of the restaurant? Arrest her and take her to prison, perhaps?

A gloved hand grasped hers, and she opened her eyes. To her surprise, Mrs. Coffinger had moved near and now gave her a comforting pat. "Don't worry, Evangeline. We will get this straightened out one way or another." She spoke to David. "And what of Miles? Did he choose the coward's way and desert us in our time of need?"

A look of disgust settled on David's face, which he quickly replaced with a politely blank expression. "No, ma'am, though to be honest I wish he had. It would have made this journey a lot more pleasant." He scanned the ship's deck, and then shouted in that direction. "Emory, would you go below and wake Mr. Coffinger?"

A member of the crew nodded and disappeared down a ladder.

"What of the minister?" Louisa searched David's face. "Were you able to find one willing to come?"

"Not a minister, no." Her face fell, but he hugged her. "Don't worry, Sweetbriar. I found someone to perform the ceremony."

A man's head appeared from the ship's berth. Evie recognized Miles's shaggy gray hair and beard, though he looked far more disheveled than usual. He must have been sleeping deeply, and obviously emerged without taking the time to make himself presentable.

"There he is."

Miles lurched through the opening in the deck as though shoved from below. His arms waved and legs danced for balance in the moment before he went sprawling. Emory appeared behind him and helped him to his feet.

"Take note, my dear," said Mrs. Coffinger with a nod in that direction. "It is impossible to make a suitably grand entrance on a ladder. One needs a staircase."

Evie couldn't help smiling at the observation. Yes, a woman of Mrs. Coffinger's temperament would insist on a grand entrance.

Louisa paid no attention to Miles. "But who will marry us if not a minister?"

"A justice of the peace." David raised his voice to be heard. "Our town is now officially named Seattle, and the Oregon Territorial Legislature has appointed our first official."

On the ship's deck, Emory let go of Miles's arm. He stumbled forward, straightened, and gave his waistcoat a tug. Half of his shirttail showed at his side and he appeared to have lost his cuff-links, for the cuffs on his wrinkled sleeves dangled open. He took a wavering step, nearly fell, and righted himself again.

Mrs. Coffinger spoke in a voice full of distaste. "How well I know that look. He's drunk."

Evie examined Miles more closely. His unsteady stance might certainly be that of a man far gone in his cups.

"And who has been appointed Seattle's first justice of the peace?" asked Arthur. "Is it you, David?"

David shook his head. "I couldn't perform my own wedding, could I?"

At that moment, Evie knew. Aghast, she followed David's pointing finger toward the inebriated Miles. "There's our new justice of the peace."

Miles stumbled forward. While everyone watched in stunned silence, he managed to climb up on the gangway. At that moment, his gaze fell on Mrs. Coffinger. He wobbled, did a double take, and then shouted in a slurred voice, "Letitia, is that really you or am I having another of those horrid hallucinations?"

Then he lost his precarious balance. With a sideways lurch he tumbled over the side of the ramp and landed with a splash in the cold waters of Elliott Bay.

Twenty

"Miles, how could you?" Evie towered over the miserable man as he slumped at a table in the restaurant, his head drooping over his hands. "Ethel and Lucy and Sarah and I left everything to come here because we trusted you to be a man of your word."

"I have kept my word." His mumble, though far from clear, was at least understandable after his dunk in the bay, several hours' sleep, and a gallon of spring water which Big Dog insisted would clear his mind more quickly than coffee. "You have your restaurant, don't you?" He lifted his head and one bloodshot eye cracked open. "And it looks very nice. You've done a remarkable job in the short time I've been gone."

"But I won't be able to keep it. How can I, when you've spent all the money and we have none with which to repay the loan and still purchase food to cook?"

"Repay two loans," added Mrs. Coffinger, who stood beside her, scowling. "The bank in Chattanooga was quite clear that our home is in danger of foreclosure if that loan is not paid soon." Her tone became piercing. "A loan of which I knew nothing."

Evie shook her head. "I don't understand. Where did all your money go, since you certainly did not spend it on our venture?"

Mrs. Coffinger's upper lip furled. "The bulk of our money was gone before you, Evangeline. The bank's records are quite thorough. Miles's poor investments have been taking their toll for years, apparently."

Miles raised his head. "To say nothing of the extravagant lifestyle you lead, Letitia."

Her bosom inflated with a hiss. "Had I but known, I could have taken measures to reduce our living expenses. Far better that than to have poverty forced upon me unawares."

He waved a hand vaguely. "We can sell the furnishings."

Mrs. Coffinger's chest deflated, and for once her arrogance fled. "Miles, you don't seem to understand." She slid onto the bench opposite the table from him and held his eyes. "They've taken most of the furnishings already. What wasn't repossessed I sold to finance my journey here. My jewelry, my china, it's nearly all gone."

An image of the big house in Chattanooga rose in Evie's mind. All those beautiful furnishings, gone?

Sorrow filled his red-rimmed eyes, and he dropped his face into his hands. "I'm sorry. Truly. I don't know how I've managed to make such a mess of things."

At the sound of a throat being cleared, Evie turned to find James standing in the doorway. Had he been eavesdropping?

"Evangeline, we need to talk."

Irritated, she snapped. "Not now, James."

"Yes, now." He crossed the floor in three strides, a determined set to his jaw. "I will not be put off any longer."

She opened her mouth to fire back a sharp retort, but when her gaze fell on Miles's lowered head, the words died on her lips. He and Mrs. Coffinger needed time alone. Instead, she sighed and allowed James to lead her outside.

For once the glade surrounding the restaurant was empty. No doubt all the new arrivals were either up at the camp or busy exploring the area. Louisa and David had disappeared hand in hand into the woods from the boat dock, and Lucy and Ethel were still down at the landing site, taking inventory of the few supplies Miles managed to obtain. Evie followed James to the totem pole, where he stopped.

"This is quite the statue," he commented, his head tilted back to see the top.

Evie was in no mood for small talk. "Please tell me whatever you have to say."

One eyebrow rose. "You've become testy since I last saw you." When she folded her arms, he ducked his head. "Oh, all right. I've brought a letter for you."

The last thing she expected to hear. "From whom?"

"See for yourself."

He extracted a crinkled envelope from his pocket. The paper was worn, as though with much handling, but the wax seal remained intact. Her name was scrawled across the front in an unfamiliar hand. She broke the seal and opened the letter.

Dear Miss Evangeline Lawrence,

I regret to inform you that your uncle, Jeremy R. Blodgett, passed away of natural causes on the eighteenth of May, in the year of our Lord 1852.

A breath caught in her throat and she wilted against the totem pole. Uncle Jeremy, dead? When her brain stopped buzzing with the news, she continued to read.

It is my understanding that he left no male heirs, nor did he settle his affairs before his passing. Therefore, as his only living relative, you are the beneficiary of his estate. At current reckoning, said estate consists of two hundred fifty undeveloped acres in Adair County, Kentucky, the house and property located at 27 Railroad Avenue in Chattanooga, Tennessee, and various accounts totaling approximately four hundred fifty dollars.

May I offer my services should you wish assistance in the management or disbursement of the above property? I shall await your reply.

> *With Regards,*
> *Edward Farthington, Esq.*
> *Chattanooga, Tennessee*

She had to read the letter three times before she fully understood the meaning. Uncle Jeremy had passed away less than a week after her arrival in Seattle. And died without appointing an heir, which meant Grandfather's house now belonged to her. And not only the house, but money and a substantial piece of property in Kentucky as well.

She became aware that James had extended his neck to its fullest and was attempting to glimpse her letter. Snatching it close to her chest, she caught him in a narrow-eyed stare.

"Do you know the contents of this letter?"

A hurt expression crossed his features. "I didn't open it, if that's what you're asking. But I heard of your uncle's death, and when your grandfather's attorney came looking for you…" He shrugged. "Has he left you the house, then?"

"Yes." She looked at the letter again, her thoughts caught in a whirlwind. "Yes, he has."

"Well, this solves our problems." He smiled broadly. "Sell the house, pay off the loan, and have enough left over to keep us comfortable for a long time."

She allowed him to see her eyebrows rising. "Us?"

"Evangeline." The smile softened, and he took her hand tenderly. Still numb over the news in the letter, Evie didn't jerk away from his touch. "I know you were upset when I mentioned delaying our marriage. I was wrong. As soon as you left I realized my mistake. I should have married you long ago. I'm sorry." He lifted her hand and pressed a kiss onto the soft skin of her wrist.

With a start, Evie realized the touch of his lips didn't infuriate her, as it would certainly have done a few hours ago. In fact, it evoked no emotion at all, save a dim sense of sorrow. Once she might have rejoiced to hear those words from him. But no longer.

Gently she extracted her hand and gave him a smile without a trace of malice. "James, I meant what I said that night. I won't marry you. I can't."

His gaze searched hers. "You've met someone else, haven't you?"

She lowered her face so he wouldn't see her tears.

With a finger under her chin, he tilted her head up. "Don't cry over me, Evangeline. In time I'll get over you." She would have corrected him, but he lifted his gaze to the treetops, a sense of adventure flickering in his eyes. "And since I've come all this way, I may decide to stay a while."

Her tears fled in surprise. "In Seattle?"

"Why not? I have nothing in Tennessee. The railroad is taking over, and there's less and less work on the river docks. But here…" His lips widened into a smile. "I've been listening to that Denny fellow talk about the lumber and the new mill they'll build. The pitiful little dock they have won't serve that kind of trade for long. They'll need a proper pier, and experienced men to manage it."

How incredibly awkward, to have her former fiancé living right here in Seattle where she might encounter him at any moment. A protest rose to Evie's lips, but died unspoken. If anyone should leave Seattle, it should be her. What did she have to keep her here now? The home over which she had mourned was restored to her. She could live there for the rest of her life, surrounded by memories of Grandfather and Mama and Papa. If Mr. Farthington could sell Uncle Jeremy's Kentucky property that would be enough to pay off the restaurant loan, as James suggested. She would happily leave the restaurant in Mrs. Coffinger's care, and when it became profitable, perhaps her share would be enough to keep her in comfort back in Tennessee.

There was something she must do first. She must speak with

Noah. When she left James behind, she hadn't given him a second thought. But she didn't love James. A lump clogged her throat. She did love Noah.

Maybe I can make him understand. I did not steal from anyone, as Sallie did. I would never steal from him.

But oh, the betrayal in his eyes yesterday on the beach. How could he ever forgive her for withholding her past from him, when he had opened his to her?

❦

The shadows that darkened the trail to the Indian camp seemed to change the mood of the forest. Evie walked quickly, her ears attuned to the sounds in the area, her gaze constantly scanning for signs of movement. Maybe she should have brought a pot and spoon from the restaurant.

Big Dog or Randall would have come with me if I'd asked.

But like a fool, she'd charged off without asking for help. Maybe she really was as bullheaded as Noah thought her. It would serve her right if she were eaten by a bear. And if she did find him safely, what would she say? Though she tried to outline her words, her mind remained a mass of whirling thoughts, none of them cohesive enough to structure into a firm plan. There *was* no plan, no list of words that had the power to convince a man to love a woman.

Maybe all that was left to say between them was goodbye.

She came upon the Duwamish camp with no warning. The women working around the first fire pit looked up from their tasks, clearly surprised to see a white woman stumble into their village alone.

One who looked familiar came toward her and asked a question in her own language. Surely everyone would be aware of the presence of a white man in the village.

Evie told her, "I'm looking for Noah."

The woman's expression cleared. She said something to her companions and then indicated that Evie should follow. That must mean he was still here. Relieved, Evie wound through the portable huts, drawing stares along the way.

When she reached the place where the big fire pit had been dug, Chief Seattle stood in the center of the clearing. She approached and stood in front of him. How had she ever thought his face impassive? All she had to do in order to know this man's feelings was look into his eyes. When she did, her heart constricted at the depths of compassion she saw there.

He smiled then, a gentle curving of his lips, and gestured with his hand toward one of the huts. When she turned, she saw a man ducking out of the low opening.

Noah.

Her throat constricted and she stumbled toward him, nearly blinded by the rush of tears that filled her eyes. He did not move, and she stopped just short of throwing herself into his arms.

"Evie, what are you doing here?" He glanced around. "Did you come alone?"

Not trusting her voice, she nodded.

He let out a sigh. "Come on. I'll take you home."

When she would have protested, she became aware of their surroundings. A good-sized crowd had gathered to watch, their expressions openly curious. Perhaps they didn't understand English, but she didn't relish being observed as she humbled herself. Nodding, she allowed him to escort her back through the camp in the direction she came.

He was silent as he led her through the trees, his shoulders stiff. Would he subject her to silence the whole way? With many hard swallows and deep gulps of air, she managed to get control of her tears by the time they stepped onto the wider trail that led to Seattle. At least then she could walk by his side and see his face instead of staring at his rigid back.

When she was certain she could speak, she blurted the words that were foremost on her mind. "I'm sorry I didn't tell you about James. I was going to, right when the ship arrived. I promise."

He walked on a few paces without answering. When he did, he didn't look at her but kept his gaze fixed ahead. "Tell me now."

Taking an unsteady breath, she told him of their engagement, of how she had come to realize that she didn't love James and to suspect that he didn't love her either. How when Noah's letter arrived and she'd overheard Miles reading it aloud while she cleaned…

"Wait." He glanced at her then, a quick flicker of the eyes that lasted only a moment. "You *worked* for Uncle Miles and Aunt Letitia?"

"Yes," she answered quietly. "I was their housemaid."

A few more steps. "So you lied when you claimed to be his business partner?"

"No! I was his business partner. Am," she corrected herself. She lowered her head, watching her feet walk down the trail. "I didn't want you to discount me as a servant. I wanted you to respect me as a businesswoman."

"I respect honesty."

The word sliced into her misery, and she could only nod. The rest of the journey she spent desperately casting about for some way to convince him of her honesty. They arrived at the restaurant, her thoughts still in turmoil. When they stepped off the trail into the glade, Noah stopped.

Evie looked up at him. "Will you come inside? I have more to tell you." The attorney's letter and all its content entailed, burned like a coal in her pocket.

Staring up at the top of the totem pole, he shook his head. "I don't think so. I've heard enough for one day."

Panic stirred to life inside her. Was he casting her aside, then? "But you don't understand. My uncle died, and I've inherited his estate. At first I thought I would go back to Tennessee, but I could stay here. I can sell the house and the property, pay off the loan, and have enough left over to build the boardinghouse we talked about."

He did look at her then. "Why should I continue a partnership with someone who isn't honest with me?"

"Because I've told you the truth." Sobs threatened to rob her of a voice, but she plowed ahead. "All of it. I have no more secrets." Desperate, she put a hand on his arm. "And I love you, Noah."

She searched his face for a sign, a glimpse of something that would give her hope that he still loved her, still cared for her. But all she could see were gray eyes clouded with doubt.

Slowly, she removed her hand. He didn't love her after all. If he did, then surely he would forgive her. The air around her darkened, and at first she thought the cause was the anguish of her thoughts. Then a heavy raindrop splashed against her cheek, followed quickly by another.

With an upward glance, Noah finally spoke. "You'd better go inside." The softness in his voice held not love, but farewell. He turned and strode away.

Evie watched until he disappeared inside the trees. Numbly, she stumbled to the restaurant and threw open the door. When she stepped inside, the storm broke. The heavens opened, and rain poured from the sky. She sank onto the nearest bench, put her hands over her face, and gave in to tears.

Twenty-One

$\mathcal{E}$thel was at the logging camp's cookhouse arranging a surprise for Evie when the rain started. The paltry amount of supplies the *Commodore* brought wouldn't keep the restaurant going more than a couple of weeks, and Mr. Coffinger had purchased all the wrong things, besides. Who could make a decent supper out of turnips and cabbage?

"Here we go." Cookee backed out of the storeroom carrying a wooden crate. "Them's canned peaches. I kin make a cobbler that'll stick to yer ribs with no more'n a can a peaches and a handful of wheat flour." With a thud, he set the crate beside the others on the rough slats that served as a table for the lumberjacks when the camp was in operation.

Ethel eyed him with disbelief. "I know my cobblers, and it takes more than peaches and flour to make a decent one."

The little man chuckled. "Well, I might throw one or two other things in there."

"Such as?"

The smile faded and he narrowed his eyes. "That there's mine to know and yours to find out. A fella can't go around givin' away all his secrets, can he?"

Cackling, he stomped back into the storeroom. Ethel gave a grunt of disgust, taking care to make it loud enough for him to hear. She saved her grin for when his back was turned. Wouldn't do to encourage him, after all.

He returned with another crate of peaches and plopped it beside the rest. "That there's the last of it. Don't know what the pusher will say 'bout handing all this over to a woman, though."

"Mr. Denny doesn't need these supplies right away, not with the logging camp temporarily closed." Ethel made note of the tally, marking two crates of peaches carefully on her paper. "By the time he's ready to start up again, Miss Evie will have made enough money in her restaurant to pay him back or replace them."

He folded an arm across his middle, propped his other elbow on it, and stroked his scraggly beard with two fingers. "Well, I'll give 'er one thing. That gal's got a lot of spunk for a Tennessee girl."

Ethel drew herself up, eyeing him down the length of her nose. "And what's wrong with Tennessee girls?"

"They's ignor'nt, for th' most part." He gave her a pointed look. "And pigheaded."

"Huh!"

She turned her back on him and marched to the open doorway. Rain fell from the sky in a true deluge. She could barely see three yards into the camp. The ground would be a muddy mess in a matter of minutes.

"Reminds me of the day we arrived," she commented without turning.

He came to stand beside her. "I remember. You and the other wimen looked like river rats and howled like a pack of banshees."

Ethel twisted her lips. "I did not howl."

"Yessiree, you did. You was cryin' like you's afraid a little rain's gonna do you in for good. And shoutin' for tea like you'd marched into a fancy restaurant or somethin'. I knew right then you was cantankerous as all git-out."

He chuckled, and though it galled her, she couldn't deny the accusation. She never had been pleasant when denied her tea.

The chuckle faded, and Cookee cocked his head to look at her sideways. "I always liked me a cantankerous woman."

Ethel looked at him. Had she heard correctly? Was that a compliment he'd just paid her? She couldn't tell from the way he was watching her. "It would take a cantankerous woman to put up with the likes of you."

"That'd be true," he admitted. "I speak my mind, I do. I need me a woman who ain't afraid to speak her mind right back." He peered at her, as if watching closely for a reaction.

A funny feeling commenced to tickle Ethel's stomach. Was Cookee trying, in his bumbling way, to tell her he had feelings for her?

"She'd have to be pigheaded too," she replied cautiously.

He threw his head back and laughter filled the cookhouse. "That she would." When the laughter died, his grin remained. "What say ye, then? You 'n' me'd have quite a time together."

At the sight of his grin, the tickle became a flutter. Her and Cookee? Well, and why not? He irked her to no end, with his brusque manner and know-it-all attitude. But he made her laugh, and in an odd way, she enjoyed spending time with him. Half the time she wanted to slap him silly, and the other half she spent laughing till her sides split. Could that become the basis of a romantic relationship? She took a new measure of him. Not a bad-looking man, if he would shave and wash his clothes every so often. The top of his head came barely to her eyebrows, and of course she outweighed him by a few stones at least.

"We'd look like Jack Sprat and his wife," she said, with a dubious frown.

"Aw, who cares? I like me a woman with some meat on her." He waggled his scraggly eyebrows at her. "Give me a nice plump hen over a scrawny ol' chick any day."

A blush warmed Ethel's cheeks. One thing was certain. Marriage to Cookee would not be a quiet, tame life. It would be full of eruptions and spats and making up.

"One thing I insist on." She narrowed her eyes. "You may not call me ignorant ever again."

He jumped to attention. "Ye have my word on that."

"In that case…" She inclined her head like a queen granting a favor to a knight, though Cookee was the least likely knight she knew. That was all right, though. She was the least likely queen in all of Seattle. "You have my permission to court me."

The joyful whoop he gave set loose a grin she couldn't have held back if she'd wanted to.

❦

Lucy was still at the dock arranging for the supplies to be transported to the restaurant when the rain started. Barely had the crew of the *Commodore* set the last box on the shore when the first fat drops landed on the top of her head. She craned her neck back. Though the sky had been overcast all day, the section directly overhead was now dark and brooding. She'd seen clouds like this a few times since her arrival in Seattle.

"Rain's coming!"

She didn't wait to see if the men who were on hand to tote the supplies up the trail took note of her warning, but dashed toward the closest trees. The deluge began while she was still ten feet outside of the dubious shelter of the forest, and she was soaked to the skin in a matter of seconds. Blinded by rain running from her hair into her eyes, she stumbled toward a tree trunk.

"Come farther in."

She heard the shout over the roar of the downpour and a moment later something was thrown over her shoulders and she was led several more yards into the forest.

"Thank you." She raised a hand to wipe the hair from her eyes so she could see her rescuer.

Her heart slammed against her ribcage, and her step faltered.

"Be careful," said James. "You'll be mud from head to toe if you fall now."

With an arm around her shoulders, he guided her to a place where a stand of cedars grew more closely together than the others, and their leaves far above provided a bit more cover. Rain still reached the forest ground, but not nearly as heavily as in the clear area by the dock. Lucy allowed herself to be led, her pulse skipping unpredictably while she tried to untie her tongue.

"There." He looked toward the treetops. "Hopefully this will blow over soon. Not sure, though. It doesn't rain like this very often back home."

"I'm from Tennessee too." She could have bit her tongue in two. Must she blurt out everything that popped into her head without thinking?

He looked at her, surprise apparent. "How do you know I'm from Tennessee?"

"Everyone does after yesterday." She ducked her head. "Everyone who was there when the *Commodore* arrived, anyway."

"Ah." His lips twisted. "So I've been pegged as Evangeline's jilted fiancé."

Jilted? A hopeful flutter arose in her heart. Rain ran down his face, and she realized she had his jacket around her shoulders.

"Here."

She lifted it to form a cover for them both, and nearly lost the ability to breathe when he moved close to hover beneath it.

"Since I saw you at the restaurant, I assume you're working with Evangeline. Did you travel with her from Chattanooga then?"

"That's right. Along with Ethel and my sister and Mr. Coffinger."

He turned his head to look at her, which in the close quarters put his face only a few inches from hers. "You do look familiar, now that you mention it. Have we met?"

"I don't think so." She was absolutely positive, though she had seen him at least a dozen times back home. The first time when she and Sarah were coming home from the dry goods store and passed the river dock. The men at work there had been laughing together, and how could she not notice the most handsome one? After that, she made a point of walking that way whenever a riverboat was in port. But she didn't need to admit that. Not yet. "I am Lucy Burrows."

"A pleasure to meet you, Miss Burrows. My name is James Garvey, recently of Chattanooga. Currently"—he gave a rueful shrug—"without permanent residence."

"Oh?" The hope in her breast rose a little higher. "Does that mean you won't be returning to Tennessee?"

"There's nothing for me there."

"I hear there are opportunities in panning for gold in California. A number of the lumberjacks recently decided to try their luck there."

"That's what it is too. Luck." With a scowl, he shook his head. "I don't put much stock in luck. I prefer to rely on determination and plain old hard work."

"If that's the case, then you've come to the right place. I've never met a more determined bunch of people than the Dennys and the men who work with them. And there's certainly enough hard work to go around."

"You know, I've been thinking the same thing since I arrived."

He smiled down at her, and Lucy had to force herself to breathe past a wave of giddiness that threatened her composure. To think that the man she secretly dreamed of in Tennessee would end up here, in Seattle, huddled beneath the same jacket with her! It was divine providence, that's what it was. And especially since the poor man's heart had been broken. Why, he needed something to work for. A goal. And maybe someone to help him accomplish it.

"Is the rain letting up any?" He extended his head to peer around the corner of the jacket toward the sky.

"No, I don't think so." Lucy smiled and settled herself a little closer to him. "I think this one might take a long time to blow over."

❦

Noah had not taken five steps away from the glade when the rain started. He barely noticed even when it pounded on his head and turned the ground beneath his boots to mush. She loved him? He didn't believe it. Back in Tennessee she thought she loved James, and what did she do to him? Deserted him. Ran off without a backward glance.

I don't know that. She said she broke their engagement before she left. That eliminated any obligation she had to tell him she was leaving.

At least, that's what she said happened. But how could he believe her?

Though the storm raged around him, Noah plunged through the forest, splashing through rivulets and puddles that formed on the ground. A tightness formed in his chest, whether from exertion or from some other cause, he dared not consider. Instead he pushed onward until he was running almost blindly up the ever-sloping terrain, breath ragged in his chest.

Somewhere along the way he realized where he was going, and he almost stopped then. Why return to his valley? There was nothing for him there. Not now.

When he topped the final ridge he halted, panting, heart thudding so hard he felt it even in the soles of his feet. Rain fell from the dark sky, swelling the stream until it overflowed its banks and lay below him like a bloated gray snake. He backed up against a tree and slid down the trunk, heedless of the wet ground. He was already so wet it didn't matter anyway.

Was he the worst judge of women who ever walked the earth? He must be, else why did he keep having his heart ripped open and handed back to him? Or maybe he just kept falling for the same type.

No. Evie was nothing like Sallie. No way could he have misjudged her so thoroughly, especially not when he'd been on guard against her from the beginning.

The thought struck him with force, and he sat back against the tree. He *had* been suspicious of her from the moment they first met in the San Francisco greengrocer store. Not because he detected any dishonesty on her part, but because his heart was still wounded from Sallie's harsh treatment. In fact, he treated her coldly and kept her at arm's length for weeks. She had not been deterred in the slightest, but only become more determined to accomplish her goals. Not at his expense, but in spite of his suspicions and refusal to help. In a man, that determination would have earned his respect.

Was it possible that he was mistrustful of Evie now not because of her behavior, but because Sallie's lies still hurt so deeply?

He rubbed at his face, wiping away water as he tried to clear his thoughts. Evie didn't exactly lie to him, not in so many words. But she had certainly withheld the truth. Wasn't that the same thing?

The downpour slowed, and within a few minutes the rain dwindled to a light drizzle. A break in the clouds directly overhead held promise that the worst of the storm was over. But the storm inside Noah raged on.

Today on the trail, Evie said she planned to tell him about her fiancé—*former* fiancé—but the arrival of the ship prevented her. When she said that, he didn't believe her. The timing was too convenient.

What if Evie had only been waiting for the right time?

He raked a hand through his rain-soaked hair, scrubbing at his scalp as if by doing so he could clear his thoughts. A ray of sunshine warmed his face, and he looked up to see the clouds beginning to recede, pushed by a breeze that stirred the treetops. As he watched, shadows covering the land below him gave way to light. He lost track of time, watching sunlight chase gloom from his valley until finally the sky showed almost as much blue as white.

The mountain, which had been hidden from view, appeared. Dense vapor still clung to the sides, wrapping the ascent in a blanket of fluffy white, but the snow-capped peak reached triumphantly above the clouds. Sunlight glittered on the distant snow like icy fire.

As his eyes feasted on the brilliance of that dazzling pinnacle, a fog lifted from Noah's thoughts.

Evie rose early in the morning after a second night spent wrestling with her thoughts and wetting her pillow with tears. She'd finally reached a decision, though she had agonized over it. After the sun rose, she would go down to the dock and arrange for return passage to San Francisco on the *Commodore*. Then she would go to Arthur Denny and ask to borrow enough money to see her safely home. She would beg if she must, and of course the attorney's letter was proof that she would soon have the means to repay him in full.

Lucy was an unmoving lump beneath the covers on the cot beside her, and Ethel's soft snore from the direction of the other gave evidence that she still slept soundly. A not-so-soft snore from the bedroom told her Mrs. Coffinger too slept on. Moving quietly, Evie donned her dress and climbed down the ladder to the restaurant below.

The room was warm from the still-burning fire in the big iron stove. Too warm, in fact. When she stoked the coals and the breakfast customers crowded in, the heat would become stifling. She crossed to the front window and pulled aside the heavy curtains to let some of the cool early morning air inside.

The sight that greeted her froze her hand in place. Not again. Three long poles leaned against the side of the restaurant, their tops propped against the frame of the window. Hadn't Chief Seattle instructed his people not to court the settler women? Or had he lifted his prohibition after yesterday, when he saw that Noah was no longer interested in her? Her heart twisted, but she ignored the pain and opened the door. If she saw any Duwamish braves hovering around, waiting to see which pole she chose, she would tell them in no uncertain terms that their romantic attentions were not welcome.

When she exited, she came to a halt and her jaw dropped. Resting against the side of her restaurant were not three poles, but at least a dozen. No, more like two dozen. The entire front of the building, end to end, was covered with poles.

At a noise from the forest, she whirled. Her head went light when she saw Noah striding across the glade toward her. A desperate hope rose in her heart when she caught sight of his tender smile. She covered her mouth with both hands, not trusting herself to speak without sobbing.

He came right up to her and stood close, looking down at her with unreadable eyes that held the darkness of the predawn sky. "I thought you were going to sleep all day."

"You've been waiting for me?" The words came out muffled behind her palms.

"For a long time." He reached up and gently took her hands in both of his. "I'm sorry, Evie. I behaved badly."

Tears stung her eyes and she shook her head violently. "No, I'm sorry. I should have…"

He stopped her with a finger against her lips. "Not now. We have a lot to discuss, but we have time." He lowered his finger and moved closer, so close his breath warmed her cheek. "A lifetime, I hope."

Emotion clogged Evie's throat. She couldn't speak. A lifetime with Noah? That was the desire of her heart.

His eyes held hers in an unbreakable gaze. "But first, you have a choice. Which pole will you choose?"

She found her voice enough to whisper, "Which one is yours?"

"They're all mine." His lips hovered over hers, and she felt his words more than heard them. "I'm not taking any chances with the woman I love."

With an overflowing heart, Evie threw her arms around his neck and pulled him into a dizzying kiss. Just before his mouth closed over hers she whispered, "I'm claiming every single one of those poles. I'm not taking any chances with you, Noah Hughes."

Epilogue

January 23, 1853
Seattle, Oregon Territory

The afternoon of Seattle's first wedding was as bright and fine a day as anyone could have hoped. Evie hurried inside the Denny cabin, her arms full of evergreen boughs, and dumped them on the table.

"That's the last of them," she announced. "I think it will be enough, don't you?"

Standing on a chair, Louisa stooped to pick one up and secure it over the window. "I'm sure it will." She settled a bow in the deep green needles and then leaned back to survey her work. "What do you think?"

"I think we would have had a lot more room in the restaurant."

Louisa made a face. "We don't need more room. We don't want the whole town in attendance, just our closest friends." She looked around the cabin. "But it is beautiful, isn't it?"

Evie planted her hands on her hips and examined the decorations. "Perfect. The whole place is lovely."

It was. She glanced around the small cabin, which looked even more festive now than it had before at Christmastime. No one ever dreamed the wedding would be delayed this long, but the past five months had been filled with the hustle and bustle of building a town and the all-important mill. Louisa and David had chosen ever-greens to decorate the wedding in honor of the beautiful trees that surrounded the little cabin David built for his sweetbriar bride. The two had gathered boughs from those very trees and just this morning Evie had helped Louisa turn their home into a cozy bower.

The half-door opened and David entered. He caught sight of Louisa on the chair and hurried to her side.

"You should have left that for me," he chided. "We can't have the bride taking a tumble on her wedding day, can we?"

"Evie," called a young voice from outside, "come see what Uncle Noah brought."

"Coming, Margaret." She started to say something to the soon-to-be-married couple, but when she saw the joy in the eyes they had fastened on one another, she held her tongue. They wouldn't have heard her anyway.

Untying her apron strings, she left the cabin. A group of guests had arrived from town. In the lead, Noah held the guide rope of a mule whose back was laden with bundles. Fixed atop was the wedding gift she and Noah were giving the bride and groom.

"It's chickens!" Margaret danced beside her. "I love chickens."

Evie hated to tell the child that the chickens would be moving to Aunt Louisa's house within a day or so when David and she had prepared a place for them. Now that Evie's chickens had multiplied and were laying regularly, perhaps she should make a gift to Arthur and Mary as well.

Noah approached, his shining eyes fixed on her. Joy that matched the newlyweds' rose in her as she and Margaret ran hand in hand to meet him.

"You look beautiful enough to be a bride yourself." His gaze roved over her as if he were starving and she a Thanksgiving feast.

Margaret tugged on his pant leg. "What about me? Am I beautiful too?" She performed a pirouette, the skirts of her new dress brushing the grass.

Noah knelt down and grinned. "You certainly are. I've never seen you look lovelier."

"Evangeline, there you are."

Evie turned to find Mrs. Coffinger, or Letitia as she now insisted on being called, bearing down on her.

"I'm sorry we're late. That tiresome Mrs. Sorrell showed up as I was locking the door and insisted she must have a sack of flour before we closed. And then while I was weighing it out, she dawdled around the store, fingering every piece of fabric in the place. I thought she'd never leave." Her immense bosom heaved with a long-suffering sigh. "But I suppose that is the cross I must bear in being the proprietor of the most successful dry goods store in town."

Evie hid a smile. For several months after she and Miles opened their store not far from the restaurant, Letitia enjoyed the distinction of owning the *only* dry goods store in town. Now that Seattle was growing, another had recently opened up down near the new pier, in anticipation of the opening of the new sawmill next month. The owners had not yet managed to see a profit, which Letitia pointed out whenever the opportunity arose.

The woman popped open a fan and began to wave it furiously in front of her face, though the temperature was certainly not warm on this January day. "And then Miles had to be dressed again."

Evie raised her eyebrows. "Dressed?"

"Oh, my dear, he was inappropriately attired. When one is officiating at a wedding, one must look the part, don't you think?"

She started to agree, but the words died on her lips when she caught sight of Miles, who brought up the rear of the party. He certainly did look the part of a justice of the peace. Not only was his black suit impeccably clean and his collar starched and crisp, but his hair had been neatly trimmed and his chin was shaved clean for the first time in Evie's memory.

She turned a look of disbelief on Letitia. "I never thought Miles would shave off his beard."

"He did not do it willingly." She sniffed and then snapped the fan closed. "Now, I must get inside and help with the decorations."

Evie stepped back to allow her to pass. Let Louisa and David be the ones to tell her she was too late to help decorate and that the wedding supper was nearly finished. She looked toward the side of the cabin, where Ethel and Cookee were busy turning a spit laden with wild ducks.

Noah came up behind her, lifted her hair, and placed a kiss on her neck that sent a delightful shiver down her spine. Giggling, she turned. "Stop that. People will talk."

"Let them." He put his arms around her and drew her close. "How about if we announce our wedding day tomorrow? I want us to be the second couple married in Seattle."

The entire town knew of their understanding, and she had fended off more inquiries than she could count from people wanting to know when they would be married. But everyone was in agreement that Louisa and David's wedding be Seattle's first. It was only fitting, since they were among the original settlers.

But so was Noah.

"I think we'd better do it first thing in the morning," she said with a laugh. "I know two other couples who may try to beat us to the honor."

She glanced first toward Ethel and Cookee, who stood closer together than was strictly necessary as they watched over the roasting ducks, and then to Lucy and James, who had arrived with Noah and the others and were now making their way, arms linked, toward the cabin.

"I'll make a sign tonight and post it on the totem pole before sunrise." Noah nuzzled her neck. "I think the day after tomorrow would be a fine day for a wedding, don't you? Before Miles's beard grows back out."

She opened her mouth to reply when a tug on her skirt stopped her. She looked down into Margaret's brown eyes.

The little girl cocked her head and creases appeared in her brow. "Are you going to smooch, or are you going to get those chickens down so I can feed them?"

Laughing, she planted a quick kiss on Noah's cheek. Then, taking the child's hand in one of hers and her beloved's in the other, she pulled them toward the cabin. "Let's go to a wedding first. *Then* we'll feed the chickens."

A Note from Lori & Virginia

The idea for the Seattle Brides series came from a television show that was one of Virginia's favorites back in the 60s. When we got together to brainstorm new story ideas, we rented *Here Come the Brides*, laughed our way through the first episode, and knew we'd found the setting for our next book. Of course, we didn't rely on the television series for our research. From there we delved into history books, journals, and true accounts of the founding of Seattle. What we learned affirmed that we had made the right choice. What a fascinating history!

Though this book is completely fiction, we've used some actual events and people's names in *A Bride for Noah*. The story's timeline for the founding of Seattle is historically accurate. Arthur, David, Mary, and Louisa were real people. Shortly after the Denny party first settled in Oregon Territory (Washington didn't become a state until several years later), Captain Howard of the *Leonesa* came looking for lumber. The settlers, who had moved there with no plans beyond establishing a town and farms, leaped at the opportunity. They volunteered to provide the lumber he wanted and did, felling trees by hand in a very short period of time. Thus began the industry that would make Seattle a profitable city.

Chief Seattle was also a real person, and we were so impressed by him that he took on an even bigger role in this story than we originally intended. He was, by all accounts, a fascinating, far-seeing, peace-loving man. In this book we used quotations from his now-famous and very moving letter to President Franklin Pierce in 1855.

Miles Coffinger's character was modeled after Doc Maynard, one of the original settlers of Seattle. The real Maynard was a great friend of Chief Seattle's and did undertake a disastrous attempt at pickling salmon. He opened the first general store in Seattle, was the city's first justice of the peace, and performed the marriage ceremony between David and Louisa. He was also quite fond of liquor, but that's where the similarities end.

Evie, Noah, and the other characters are all fictional. The Indian marriage poles were an actual tradition of the Duwamish tribe of that era, but in reality it was Louisa Boren who found three poles leaning against her cabin. We decided that incident was too much fun not to use in our story, and hope you'll forgive us for delivering the poles to Evie instead of Louisa.

We hope you enjoyed reading *A Bride for Noah* as much as we enjoyed writing it! We'd love to hear what you think. Visit us online at www.loricopelandandvirginiasmith.com, where you can send us a message and also learn about the other books we've coauthored.

Happy reading!

Lori & Virginia

Chief Seattle's Letter

As we conducted the research for A Bride for Noah, *we came across a letter that was purported to have been written by Chief Si'ahl (Seattle) to President Franklin Pierce in 1855. A lot of controversy surrounds this letter. Some say it was not a letter at all, but a speech. Others say the letter was not written by the chieftain, but by a scriptwriter in the 1970s. Regardless, we were moved by the eloquence of the writing and the character of the individual who penned it. There is no doubt that the real Chief Seattle was a man of intelligence and was committed to peace with the white settlers who arrived in the land long held by his tribe. We thought you'd enjoy reading the letter that inspired us.*

The President in Washington sends word that he wishes to buy our land. But how can you buy or sell the sky? the land? The idea is strange to us. If we do not own the freshness of the air and the sparkle of the water, how can you buy them?

Every part of the earth is sacred to my people. Every shining pine needle, every sandy shore, every mist in the dark woods, every meadow, every humming insect. All are holy in the memory and experience of my people.

We know the sap which courses through the trees as we know the blood that courses through our veins. We are part of the earth and it is part of us. The perfumed flowers are our sisters. The bear, the deer, the great eagle, these are our brothers. The rocky crests, the dew in the meadow, the body heat of the pony, and man all belong to the same family.

The shining water that moves in the streams and rivers is not just water, but the blood of our ancestors. If we sell you our land, you must remember that it is sacred. Each glossy reflection in the clear waters of the lakes tells of events and memories in the life of my people. The water's murmur is the voice of my father's father.

The rivers are our brothers. They quench our thirst. They carry our canoes and feed our children. So you must give the rivers the kindness that you would give any brother.

If we sell you our land, remember that the air is precious to us, that the air shares its spirit with all the life that it supports. The wind that gave our grandfather his first breath also received his last sigh. The wind also gives our children the spirit of life. So if we sell our land, you must keep it apart and sacred, as a place where man can go to taste the wind that is sweetened by the meadow flowers.

Will you teach your children what we have taught our children? That the earth is our mother? What befalls the earth befalls all the sons of the earth.

This we know: the earth does not belong to man, man belongs to the earth. All things are connected like the blood that unites us all. Man did not weave the web of life, he is merely a strand in it. Whatever he does to the web, he does to himself.

One thing we know: our God is also your God. The earth is precious to him and to harm the earth is to heap contempt on its creator.

Your destiny is a mystery to us. What will happen when the buffalo are all slaughtered? The wild horses tamed? What will happen when the secret corners of the forest are heavy with the scent of many men and the view of the ripe hills is blotted with talking wires? Where will the thicket be? Gone! Where will the eagle be?

Gone! And what is to say goodbye to the swift pony and the hunt? The end of living and the beginning of survival.

When the last red man has vanished with this wilderness, and his memory is only the shadow of a cloud moving across the prairie, will these shores and forests still be here? Will there be any of the spirit of my people left?

We love this earth as a newborn loves its mother's heartbeat. So, if we sell you our land, love it as we have loved it. Care for it, as we have cared for it. Hold in your mind the memory of the land as it is when you receive it. Preserve the land for all children, and love it, as God loves us.

As we are part of the land, you too are part of the land. This earth is precious to us. It is also precious to you.

One thing we know—there is only one God. No man, be he Red man or White man, can be apart. We are all brothers after all.

Discussion Questions

1. What makes Evie realize that she does not love her fiancé? Why do you think Evie agreed to marry James in the first place?

2. When Evie meets Noah, she does not reveal her background as the Coffingers' housemaid. Why? Is withholding the truth the same thing as a lie?

3. When the ladies arrive in Seattle, they sit down and cry. That was a fictitious account of an actual event. Why were they upset?

4. Which of Evie's characteristics does Noah dislike? Which does he admire?

5. For the first part of their relationship, Evie and Noah are at odds with each other. What happens to cause them to join forces?

6. Describe Miles. What do you find appealing and displeasing about him?

7. Was Noah justified in questioning Evie's honesty?

8. Chief Seattle asks Noah, "Why do you think you will hear God here (in the Duwamish village) when you don't listen to Him there (in the white man's settlement)?" Are there places where you hear from the Lord more clearly than others? Why?

9. Mrs. Coffinger underwent a change between the beginning of the book and the end. To what do you attribute this change?

10. What does Mount Rainier represent to Noah? How does the mountain help clear his thoughts about a relationship with Evie?

11. At first appearances, Ethel and Cookee are an unlikely couple. Do they have a chance at romance?

12. With which character in *A Bride for Noah* did you most identify?

*L*ori Copeland is the author of more than 90 titles, both historical and contemporary fiction. With more than 3 million copies of her books in print, she has developed a loyal following among her rapidly growing fans in the inspirational market. She has been honored with the Romantic Times Reviewer's Choice Award, The Holt Medallion, and Walden Books' Best Seller award. In 2000, Lori was inducted into the Missouri Writers Hall of Fame. She lives in the beautiful Ozarks with her husband, Lance, and their three children and five grandchildren.

*V*irginia Smith is the author of more than twenty inspirational novels and over fifty articles and short stories. An avid reader with eclectic tastes in fiction, Ginny writes in a variety of styles, from lighthearted relationship stories to breath-snatching suspense. She and her husband divide their time between their homes in Utah and Kentucky.

To learn more about books by Lori Copeland and Virginia Smith
or to read sample chapters,
log on to our website: www.harvesthousepublishers.com

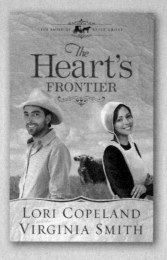

The Heart's Frontier

Lori Copeland & Virginia Smith

An exciting new Amish-meets-Wild West adventure from best-selling authors Lori Copeland and Virginia Smith weaves an entertaining and romantic tale for devoted fans and new readers.

Kansas,1881—On a trip to visit relatives, Emma Switzer's Amish family is robbed of all their possessions, leaving them destitute and stranded on the prairie. Walking into the nearest trading settlement, they pray to the Lord for someone to help. When a man lands in the dust at her feet, Emma looks down at him and thinks, *The Lord might have cleaned him up first.*

Luke Carson, heading up his first cattle drive, is not planning on being the answer to anyone's prayers, but it looks as though God has something else in mind for this kind and gentle man. Plain and rugged—do the two mix? And what happens when a dedicated Amish woman and a stubborn trail boss prove to be each other's match?

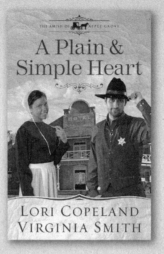

A Plain and Simple Heart

LORI COPELAND & VIRGINIA SMITH

A Plain and Simple Heart, an exciting new Amish-meets-Wild West adventure from bestselling authors Lori Copeland and Virginia Smith, weaves an entertaining and romantic tale for devoted fans and new readers.

1884—Several years earlier, young Rebecca Switzer lost her heart to Jesse Montgomery, a rugged but dissolute cowboy on a dusty cattle trail near the Amish settlement of Apple Grove. Now she is grown up, and when she hears one day that he has been spotted nearby, her desire is plain and simple: She must see him.

Sheriff Colin Maddox is counting the days until he can leave law enforcement and follow his dream of starting a church. When a lovely woman, new to town and looking travel weary and a bit lost, gets caught up in the middle of a temperance riot, she is arrested along with the leaders. He can hardly believe she is what she claims—a Plain and simple woman. Nor can he believe how quickly he loses his heart to her. Can Colin convince her to forget Jesse and give him a chance?